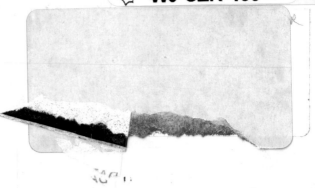

C

D

S

M

ALFRED HITCHCOCK'S

MONSTER MUSEUM

Here is a collection of Alfred Hitchcock's favorite monsters, gathered in one book so that others may share his enjoyment of them. "As you read on," says Mr. Hitchcock in his introduction, "just keep firmly in mind that these are *stories,* and you will be fine."

The Master of Suspense presents this book in the scary tradition of his earlier anthologies for young readers, *Alfred Hitchcock's Haunted Houseful* and *Alfred Hitchcock's Ghostly Gallery.*

ALFRED HITCHCOCK'S
MONSTER
MUSEUM

Illustrated by EARL E. MAYAN

RANDOM HOUSE • New York

*The editor gratefully acknowledges
the invaluable assistance of Robert Arthur
in the preparation of this volume*

The editor wishes to thank the following, for permission to reprint:

Milton Amgott for "Shadow, Shadow on the Wall" by Theodore Sturgeon. Copyright 1950 by Greenleaf Publishing Company. Reprinted from *Imagination*.

Arkham House for "Slime" by Joseph Payne Brennan. Copyright 1953 by Weird Tales. Reprinted from *Nine Horrors and a Dream* by Joseph Payne Brennan. And for "The Desrick on Yandro" by Manly Wade Wellman. Copyright 1952 by Fantasy House, Inc. Reprinted from *Who Fears the Devil*.

Jerome Bixby for "The Young One" by Jerome Bixby. Copyright 1953 by Ziff-Davis Publishing Company. First published in *Fantastic*.

Brandt & Brandt for "The King of the Cats" by Stephen Vincent Benét. Copyright 1929 by Stephen Vincent Benét, Copyright Renewed © 1957 by Rosemary Carr Benét. Reprinted from *The Selected Works of Stephen Vincent Benét*.

Curtis Brown, Ltd. for "The Wheelbarrow Boy" by Richard Parker. Copyright © 1953 by Fantasy House, Inc. Reprinted from *The Magazine of Fantasy and Science Fiction*.

Miriam Allen deFord for "Henry Martindale, Great Dane" by Miriam Allen deFord. Copyright © 1954 by Galaxy Publishing Corporation. Reprinted from *Beyond*.

Barthold Fles for "The Day of the Dragon" by Guy Endore. Copyright 1934 by Guy Endore. First published in *Bluebook*.

Littauer and Wilkinson for "Doomsday Deferred" by Will F. Jenkins. Copyright 1949 by Will F. Jenkins.

Harold Matson Company, Inc. for "Homecoming" by Ray Bradbury. Copyright 1946 & 1947 by Street & Smith Publications, Inc. Copyright 1943, 1944, 1945, 1946, 1947, 1954, 1955 by Ray Bradbury.

McIntosh & Otis, Inc. for "The Man Who Sold Rope to the Gnoles" by Idris Seabright. Copyright 1951 by Mercury Press, Inc. Reprinted from *The Magazine of Fantasy and Science Fiction*.

Paul R. Reynolds Inc. for "The Microscopic Giants" by Paul Ernst. Copyright 1936 by Beacon Magazines, Inc. Reprinted from *Thrilling Wonder Stories*.

INTRODUCTION
A Variety of Monsters

This seems to be the Age of the Monsters. Monsters are all around us. They abound on the motion picture-screens, coming from the depths of the sea, from under the Arctic ice, from outer space, or other such unexplored regions. They are likewise to be found plentifully on the face of the ingenious device known as the television picture tube. Here they are usually similar to their brothers on the movie screens except, for obvious reasons, smaller.

As if this were not enough, they leap out at us from comic books by the dozen. And to my horror I learn that they have now invaded the playroom and the nursery. There are actually on sale Make-Your-Own-Monster kits, so everyone can have a pet monster around the house to tell his troubles to.

I have only one word to describe this latest development.

The word is—*monstrous*. Why, next, someone will be starting a ·Monster Pen Pal Club!

As one who has known and been fond of many fine monsters of the motion-picture variety, I find today's crop of monsters lacking in variety or imagination. After all, a monster does not have to be a beast so large he wipes out a suburb every time he lashes his tail. Nor does he have to be a roughly human-shaped creature with his head bolted to his neck.

Indeed, no! I contend that a monster can be only a shadow on the wall—but what a shadow! He can be a wheelbarrow which is really a boy but won't admit it. He can be a pleasant-mannered gentleman named Henry, who wears the shape of a Great Dane. He can be a giant mere inches tall.

How can a giant be only inches tall? My dear young friends, you must read the following pages to find out. If you do so, you will also meet a polished gentleman with a tail like a cat, as well as a group of gnoles who have eyes like emeralds and some curious habits with regard to rope.

As if this were not enough, you will also meet those sinister creatures, the Flat, the Culverin, the Behinder and the Bammat. And I will wager you have never met *them* before.

Into this group of my favorite monsters, which I have gathered here thinking you may share my enjoyment of them, I have thrown a dragon or so, some werewolves, and a few such others just for flavoring. As you read on, just keep firmly in mind that these are *stories*, and you will be fine.

So, onward, young friends. The monsters are coming!

Alfred Hitchcock

CONTENTS

The Day of the Dragon

GUY ENDORE

No, in those days no one ever thought of such a peril to the existence of the human race. I was young then, but I recall the times distinctly. Scientists at their annual meetings used to discuss the probability of the termination of the triumphant progress of the human race, but that it should come about in this fashion—this terrible and at the same time ridiculous fashion—*that,* no one ever imagined.

At the present writing it does seem that the complete extinction of all mankind will be delayed, for there must be quite a number of small communities that have found refuge in mines and caves. And though it is long since we have had any word from them, yet in big cities such as Paris, Berlin and London, where there are impregnable subway systems, men and women can still hold out against the terror that ravages the open country. But how long can we last?

Few people, I suppose, are more capable than I of recapitulating the whole story from its completely insane inception of which I believe I was, and remain, the only living witness. I have heard lately so many different versions of how it all began that I want to say this: they are for the most part far from the truth. But it is

1

a very human necessity to demand an explanation of some
sort. . . .

Well, as I say, in those days scientists used to imagine many
perils to mankind. Some foresaw vast cataclysms; others predicted
more subtle scourges. Very frequent was the prophecy that insects
would succeed to the rule of the earth. I can still recall clearly a
very stirring lecture delivered by a great entomologist. He began
by pointing out that though new species of insects were being
discovered at the rate of ten thousand a year, and over half a
million kinds were already listed, yet by virtue of the processes of
evolution, he felt that the insects were increasing their species at
a faster rate than they were being catalogued, certainly faster than
their widely varying habits were capable of being studied. So
that, in short, as far as insects were concerned, science was playing a losing hand.

He pictured vividly the hordes of insects that attacked our food
crops in those days, the blights, the scales, the weevils, the fruit-
flies and moths of all kinds. The listeners shivered as they heard
tales of vast clouds of grasshoppers leaving whole countries bare,
all growing things nibbled down to the last stalk; tales of permanent battlelines of the entrenched farmer, the gardener, the
orchard grower, fighting off with poisonous gases the perpetually
renewed attacks of their inexhaustible insect enemies.

What, the lecturer queried, might happen in a moment of in-
attention? What, if by mischance some natural enemy of a given
insect were to cease its alliance with man and allow this insect
to breed in such multitudes as to ruin crops all over the world?
Imagine, the lecturer told us, months of famine during which
whole races would perish and others lapse into savagery and can-
nibalism. Was that to be the end of our proud civilization? Our
puny chemicals would soon be found ineffective against these
armored beasts, whose small size and vast numbers are so much
in their favor.

"But," so this lecturer affirmed, "the peril from such disorgan-
ized swarms is small compared to that offered by those practically
civilized insects, the ants, whose numerous varieties are already

so high on the rungs of the ladder of progress. The ant cultivates plants, keeps domestic animals, has masons and bridge-builders, law-makers and rulers, soldiers and captains. What if some Napoleon of the ant-world were to arise and were to ally all the many species of ants into a great confederacy, the object of which would be the subjugation of the earth? What if ant-scientists were to discover some glandular extract that would cause them to grow to enormous size? Have not bees and many other insects already developed something analogous? What is to prevent them from doing this, then waxing big as rats, to move against mankind in order to enslave and domesticate it? What a comi-tragedy! Man ending his history in the stalls of vast pyramidal ant-hills—the ant's bond-servant, his domestic animal!"

Curious, now I think of it, how man has come to a pass that is nearly, if not quite as ridiculous. I must say this lecturer had a pretty clear idea of what would happen, but how it was to come about—that was another matter. He had his guess, to which he was entitled. The guesses of others took different directions. I shan't dwell upon them at length. Now it was the sun that was to become exhausted, whereupon our planet would grow cold, the vast seas frozen to the very bottom and all life refrigerated to death in perfect cold-storage embalming. Again it was the earth that was to cease to revolve, leaving one-half of itself parched in perpetual high-noon sunshine, the other frozen in eternal midnight. Or else it was a comet that was to strike our earth and shatter it into a million inconsequential planetoids.

To such cataclysmic horrors others opposed more subtle dangers. Did not the statistics on insanity show that its rate of increase was such that it would not be long before the whole world was a raving madhouse, in which such poor normal beings as might remain would have a far from enviable fate? Would not, so other students asked, the increasing use of fuel disturb the balance of the atmosphere? Would not the use of oil by motor-ships give rise to a scum of oil on the seas? In short, were we not about to blanket the earth and the waters and shut out the health-giving ultra-violet rays without which life is impossible?

Ah, but that we should be attacked and destroyed by a legendary animal —no, that I never heard from the mouth of any of these scientists. Why, such an animal does not even exist, they would have said. Ridiculous! A fabulous monster? Why, that's pure myth! Oh, good enough, I suppose, for fairy-tale writers and for artists with lively fancies. But we serious——

Well, it was out of just such legends that it came about. That sounds strange and impossible, but it is true. Listen:

In the old days, in the golden era when mankind walked out carefree into the great light, where the laughing sun played on the pied fields, and the good breeze blew—I was then a reporter; and I well remember the time I was called upon to do a story on a live toad said to have been immured for a billion years in rock. That was the beginning of it.

In some upstate county, this toad hopped out of a kind of natural bubble in the stone, hopped out just as the stone-cutter's chisel broke through into the air-hole. And the workman, flabbergasted, ran to the editor of the village paper and there gasped out his tale. A local amateur geologist claimed that the rock of this region had been laid down a billion years or more ago, and that the toad must therefore be a billion years old or more. But the editor of the paper called the stone-cutter a fool for not having caught the toad. A group of people, however, who had gone out to investigate found a toad not ten feet away from the cuplike depression, the stone-bubble, and there was no reason to think that this was any other but the long-lived toad, just out from a billion years of solitary confinement.

The story, though old and often scorned, got about. The toad was exhibited in the village drugstore, where he contentedly accepted a tribute of live flies; and a reporter from a near-by town called to write up the tale and take pictures of the toad and the quarryman. And so the story came to New York. The Sunday rotogravure ran pictures of the event and such was the interest stirred up that I was asked to collect opinions from the wiseacres of the Museum and the local colleges and scientific institutes.

Naturally I took advantage of this assignment to look up my

old teacher, Crabshaw. We used to call him Fossil Crab's Paw. If you said it rapidly it sounded so much like Professor Crabshaw, that we dared to say it to his face, and being young and silly, we thought it a very brave and clever thing to do. I thought it would be good fun to see old Crabshaw again.

But it did not prove to be such fun, for the once so familiar biologic laboratory on the top floor made me melancholy. And the memory of many drowsy afternoons spent here, dissecting cockroaches and rats, afflicted me.

The dissecting-room was empty, but there in the rear was old Professor Crabshaw's office. I could see him sitting at his desk, bent over a pile of examination papers. He was more seedy than ever and I swear he wore the same acid-stained smock, even as his meek face bore the same old pale and drooping whiskers.

The honors and awards of being a scientist had passed over Professor Crabshaw and left him practically where he had started. He was still an instructor, overworked and poor. And yet he had done some fair work. He used to tell, with considerable pride, how his work on the surface-tension of various fluids taken from protozoa of different types had suggested to him the possibility of constructing a synthetic cell. This suggestion had been taken up by a later worker and carried to success, reaping fame and rich material rewards, but not for Crabshaw.

I introduced myself to the Professor and reminded him that I had once been a student in his class. He smiled and bade me be seated. That he was pleased to have a great newspaper ask him for his opinion, was evident.

"Of course there's no truth in it. Just another popular fallacy like horsehair snakes. The toad no doubt lived near by. You say yourself that it differs not at all from the present species common to that region. That explains the whole story, which after all relies almost entirely on the say-so of the quarryman, who was probably frightened out of his wits when a toad hopped past his chisel."

"May I quote you?" I asked.

It was in his answer to this that Professor Crabshaw revealed all the meekness of his nature, all the years in which the better diplomats in his science had advanced to more important posts, while he, the patient worker, had remained behind to correct examination papers.

"I'm afraid I can't permit that. You may say—ah—that a professor at a local college—ah—a well-known biologist—of note— well, any sort of paraphrase." He smiled, pleased at his own flattery of himself, and content to visualize himself praised, even anonymously.

As I left, I imagined him secretly hoping I might forget his injunction and publish his name. But we published nothing, for it was decided to have a feature article on the subject in the Sunday magazine section. When the editor of the Sunday magazine told me this, I suggested Professor Crabshaw as a likely person to do the article. The moment I did so, I regretted it. No one could have been more unsuited to the task. But I consoled myself with the thought that he would surely refuse to write for a cheap paper.

But I was mistaken. He accepted, so I learned, and with great pleasure. Had he been seduced by the need of the two hundred dollars, which was the magazine's price for the article? I confess I was rather worried, for I felt myself responsible for the whole business.

I therefore called him up on the telephone and began by explaining that it was I who had recommended him.

"I thought as much," he replied; "and you must have lunch with me. Can you meet me at the Faculty Club at once?"

I accepted, thinking that my business would be settled better across a table.

Professor Crabshaw was prompt to the appointment. With him was his wife, a buxom, frowsy person, whose not unkindly face showed plainly the effects of years of disappointed hopes.

She was voluble in her thanks to me. It was so kind of me to have recommended Paul! That it was the two hundred dollars that magnetized her was easy to guess. Her conversation at the luncheon was of nothing but money.

"Look," she said, "there's Professor Slocum. Of course you've

heard of him. Economics, you know. They say he's made a fortune in Wall Street. Those economists have secrets. You should
see his new roadster.

"And that's Professor Dillinger, yes, the man with the little
beard. He's rich. That's his wife there, the tall one with the permanent. He's got political connections. They say he's the brains
for the sugar lobby."

"Now, Lizzy——" Crabshaw objected.

"But it's true. Just take a look at Professor Wailson. Just
because he discovered that the mob reacts like a spoiled baby,
he got himself a hundred-thousand-dollar-a-year job with an ad-
vertising house. . . . Oh, Paul, why haven't you ever discovered
something brilliant like that? But of course, what can one do with
protozoa? I always say there's no profit to be made out of raising
such tiny bits of things."

"Well, I did once discover——" Crabshaw began meekly.

"Yes, Paul, we know all about that," his wife said severely.

"But, Lizzie, I was only going to explain to Mr.——"

"Paul, how often must I tell you to call me Elspeth? You know,"
she said, turning to me, "that I've always felt that if Paul would
only get used to calling me Elspeth, instead of Lizzie, he'd make
at least a thousand dollars more a year."

I saw that this conversation was becoming very painful to
Crabshaw, so I began to question him about the article.

"What have you planned to say?"

"Well, I've begun with an examination of the much-disputed
topic of what constitutes scientific evidence. Then taking up the
story of the toad, I show that the proper evidence is lacking. And
I conclude with a discussion of the life-habits of the toad and the
experiments that have been made on prolonging the hibernation
of various animals, demonstrating that they cannot survive much
beyond their usual period."

This was, of course, precisely what I had been afraid of: a
rather dull, scientific, educational tract.

"That's fine," I said. "Hm—but I'm just a little afraid it may
not appeal to the reading public of our paper. Now, if you're

seriously thinking of writing this sort of article, you'll have to come down a bit. Meet the public halfway. Its interest would be more aroused by a toad that has actually lived a billion years. Give the toad a chance to do his stuff."

"But toads don't live a billion years," Crabshaw exclaimed. "It's preposterous!"

"That's it!" I cried. "That's precisely it. The more preposterous, the better. You are a scientist, and you can give the preposterous that scientific veneer that will make it acceptable."

"But——" objected Crabshaw, his jaw hanging.

His wife cut him short: "Of course you can, Paul. Think of it: two hundred dollars every time you write an article! Why, that's almost a month's salary."

"Even more than that, Mrs. Crabshaw," I said, "if the articles should ever come into demand and editors compete for your husband's product."

Professor Crabshaw looked most woebegone, but we two had no pity on him. I saw that in gaining an ally in Mrs. Crabshaw I had the matter clinched. And indeed, the article turned out to be all that could be expected of the most experienced yellow journalist. We ran it under big headlines: "GREAT SCIENTIST CHAMPIONS BILLION-YEAR-OLD TOAD," by *Professor Paul Crabshaw, internationally famous biologist.*" And we had enormous pictures of toads along with a strip of vignettes showing *"our artist's conception of history and the toad,"* in which, above repeated pictures of the toad immured in his rock-prison, were depicted prehistoric animals, the glacial period, early apelike man, first signs of civilization in Egypt, then the Jews captive in Babylon, then Christ on the cross, and following that, Columbus in his caravel, Napoleon, and then the final picture typifying the most up-to-date scene: The President of the United States surrounded by a draped flag and a spread-eagle. In the article itself Professor Crabshaw adduced numerous reasons, all couched in the form of striking anecdotes, and designed to prove the possibility of a billion-year-old toad.

It really made great yellow journalism, but it made mighty

poor science for a college professor, and the higher powers were down upon him at once.

But that meant nothing to the editor of the Sunday magazine. A few weeks later, when passengers came home with a tale of having sighted a sea-serpent, that hoary legend was sent to Professor Paul Crabshaw for confirmation, and again he made good, no doubt goaded by Lizzie.

In a short time the articles of Crabshaw had become indispensable and were a regular feature, for which we paid increasing prices. There followed articles on boys brought up by wolves, living in the forest and running on all fours, and articles on the plagues of Egypt and—well, that sort of thing.

For several years this continued, during which Lizzie sure enough blossomed into Elspeth, with facials, permanents and better clothes to make her look the part. I used to meet them now and then for lunch at the Faculty Club, where Professor Crabshaw, at his wife's behest, still went, though he could feel that his colleagues had lost their respect for him.

"But I'm preparing my revenge," he confided to me one day. "I'm going to electrify the world. You just watch and see. I'm going to prove that marvelous things can and do happen. And that will be my vindication for that tripe on 'Was Jonah Swallowed by a Whale?' and 'What Will Man Look Like Fifty Thousand Years From Now?'"

"Tell me more," I begged.

He shook his head. And Elspeth said: "He won't even show me what he's doing. But he's got himself a laboratory or something off in New Jersey and he goes there every day now."

One morning Crabshaw called me up and insisted that I must come up to see him at once, that he had something quite marvelous to show me. There was a note of exultation in his voice that made me drop my work and obey him.

When I arrived, he wrung my hand in his thin, nervous fingers, then, skipping ahead of me like a French dancing-master, he led me into his study.

"Now," he said, when I was seated, "my great day is at hand!"

And with a smile that freed and relaxed all the long-frozen wrinkles of his face, he declared proudly: "I was fired last night."

Seeing my look of astonishment, he continued: "No, not fired precisely, but given an ultimatum in something of this manner." Then old Crabshaw pulled in his little chin, tried to look cocky and arrogant and paunchy and said: "Here stood Prexy, just like this; he said 'Mr. Crabshaw' (you see it was no longer *Professor* but just *Mister*), 'Mr. Crabshaw, I think the moment has come for you to decide what subject you are most interested in, science or fiction-writing!'

"I answered him back hotly: 'Mr. President, you have no right to set a limit to scientific investigation.' And he answered: 'No, but we do try to keep our departments of science and of *belles-lettres* distinct.'

"Then I said: 'Mr. President, if you want to be shown that I am not romancing but have made one of the greatest contributions ever made to biology, I invite you over to my New Jersey laboratory tomorrow. You will see mythology come to life. I have invited several of my skeptical colleagues to come with me and if you wish to be fair to me, I shall have the honor of calling for you at three tomorrow!'

"He refused at first, but upon my insistence that I deserved a fair trial, he consented. It is past two now and we must leave soon. You will go along as a member of the press and you will write this up for your paper. So get out your pencil and make notes of what I'm going to tell you. This will be the biggest scoop of your life and will serve to repay you some for what you did for me."

"But——" I began.

"Let's not argue now," he said hastily. "We haven't the time. Listen carefully. I was going to make an article of this myself, but on second thought I decided that the first report ought to come from someone else. I would never be credited by serious readers: for it is more fantastic than anything I have ever written and yet every word of it is true.

"Let me begin at the beginning, however. You knew, did you

not, that for some time I have been suffering under the slights of my fellow-scientists? I confess I did write many silly articles, but, if science would not butter my bread, then I had to do something else. So for a long time I have been scheming to rehabilitate myself. At first all I could do was hope and pray that something might happen that would, of itself, lift this reproach from me, some striking event that would, so to speak, give a little basis for my flights of fancy.

"Then I myself began to cudgel my brains to scheme out something of my own. After several false attempts that I need not discuss here, I recalled something I had known for many years. And I wondered if there might not be a possibility for me in this bit of knowledge. Perhaps you can still recall my classroom lecture on the nature of the reptilian heart? Well, in brief, it is, compared to the mammalian heart, the human heart for example, an incomplete organ. In a way, it is a malformation. For it is so constructed that the blood vessels of the animal are never filled with freshly oxygenated blood. The old stale blood, replete with body poisons, mixes in the chambers of the heart with the bright, clean blood from the lungs and is pumped back through the body again, only half cleansed.

"Scientifically, we express that by saying that the septum between the ventricles, the wall that should be there to keep the two blood streams separated, is incompletely formed. The animal thus suffers all its lifetime from auto-intoxication, and is by nature sluggish. Suffers is perhaps the wrong word, for its whole organism is evidently attuned to this sub-normal state. The alligator is, then, to speak roughly, a life-long congenital cardiac, incapable of great activity except in infrequent spasms. His race is an invalid race, each member born an invalid and remaining an invalid throughout its existence.

"And does not the alligator give us an example of how the cardiac should live? No physician could prescribe anything finer for his patients than the alligator's calm, docile, peaceful, snoozy sort of life. Notice the alligators at the aquarium. They may look fierce, but they are condemned invalids and no matter how long they live, they will continue to practice extreme caution, sparing their poor circulatory systems, lying all day in bed, that is to say in the warm mud, and doing very little more than sending out an occasional blink of the eyelid.

"Well," Crabshaw went on before I could interrupt, "it occurred to me one day to see what would happen if that bad heart condition of the alligator were cleared up or at least improved by stretching that incomplete septum to form a dividing wall between the venous and the arterial blood streams. I immediately procured a lot of baby alligators and set to work to find out.

"My method was simple. I just chloroformed my patient and operated on him, following as well as I could, the directions given in a textbook on surgery.

"My mortality rate was enormous. No doubt my surgical technique was atrocious. But then, I'm no surgeon and don't pretend to be one. It seemed that the heart condition only grew worse after the incomplete septum was stretched out. The poor alligators just turned up their pale and swollen bellies and gave up their alligatorish ghosts; many of them did not even bother to recover from the effects of the chloroform.

"I, myself, was frequently on the point of throwing up the sponge, when patient Number 87 gave me the courage to carry on. For several hours after the operation, that fellow ran about the room like a frisky puppy. I am sure that no one in the world has ever witnessed such speed and agility on the part of an alligator. I tell you, he ran about like a chipmunk, dived in and out of the water tank, leaped, frolicked and dashed about in a reckless, gleeful manner that was a marvel and a delight to behold. Then suddenly, over he turned, wriggled his paws madly, like a toy train upset, the wheels of which continue to spin until the spring has unwound.

"Number 87 revived my courage. I determined to fight on and as I say, I gradually grew more skillful and altered my technique by constant improvement as I studied the matter. Finally, I determined to try somewhat larger specimens than those I had hitherto been working on and do more thorough and careful operations. Out of ten trials, I achieved two amazing successes. Whereupon I ceased to operate on further specimens and studied those two.

"I noted, in the first place, that they devoured from four to eight times as much food as ordinary alligators of their age. But then they were never still for a moment, whereas their ailing brothers slept most of the day. Indeed, my two alligators grew so fast that I realized that something had to be done quickly or they would soon outgrow my little laboratory. At that time I worked in a store I had rented—a former sea-food shop—in which the left-over equipment provided me with excellent facilities for the performance of my experiments. I say it behooved me now to hasten, lest I be caught in a jam, for at their rate of growth I realized that I would soon be unable to move them. Fortunately, I was able to locate and rent, for a reasonable price, a former platinum refinery in New Jersey, a large single-story brick building, a shed rather, which was particularly suited to my purposes since the windows were all heavily barred with iron.

"I had some trouble crating and moving my pets. I had to creep up on the beasts and spray them with chloroform, and that was dangerous business, for I very nearly chloroformed myself. I should have had help, but I wanted no inkling of my work to reach the outside world. And those alligators were quick as birds and big too, as large I should say as young calves. They had grown to four times their original size in six days' time. And could they fight and squirm!

"Well, anyway, that's all over and I now have my two pretty ones in their new home, which was at that time comfortably arranged to house them. Yes, I say pretty ones, for they were sleek and shiny and the way they flirted their tails and skimmed along the floor with their paws moving so fast you could hardly see them, was a pleasure; and their eyes were never closed. . . . I had built a big tank for them and you should have seen them swim and dive and go leaping out of the water and come falling back with loud smacking splashes, like dolphins or seals. And taking such joy in life! I wish I could show you that, but they have outgrown that tank now. I must build them a new one.

"I tell you I used to watch them by the hour and say to myself, 'You're a public benefactor, you are. Here are the first two healthy alligators in the world! Why has man been so cruel as to reserve his medical knowledge so much for himself and his domestic animals? Wild life, too, needs some attention.' You see, I hadn't then an inkling of what I had really succeeded in doing, but I was right nevertheless in one respect. I had given health to two alligators and I was the first privileged human being to observe what a healthy alligator was like.

"I noticed many peculiarities that set off my healthy two from the rest of the sickly breed of alligators. They began, for example, to show a better growth in the chest. They swelled out something like geckos. You know how geckos look, those small lizards. And with a better growth of the chest cavity went a different carriage of the head. The head rose from the ground—from which the ordinary alligator does not seem to have the strength to raise it— and was held up a bit, thus contriving to give the beasts the appearance of a neck. That bad posture that one notices in all alligators, crocodiles and gavials and related species, is plainly just another symptom of their congenital heart trouble. They are all stricken down with severe auto-intoxication. It is to be noticed, by the way, that they all have a bad breath. My alligators had a sweet breath.

"The next noteworthy change in outward appearance was the heavier growth of those spinal processes. In fact, in the common diseased alligator, there are no spinal processes to speak of, though along the tail are to be found some heavy skin-growths forming a serrated ridge and indicating perhaps what nature intended the beast to have there and which is actually to be seen on my two specimens, namely, ridges that are part of the spine and that reach luxurious proportions. The tail, too, grew larger and longer each day and there is nothing prettier to see than the way it curls and rolls in rich serpentine curves and even in complete circles. You won't be able to see that now, because the quarters have become so cramped, but you will see how instead of terminating in a weak point, my healthy alligators have developed a flat arrowhead on the end, something like the whale's tail, only sharper.

"Mind you, those beasts of mine were now consuming each a good-sized sheep. And demanding more every day! And though big around as cows and, of course, two or three times as long, they were still but tots, so to speak, being but a few months old and still in the process of development. Especially curious was the ridge that grew along the back, and which, between the shoulder blades and the hips, if I may be permitted such loose anatomical designations, seemed to rise higher each day and to have greater internal structural support, for not only did the spine enter into its formation, but the ribs actually grew out of the body and provided buttresses for it. For some weeks my patients appeared as if a heavy mushroom-like parasol were sprouting out of their backs.

"'Now whatever can that be?' I used to wonder and continued to watch. But there were so many interesting things to see. I must explain that with my beasts the size of elephants, I ceased to be able to examine them very closely. I'll tell you the way I go about it: the factory is along a rarely used unsurfaced road in a remote part of the country, and I drive up there every day, formerly in my old used car, but now in a truck specially purchased, and loaded down with a couple of sheep or pigs fresh from the slaughterhouse and with several tubs of fish. Before I installed a differential pulley, I had to drag all this up to the roof and dump the whole business through a ventilator on it. I don't dare enter the place. Why, it was even dangerous to do that much, for their lashing tails with that heavy and sharp arrowhead termination used to come whipping around and crash through the window or rather whatever fragments of glass and iron bars remained in the window, and come out thumping and feeling around on the roof. I guess they were curious to find out what was all the disturbance up there. Or perhaps they knew it was feeding time and they just wanted to show their appreciation of my solicitude. I often did think they felt gratitude for me, their deliverer from the oppression of heart trouble.

"Oh yes, I forgot to tell you how they began to show knobs on their snouts and how these knobs kept growing out and formed what I can only describe as feelers or whiskers, heavy things, flexible and curling like the trunk of an elephant, only thinner and covered with a leathery integument. Well, one of those feelers came whipping out of the ventilator one day and gave me a caress that tore through all my clothes and left a deep, bloody scar. As I say, I suppose it was a caress, but I was so frightened that I jerked back. I believe that if it had been ill-meant I wouldn't be here to tell about it. Yes, I'm pretty nearly positive of the fact that they like me.

"Of late it has grown more and more difficult to get a good glimpse of them. It's been getting more and more dangerous to go near that building and before I rigged up my rope system, I used to climb up to the roof by a ladder placed against the rear of the building where there aren't any windows, and once on the roof, I'd make sure that nothing was protruding from the ventilator and then I'd rush up and cast down my load and rush right back with another load. Once they were busy eating, it was fairly safe.

"Now and then I'd put my eye to a little opening I'd found and peer through. There were my beasts, growing larger every day, greater now than elephants in the bulk of their torso and with that parasol-like growth on their backs expanding and expanding, and shaping itself out into two vast ovals, one on each side. Then, one day, it came over me, suddenly, what these were: wings! Yes, sir: wings!

"And suddenly, too, that day I realized what I possessed there, locked up in that old factory, and I ran back to my car and drove at breakneck speed to New York and to the library. Why, of course, what else but dragons! And the stories and pictures of those fabulous beasts proved to me that my alligators were not the only healthy alligators that had ever existed. There had been at various times, but mostly in prehistoric days, other rare specimens of healthy alligators. How else explain the fact that people

had seen precisely such monsters as I have out there, and preserved the record of their appearance in story and art? Why,
those Chinese dragons you see embroidered in silk were as like
mine as two peas. Undoubtedly there appears now and then, but
exceedingly rarely, a sport or variant among the alligators or
crocodiles, provided by chance with a healthy heart, and so free
from auto-intoxication.

"But to get back to the progress of my pets. They continued to
develop and pretty soon I began to see their wings unfold, with
those enormous ribs of theirs strengthening them like ribbed
Gothic vaulting. Hunched they are at the shoulders, and then
smoothing down flat to the rear and wrapping against the lower
body like enormous shields. You can see that they are aching,
now, to try out the wings—but there is no room in the factory.
But now and then they do a little tentative flapping, you know
like chickens, and then they subside, sadly. I tell you it breaks my
heart to see them so confined. But that will be remedied. Now
they have begun to look awkward on the ground, trailing their
immense wings, their size preventing them from frisking around
as they used to do. They move back and forth like caged beasts
and I can see that their tempers are getting short and ugly."

He paused suddenly and looked at his watch. "Come, we've no
time to waste. I'm to call for the delegation at a quarter to three
and then be at the President's house at three sharp."

"Say!" I exclaimed. "This is all so terribly exciting that my
head is simply whirling. What a story this is going to make! We'll
run a whole page of pictures!" I was so carried away by Crabshaw's vivid story that I never for a moment doubted its veracity.

"Pictures?" Crabshaw cried. "Pictures? Of course! Why did I
never think of that? But I have been so feverishly excited. We
must take some now. Wait, let me get our camera. Pshaw! I wish
I had kept a photographic record of their development. Well,
that will have to wait for the next group I operate on."

I suggested calling up for one of our news photographers, but
he vetoed the idea. For the present, he wanted no outsider except
me.

We drove out in a limousine Crabshaw had hired for the occasion. There was a curious strained atmosphere among the occupants of the car. At first there had been solemn politeness, the stilted courtesy of duelists, which now and then one of the former colleagues of Crabshaw would try to break by a weak attempt at humor. Crabshaw brushed these attempts aside and set the conversation on the recent spell of hot weather, or the latest political news, and in that fashion the conversation limped along until we had driven far out into New Jersey and had gone off the traveled highway and were bumping along a forest road much in need of repair.

The professors sat with their hats on their knees, the President wiped the copious sweat from his brow, and Crabshaw, thin and alert, kept leaning forward to give the driver directions.

Suddenly Crabshaw gave a cry. The car drove out into an open space and stopped abruptly. Before us were the heaped ruins of what had once been a red brick building of some size.

Disregarding our solicitous inquiries, Crabshaw continued to yell: "They've escaped! They've broken out! They're gone!" We could not get any other intelligent statement from him.

He ran out and scrambled up over the masses of wreckage, the heaps of brick, the twisted girders, and continued to let forth one piercing scream after another. We sat in the car for a while, overcome by a powerful stench that, along with the heat of the day, robbed our lungs of the breath they craved.

The President, holding his kerchief to his nose, a gesture that his professional satellites imitated at once, made a muffled nasal remark: "Our friend has histrionic talents, too. Whew! If you agree with me, gentlemen, that we have seen enough, let us be off. I can't breathe here."

"Nor I . . . nor I," said the obedient professors.

But I followed Crabshaw up the heap of wreckage and looked down upon the interior of the building, where vast mounds of trampled filth lay so thick that it almost obscured the existence of a flat concrete floor beneath. And the odor was like that of the monkey-house at the zoo, only many times worse.

The President cried out: "Crabshaw, I insist upon being driven back to my residence at once. Otherwise I shall commandeer this car and leave you here."

Crabshaw, his eyes popping out of his head, his voice cracked with sobs, shouted back: "Come on up here, you fools! There's evidence left here, at any rate. Look at those foot-prints!"

Two of the professors, more curious and bolder than the rest, mounted to where we stood and looked down upon the scene below. But they had eyes only for the filth and not for its meaning or origin.

"The Augean stables had nothing on this," one of them began.

"See those prints?" Crabshaw cried.

"I insist, Crabshaw," bellowed the President, whereupon one of the professors dutifully declared:

"I've seen enough," and the other echoed that flat statement.

It made no difference to them how Crabshaw swore and begged and whined, with the tears flying from his eyes, his mouth sputtering: "Here you, Professor Albert, world-famous paleontologist, why don't you measure these foot-prints? What animal do they come from? Did you ever see such enormous holes as these claws have dug? And you, Professor Wiener! Why do you stand like dummies? Do you turn up your noses because the evidence is not a million years old? Why, if this were in the rocks of Montana, you'd be all over the ground, sniffing and measuring and preparing to write huge tomes. What's the matter with you now?"

Gently I led the hysterical man down from his mound of bricks and pulled him into the car. On the drive home he remained silent except for an occasional attempt to arouse the others with a sarcastic or pleading remark. To these the President answered once, without looking at poor Crabshaw:

"I've never been so hood-winked before . . . so grossly insulted!"

And the scientists repeated: "A plain fraud!"

"A salted mine," said another, and one mentioned Cesnola and the fake antiquities he palmed off on the Metropolitan Museum, and another mentioned Glozel, and a third thought of the Louvre and the crown of Artaphernes, and then they reminded themselves of the Cardiff giant. . . .

In short, they passed in sarcastic review all the trickeries ever perpetrated upon science.

But all things have an end; eventually we unloaded our cargo of scoffers and proceeded on to Crabshaw's apartment. The life had gone out of that man so that I could not desert him, but must see him safely home. As we rode on to his apartment, I heard newsboys crying extras. Though the moment was hardly propitious, I felt that my profession demanded a copy. I stopped the car and called to one of the boys. No sooner had I spread out the sheet than I gave Crabshaw a mighty slap on the shoulder, for I confess that my own first emotion was one of exultation:

"Look, man! Read this!" I cried.

MONSTERS ATTACK ATLANTIC CITY

FOUR BATHING BEAUTIES AMONG MISSING

MANY SPECTATORS AT BATHING BEAUTY CONTEST ARE SLAIN AND MANY MAIMED BY FLYING MONSTERS

As usual the actual news report was meager, for extras often have nothing more than a headline to sell. It is published while the reporters hustle out to secure more complete information. The body of the article repeated in various forms the following story:

> Conflicting reports by telephone from Atlantic City tell of enormous flying monsters, birds or airplanes (eyewitnesses are not in agreement on this point), attacking the crowd assembled to watch the final awards in the nation-wide competition for the nomination of Miss America. Two or more scarlet-colored birds of vast size swooped down on the panic-stricken multitude, who dashed for cover in all directions. One informant declares he was reminded of the airplane attacks on infantry that were a feature of the World War.

Whatever they were, beast or machine, they mutilated dozens of bystanders—and were gone. Their appearance and disappearance were so rapid, their speed so enormous, that no one seems to have retained a clear notion as to precisely what happened. The monsters seem to have swooped down out of the clouds and back again, carrying off some of the victims and leaving the boardwalk strewn with the dead and the dying.

The earliest reports from the hastily organized volunteer ambulance and medical corps——

I grew more and more serious as I read of the victims. But Crabshaw only expanded. He slapped his knee:

"Ha, ha! Those healthy youngsters! What an appetite! Think of that! Just swooped down from the clouds"—he illustrated the maneuver with a swoop of his hand—"snatched up those beauties and climbed right back out of human sight. Wow! Think of it, man!" And he gave me a jovial dig in the ribs.

"I'm thinking of it, all right," I said soberly.

But he was so delighted that he actually began to caper around in the car. It was droll, but I could not laugh. I thought of the dead and dying out there on the boardwalk and the four young girls who had come to exhibit their youth and beauty and who had been snatched up beyond the clouds and devoured.

"Stop! Stop the car!" Crabshaw shouted. "We must get dozens of those papers and clip out those articles and send them to those benighted professorial asses who came out there and refused to use their five senses."

"Do nothing of the kind!" I cried and pulled Crabshaw back to his seat. "Listen to me, you fool. Do you want the whole world on your neck? Don't you realize what your dragons have done? They've killed, or injured for life, scores of people. What will the world say of Professor Crabshaw when it learns that his petty desire for vindication in the eyes of his colleagues has caused wholesale murder? Take my advice and keep quiet about this and pray that it may blow over. Or enjoy your bloody triumph if you like, but beware of proclaiming it. As far as I am concerned, not a word of your connection with this gruesome business at Atlantic City will get into the newspapers."

That sobered him. But only for a moment; then he wagged his head, tickled silly by the accomplishment of his pets. "Husky youngsters!" he muttered over and over again to himself. Then he exclaimed out loud: "Husky youngsters! Gad! What will they do when they are full-grown, can you imagine? Why, they're only kids now. They're not a year old yet. And just out of the hospital, so to speak. Why, come to think of it, this is the first day they flew. Say, what do you suppose they'll do when they are as big as battleships? Bigger, maybe. Wow!"

And he went on ruminating gleefully: "Flying so perfectly on their first essay! Where is the human aviator who could equal that! And say! By gosh, I never thought of that. Do you recall all the stories of the dragons demanding a tribute of fair maidens? Well, there you see it. First thing they do is go after the beautiful virgins. Ha-ha! Just another proof for you that those old artists and poets were not just imbeciles, but as good scientific observers as any of us moderns. Fairy tales, eh? I tell you, Mr. President, those fairy tales are true. And Crabshaw's fancies are as good as any of your old stodgy facts. Maybe better, because dreams come true, while facts are always being challenged and disproved."

He went on thus while the car drove to his home. Just as we reached there, he let out a scream that nearly stopped my heart beating.

"What's the matter now?" I gasped.

"Never thought of it!" he shouted. "Never once occurred to me. Oh, this is rich! Just too perfect! Male and female created He them. Yes sir! One male and one female. Think of it, man. Think of the race that will come from those beasts! Why—why, it——" He stood there with an ecstatic smile on his uplifted face. It was as if he felt himself akin to the Creator and was calling down a blessing upon the Adam and Eve of the new race of dragons.

It occurred to me later, where I had heard people talk just like Crabshaw during that ride home. Parents, hardworking parents of the poorer classes, who raise up their children to take the place in the world that they, the parents, would have liked to occupy, they speak thus. And for Crabshaw, his dragons, so strong, so unassailable, were his sons who were going to wipe out with their strength all the disappointments that he had been forced to swallow.

No sooner had we alighted and dismissed the car than he declared: "I'm not going upstairs. Please, do me a favor: go up and tell Elspeth not to expect me until late. Say nothing about the dragons, of course."

"And what are you going to do?" I asked, displeased at his request.

"I've got something I must take care of," he said mysteriously. And then, sensing that I was about to object, he pleaded quickly: "Go, please! Good Lord, am I to be balked all my life?"

I realized vaguely what he wanted to do, but his last words made me give in to his plea. And then what good would it have done to have refused him? He would have put through his plan anyhow. The manner in which he clutched his camera under his arm, and the light of fanatic determination in his eyes, were indicative of a firm resolve to go back to the ruined factory in New Jersey, no doubt driving there in his own little car, in the hope that the darling alligators whom he had nursed to health from their original heart trouble would return to roost there and he would be thus enabled to secure photographs of them.

I let him go and regretted it; but I hold myself blameless, for short of locking him up behind iron bars, nothing could have restrained him. I went up and made some excuse to Elspeth and then left to catch up on my neglected work. Of the unsuccessful dragon expedition, I said nothing to anyone. To have done so would have been to expose Crabshaw. I was rather surprised to find that the professors at the University suspected nothing of his connection with the disaster at Atlantic City, but on second thought, this was only natural: such a connection must have appeared extremely far-fetched and to have propounded it would have been to expose one's self to ridicule if it were proved false and again to ridicule, were it proved true. In any case, the great publicity would have been Crabshaw's. Such must have been the motives of the professors in keeping quiet, if indeed they had any thoughts on the matter at all. Afterwards, true enough, all sorts of crazy things were propounded by professor and layman alike, and Crabshaw's name was mentioned, but those who had been in a position to assure themselves of the justice of Crabshaw's claims and had neglected to do so, had nothing to gain by speaking up; on the contrary——

When I called up Crabshaw on the afternoon of the following day, Elspeth answered, extremely agitated.

"What do you know about this?" she asked. "Where is Paul?"

"Why? Didn't he come home?" I asked, my heart sinking at the thought of Crabshaw alone with the dragons.

"No, he didn't come home," she answered. "But that's not what puzzles me so much as where he has been. I'm afraid there's some sort of hoax afoot. Since yesterday I have had three cablegrams, ostensibly from him, all sent collect."

"Cablegrams?"

"Yes. One from London that came last night. The second one came early this morning and was from Alexandria. And I just had another, just this moment. From Singapore, Malay States."

"Well, what does he say?"

"He says the same thing in each one: DON'T WORRY STOP AM SAFE STOP BE HOME SOON.

"Well, that sounds encouraging," I said, for want of any better comment.

Elspeth, however, declared: "Well, I can tell you this: I don't believe they come from Paul. He can't be all over the world in one night. And I'm not going to pay for any more of them! Perhaps you can tell me what it's all about. What did you two do yesterday?"

"Why, nothing," I said and blandly made whatever excuses I could think of quickly and then hung up. Actually, of course, I had a good notion of what had happened. It was plain that he was riding through the clouds on the back of one or the other of his flying alligators, and could stop them where he pleased. Flying from continent to continent, and over the oceans. . . . Well, glory be to you, Paul! Now you are truly vindicated. Now you have your apotheosis. All the world will bow to you when you come alighting in the middle of Broadway on your pet dragon!

I thought for a moment of proclaiming the arrival of Paul Crabshaw from a round-the-world hop done in one day. But fortunately I thought better of it—in view of the recent disaster at Atlantic City, of which the papers were now full. But I could not restrain my mind from waxing enthusiastic over the fact that it was plain that Paul had tamed the monsters. What would not mankind be able to do with these domesticated dragons, who were so superior to airplanes? Perhaps Paul had struck the right track, the new road, along which mankind was to progress by breeding or otherwise developing animals to do the work of machines.

But we waited in vain for Paul Crabshaw to return. Elspeth paid for several more cablegrams from South America, from Africa and from other outlandish places. Then the cablegrams ceased, which both pleased and disappointed the economical Elspeth. And after that we never heard of Paul again. . . .

As for the rest, it is history. The bruit of the Atlantic City disaster died down and for several years we heard nothing more of monsters. Elspeth, bereaved, had gone away to nurse her sorrow and Paul Crabshaw's disappearance was soon forgotten. I used to ponder over the probable fate of the dragons. Evidently their mighty hearts had given way and they had fallen into the sea along with their doctor.

But they had only retired to remote regions, there to breed thousands of their kind. For soon the world awoke to the fact that it was positively infested with dragons. There were, at first, rumors of dragons devouring the natives of interior Africa. This was presumed to be false, like so many other jungle stories. And then there were rumors of dragons in South America and China. These were dismissed as tropically over-heated imaginations and mere Chinese fantasies. And then there were dragons in Europe, in France, in England, in the United States, in New York—and no one could doubt the truth of it any more. The world was a prey to man-eating dragons!

Too late then to fight the vermin that had obtained such a foothold in our world. Alas—no longer *our* world, but the world of the dragons who have become supreme! Step by step, we have retreated and given up the globe which we had brought so near to complete civilization, given it up to our successors in time. The human history of the earth is closing its books.

Too late then for me to tell what I knew, and when I did, I found no one to believe me. No one would try my simple explanation and see if alligators could really be cured of their heart trouble and become dragons. The mere suggestion was dismissed at once on the grounds that acquired characteristics were not inherited, whereas these dragons bred true. In short, the idea was too ridiculous to be discussed seriously. The explanation that science handed down was that some dragon eggs, remaining for millions of years in the cold storage of the Arctic, had by chance been caught in the sweep of the glacier, had been carried down in the slow glacial movement to the sea, had thence, along with an iceberg, been carried off to sea and had floated down into the warmth of the tropics. On some tropical island shore the dragon eggs, still by miracle unbroken and unspoiled, had slowly been brooded to life by the warmth of the sun. This theory fitted in well with old tales of gigantic roc eggs and was generally accepted by science and laity alike.

I did not press my point, for what could be the value, at this late date, of knowing how to transform a comparatively harmless alligator into a dragon? Making more dragons, even in the name of research, was the silliest ever of all schemes to carry coals to Newcastle. Why, the world was full of them! Not a city, not a village, not the remotest hamlet but suffered their depredations. The dread fowl came down like a hawk upon chickens and carried off men, women and children, as well as cattle, and left only its horrid droppings as a final insult to the tragic survivors.

In vain mankind prayed. In vain ministers sermonized on the

Beast of the Apocalypse, the beast whose number was 666. In vain we turned to anti-aircraft guns, to explosive bullets, to poison gases, to gigantic traps. In vain, our most courageous aviators mounted the skies in pursuit of them. A thrash of their tails and man and his machine tumbled to the earth, while his bullets rattled harmlessly off the armor-like hide of the beast. It was useless to fight. We were beaten. And the wise ones were those who scurried off soonest to the best caves and mines. Farmers burrowed underground and tilled their fields in the darkest nights and did not trouble themselves to grow any more food than they could use. Famine added itself to the miseries of mankind. Our supply of coal gave out. Our electric power houses ceased to function. Turbines still ran while there were volunteers to brave the danger of running them and of repairing power lines. As long as our machines still held together they were used, but repairs grew more and more impossible. To work in the daylight was suicidal. At night, light was forbidden, for it immediately attracted a dragon out of the sky.

Evidently they bred rapidly. Not twenty years after Crabshaw's first specimen, thousands were counted. And the world of human life perished before their insatiable hunger, as once the world of animal life had perished before our advance. What we had done to buffalo and passenger pigeons was repaid by us in full measure.

Oh, where is now the Saint George that is to rid us of our scourge? Where the scientist with serum or innoculation that should wipe out these dragons? What? Will science fail us? Are we doomed, we, the last remnants of the human race who now exist in perpetual fear? At first how many and how bright were the reports of what we would do to the dragons: Reports of new types of guns. Of great steel spring nets. Of new and most potent gases, harmless to man but deadly to the great saurians. Of disease germs that were to be spread among them and wipe them out in one vast epidemic. Of poisoned bait. . . . Alas, all, all failed! Until even the most optimistic of us have lost heart. . . .

We ceased to hope and made the best of things, and quietly

blessed those valiant old New Yorkers who had constructed that so often ridiculed megalopolis with its impregnable fortress of skyscrapers and its marvelous network of underground passageways where we, besieged mankind, can make our last stand. Here we are safe for a time. That is to say, until famine gets us. We stave off that as best we can by utilizing every roof-top and planting countless window-boxes and developing whatever mushroom and other fungus growths will thrive in the dark. Here and there too, we grow food under ultra-violet light, but current is almost priceless. How long can we last, seeing that our existence is ultimately dependent on the constant excursions of volunteer corps who are ever risking their lives for the community? Our numbers grow daily less. A few, we are told by rare travelers, survive in the far north where dragons rarely go. A few survive in mines. No doubt there must be other communities, say in London, and Berlin and other places where there are extensive subways, but it is years since we have had any communication with them.

What is to be the end of all this, I ask myself. Are we to perish utterly? I think I shall cause this tale to be engraved on stone so that if ever the human race arises again, it may read and know how the damnable inferiority complex of one Paul Crabshaw made all mankind the prey of fabulous monsters.

The King of the Cats

STEPHEN VINCENT BENÉT

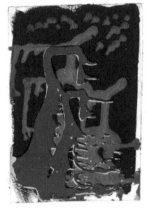

"But, my *dear,*" said Mrs. Culverin, with a tiny gasp, "you can't actually mean—a *tail!*"

Mrs. Dingle nodded impressively. "Exactly. I've seen him. Twice. Paris, of course, and then, a command appearance at Rome—we were in the Royal box. He conducted —my dear, you've never heard such effects from an orchestra— and, my dear," she hesitated slightly, "he conducted *with it.*"

"How perfectly, fascinatingly too horrid for words!" said Mrs. Culverin in a dazed but greedy voice. "We *must* have him to dinner as soon as he comes over—he is coming over, isn't he?"

"The twelfth," said Mrs. Dingle with a gleam in her eyes. "The New Symphony people have asked him to be guest-conductor for three special concerts—I do hope you can dine with *us* some night while he's here—he'll be very busy, of course—but he's promised to give us what time he can spare——"

"Oh, thank you, dear," said Mrs. Culverin, abstractedly, her last raid upon Mrs. Dingle's pet British novelist still fresh in her mind. "You're always so delightfully hospitable—but you mustn't wear yourself out—the rest of us must do *our* part—I know Henry and myself would be only too glad to——"

"That's very sweet of you, darling." Mrs. Dingle also remembered the larceny of the British novelist. "But we're just going to give Monsieur Tibault—sweet name, isn't it! They say he's descended from the Tybalt in 'Romeo and Juliet' and that's why he doesn't like Shakespeare—we're just going to give Monsieur Tibault the simplest sort of time—a little reception after his first concert, perhaps. He hates," she looked around the table, "large, mixed parties. And then, of course, his—er—little idiosyncrasy ——" she coughed delicately. "It makes him feel a trifle shy with strangers."

"But I don't understand yet, Aunt Emily," said Tommy Brooks, Mrs. Dingle's nephew. "Do you really mean this Tibault bozo has a tail? Like a monkey and everything?"

"Tommy dear," said Mrs. Culverin, crushingly, "in the first place Monsieur Tibault is not a bozo—he is a very distinguished musician—the finest conductor in Europe. And in the second place——"

"He has," Mrs. Dingle was firm. "He has a tail. He conducts with it."

"Oh, but honestly!" said Tommy, his ears pinkening. "I mean —of course, if you say so, Aunt Emily, I'm sure he has—but still, it sounds pretty steep, if you know what I mean! How about it, Professor Tatto?"

Professor Tatto cleared his throat. "Tck," he said, putting his fingertips together cautiously, "I shall be very anxious to see this Monsieur Tibault. For myself, I have never observed a genuine specimen of *homo caudatus,* so I should be inclined to doubt, and yet . . . In the Middle Ages, for instance, the belief in men—er— tailed or with caudal appendages of some sort, was both widespread and, as far as we can gather, well founded. As late as the Eighteenth Century, a Dutch sea-captain with some character for veracity recounts the discovery of a pair of such creatures in the island of Formosa. They were in a low state of civilization, I believe, but the appendages in question were quite distinct. And in 1860, Dr. Grimbrook, the English surgeon, claims to have treated no less than three African natives with short but evident

tails—though his testimony rests upon his unsupported word. After all, the thing is not impossible, though doubtless unusual. Web feet—rudimentary gills—these occur with some frequency. The appendix we have with us always. The chain of our descent from the ape-like form is by no means complete. For that matter," he beamed around the table, "what can we call the last few vertebrae of the normal spine but the beginnings of a concealed and rudimentary tail? Oh, yes—yes—it's possible—quite—that in an extraordinary case—a reversion to type—a survival—though, of course——"

"I told you so," said Mrs. Dingle triumphantly. *"Isn't* it fascinating? Isn't it, Princess?"

The Princess Vivrakanarda's eyes, blue as a field of larkspur, fathomless as the centre of heaven, rested lightly for a moment on Mrs. Dingle's excited countenance.

"Ve-ry fascinating," she said, in a voice like stroked, golden velvet. "I should like—I should like ve-ry much to meet this Monsieur Tibault."

"Well, *I* hope he breaks his neck!" said Tommy Brooks, under his breath—but nobody ever paid much attention to Tommy.

Nevertheless as the time for Mr. Tibault's arrival in these States drew nearer and nearer, people in general began to wonder whether the Princess had spoken quite truthfully—for there was no doubt of the fact that, up till then, she had been the unique sensation of the season—and you know what social lions and lionesses are.

It was, if you remember, a Siamese season, and genuine Siamese were at quite as much of a premium as Russian accents had been in the quaint old days when the Chauve-Souris was a novelty. The Siamese Art Theatre, imported at terrific expense, was playing to packed houses. "Gushuptzgu," an epic novel of Siamese farm life, in nineteen closely-printed volumes, had just been awarded the Nobel prize. Prominent pet-and-newt dealers reported no cessation in the appalling demand for Siamese cats. And upon the crest of this wave of interest in things Siamese, the Princess Vivrakanarda poised with the elegant nonchalance of a

Hawaiian water-baby upon its surfboard. She was indispensable. She was incomparable. She was everywhere.

Youthful, enormously wealthy, allied on one hand to the Royal Family of Siam and on the other to the Cabots (and yet with the first eighteen of her twenty-one years shrouded from speculation in a golden zone of mystery), the mingling of races in her had produced an exotic beauty as distinguished as it was strange. She moved with a feline, effortless grace, and her skin was as if it had been gently powdered with tiny grains of the purest gold—yet the blueness of her eyes, set just a trifle slant-ingly, was as pure and startling as the sea on the rocks of Maine. Her brown hair fell to her knees—she had been offered extra-ordinary sums by the Master Barbers' Protective Association to have it shingled. Straight as a waterfall tumbling over brown rocks, it had a vague perfume of sandalwood and suave spices and held tints of rust and the sun. She did not talk very much—but then she did not have to—her voice had an odd, small, melo-dious huskiness that haunted the mind. She lived alone and was reputed to be very lazy—at least it was known that she slept dur-ing most of the day—but at night she bloomed like a moonflower and a depth came into her eyes.

It was no wonder that Tommy Brooks fell in love with her. The wonder was that she let him. There was nothing exotic or distinguished about Tommy—he was just one of those pleasant, normal young men who seemed created to carry on the bond business by reading the newspapers in the University Club dur-ing most the day, and can always be relied upon at night to fill an unexpected hole in a dinner-party. It is true that the Princess could hardly be said to do more than tolerate any of her suitors —no one had ever seen those aloofly arrogant eyes enliven at the entrance of any male. But she seemed to be able to tolerate Tommy a little more than the rest—and that young man's infat-uated day-dreams were beginning to be beset by smart solitaires and imaginary apartments on Park Avenue, when the famous M. Tibault conducted his first concert at Carnegie Hall.

Tommy Brooks sat beside the Princess. The eyes he turned

upon her were eyes of longing and love, but her face was as im-
passive as a mask, and the only remark she made during the
preliminary bustlings was that there seemed to be a number of
people in the audience. But Tommy was relieved, if anything, to
find her even a little more aloof than usual, for, ever since Mrs.
Culverin's dinner-party, a vague disquiet as to the possible impression which this Tibault creature might make upon her had
been growing in his mind. It shows his devotion that he was present at all. To a man whose simple Princetonian nature found in
"Just a Little Love, a Little Kiss," the quintessence of musical
art, the average symphony was a positive torture, and he looked
forward to the evening's programme itself with a grim, brave
smile.

"Ssh!" said Mrs. Dingle, breathlessly. "He's coming!" It seemed
to the startled Tommy as if he were suddenly back in the
trenches under a heavy barrage, as M. Tibault made his entrance
to a perfect bombardment of applause.

Then the enthusiastic noise was sliced off in the middle and a
gasp took its place—a vast, windy sigh, as if every person in that
multitude had suddenly said, "Ah." For the papers had not lied
about him. The tail was there.

They called him theatric—but how well he understood the
uses of theatricalism! Dressed in unrelieved black from head to
foot (the black dress-shirt had been a special token of Mussolini's
esteem), he did not walk on, he strolled, leisurely, easily, aloofly,
the famous tail curled nonchalantly about one wrist—a suave,
black panther lounging through a summer garden with that little
mysterious weave of the head that panthers have when they pad
behind bars—the glittering darkness of his eyes unmoved by any
surprise or elation. He nodded, twice, in regal acknowledgment,
as the clapping reached an apogee of frenzy. To Tommy there
was something dreadfully reminiscent of the Princess in the way
he nodded. Then he turned to his orchestra.

A second and louder gasp went up from the audience at this
point, for, as he turned, the tip of that incredible tail twined with
dainty carelessness into some hidden pocket and produced a
black baton. But Tommy did not even notice. He was looking at

the Princess instead.

She had not even bothered to clap, at first, but now—He had never seen her moved like this, never. She was not applauding, her hands were clenched in her lap, but her whole body was rigid, rigid as a steel bar, and the blue flowers of her eyes were bent upon the figure of M. Tibault in a terrible concentration. The pose of her entire figure was so still and intense that for an instant Tommy had the lunatic idea that any moment she might leap from her seat beside him as lightly as a moth, and land, with no sound, at M. Tibault's side to—yes—to rub her proud head against his coat in worship. Even Mrs. Dingle would notice in a moment.

"Princess——" he said, in a horrified whisper, "Princess——"

Slowly the tenseness of her body relaxed, her eyes veiled again, she grew calm.

"Yes, Tommy?" she said, in her usual voice, but there was still something about her . . .

"Nothing, only—oh, hang—he's starting!" said Tommy, as M. Tibault, his hands loosely clasped before him, turned and *faced* the audience. His eyes dropped, his tail switched once impressively, then gave three little preliminary taps with his baton on the floor.

Seldom has Gluck's overture to "Iphigenie in Aulis" received such an ovation. But it was not until the Eighth Symphony that the hysteria of the audience reached its climax. Never before had the New Symphony played so superbly—and certainly never before had it been led with such genius. Three prominent conductors in the audience were sobbing with the despairing admiration of envious children toward the close, and one at least was heard to offer wildly ten thousand dollars to a well-known facial surgeon there present for a shred of evidence that tails of some variety could by any stretch of science be grafted upon a normally decaudate form. There was no doubt about it—no mortal hand and arm, be they ever so dexterous, could combine the delicate elan and powerful grace displayed in every gesture of M. Tibault's tail.

A sable staff, it dominated the brasses like a flicker of black lightning; an ebon, elusive whip, it drew the last exquisite breath of melody from the woodwinds and ruled the stormy strings like a magician's rod. M. Tibault bowed and bowed again—roar after roar of frenzied admiration shook the hall to its foundations— and when he finally staggered, exhausted, from the platform, the president of the Wednesday Sonata Club was only restrained by force from flinging her ninety-thousand-dollar string of pearls after him in an excess of aesthetic appreciation. New York had come and seen—and New York was conquered. Mrs. Dingle was immediately besieged by reporters, and Tommy Brooks looked forward to the "little party" at which he was to meet the new hero of the hour with feelings only a little less lugubrious than those that would have come to him just before taking his seat in the electric chair.

The meeting between his Princess and M. Tibault was worse and better than he expected. Better because, after all, they did not say much to each other—and worse because it seemed to him, somehow, that some curious kinship of mind between them made words unnecessary. They were certainly the most distinguished-looking couple in the room, as he bent over her hand. "So daringly foreign, both of them, and yet so different," babbled Mrs. Dingle—but Tommy couldn't agree.

They were different, yes—the dark, lithe stranger with the bizarre appendage tucked carelessly in his pocket, and the blue-eyed, brown-haired girl. But that difference only accentuated what they had in common—something in the way they moved, in the suavity of their gestures, in the set of their eyes. Something deeper, even, than race. He tried to puzzle it out—then, looking around at the others, he had a flash of revelation. It was as if that couple were foreign, indeed—not only to New York but to all common humanity. As if they were polite guests from a different star.

Tommy did not have a very happy evening, on the whole. But his mind worked slowly, and it was not until much later that the mad suspicion came upon him in full force.

Perhaps he is not to be blamed for his lack of immediate comprehension. The next few weeks were weeks of bewildered misery for him. It was not that the Princess's attitude toward him had changed—she was just as tolerant of him as before, but M. Tibault was always there. He had a faculty of appearing, as out of thin air—he walked, for all his height, as lightly as a butterfly—and Tommy grew to hate the faintest shuffle on the carpet that announced his presence.

And then, hang it all, the man was so smooth, so infernally, unruffably smooth! He was never out of temper, never embarrassed. He treated Tommy with the extreme of urbanity, and yet his eyes mocked, deep-down, and Tommy could do nothing. And, gradually, the Princess became more and more drawn to this stranger, in a soundless communion that found little need for speech—and that, too, Tommy saw and hated, and that, too, he could not mend.

He began to be haunted not only by M. Tibault in the flesh, but by M. Tibault in the spirit. He slept badly, and when he slept, he dreamed—of M. Tibault, a man no longer, but a shadow, a spectre, the limber ghost of an animal whose words came purringly between sharp little pointed teeth. There was certainly something odd about the whole shape of the fellow—his fluid ease, the mould of his head, even the cut of his fingernails—but just what it was escaped Tommy's intensest cogitation. And when he did put his finger on it at length, at first he refused to believe.

A pair of petty incidents decided him, finally, against all reason. He had gone to Mrs. Dingle's, one winter afternoon, hoping to find the Princess. She was out with his aunt, but was expected back for tea, and he wandered idly into the library to wait. He was just about to switch on the lights, for the library was always dark even in summer, when he heard a sound of light breathing that seemed to come from the leather couch in the corner. He approached it cautiously and dimly made out the form of M. Tibault, curled up on the couch, peacefully asleep.

The sight annoyed Tommy so that he swore under his breath and was back near the door on his way out, when the feeling we all know and hate, the feeling that eyes we cannot see are watching us, arrested him. He turned back—M. Tibault had not moved a muscle of his body to all appearance—but his eyes were open now. And those eyes were black and human no longer. They were green—Tommy could have sworn it—and he could have sworn that they had no bottom and gleamed like little emeralds in the dark: It only lasted a moment, for Tommy pressed the light-button automatically—and there was M. Tibault, his normal self, yawning a little but urbanely apologetic, but it gave Tommy time to think. Nor did what happened a trifle later increase his peace of mind.

They had lit a fire and were talking in front of it—by now Tommy hated M. Tibault so thoroughly that he felt that odd yearning for his company that often occurs in such cases. M. Tibault was telling some anecdote and Tommy was hating him worse than ever for basking with such obvious enjoyment in the heat of the flames and the ripple of his own voice.

Then they heard the street-door open, and M. Tibault jumped up—and jumping, caught one sock on a sharp corner of the brass fire-rail and tore it open in a jagged flap. Tommy looked down mechanically at the tear—a second's glance, but enough—for M. Tibault, for the first time in Tommy's experience, lost his temper completely. He swore violently in some spitting, foreign tongue—his face distorted suddenly—he clapped his hand over his sock. Then, glaring furiously at Tommy, he fairly sprang from the room, and Tommy could hear him scaling the stairs in long, agile bounds.

Tommy sank into a chair, careless for once of the fact that he heard the Princess's light laugh in the hall. He didn't want to see the Princess. He didn't want to see anybody. There had been something revealed when M. Tibault had torn that hole in his sock—and it was not the skin of a man. Tommy had caught a glimpse of—black plush. Black velvet. And then had come M. Tibault's sudden explosion of fury. Good *Lord*—did the man wear

black velvet stockings under his ordinary socks? Or could he—
could he—but here Tommy held his fevered head in his hands.

He went to Professor Tatto that evening with a series of hypothetical questions, but as he did not dare confide his real suspicions to the Professor, the hypothetical answers he received served
only to confuse him the more. Then he thought of Billy Strange.
Billy was a good sort, and his mind had a turn for the bizarre.
Billy might be able to help.

He couldn't get hold of Billy for three days and lived through
the interval in a fever of impatience. But finally they had dinner
together at Billy's apartment, where his queer books were, and
Tommy was able to blurt out the whole disordered jumble of his
suspicions.

Billy listened without interrupting until Tommy was quite
through. Then he pulled at his pipe. "But, my dear *man*——" he
said, protestingly.

"Oh, I know—I know——" said Tommy, and waved his
hands, "I know I'm crazy—you needn't tell me that—but I tell
you, the man's a cat all the same—no, I don't see how he could
be, but he is—why, hang it, in the first place, everybody knows
he's got a tail!"

"Even so," said Billy, puffing. "Oh, my dear Tommy, I don't
doubt you saw, or think you saw, everything you say. But, even
so——" He shook his head.

"But what about those other birds, werwolves and things?"
said Tommy.

Billy looked dubious. "We-ll," he admitted, "you've got me
there, of course. At least—a tailed man *is* possible. And the yarns
about werwolves go back far enough, so that—well, I wouldn't
say there aren't or haven't been werwolves—but then I'm willing
to believe more things than most people. But a wer-cat—or a
man that's a cat and a cat that's a man—honestly, Tommy——"

"If I don't get some real advice I'll go clean off my hinge. For
Heaven's sake, tell me something to *do!*"

"Lemme think," said Billy. "First, you're pizen-sure this man
is——"

"A cat. Yeah," and Tommy nodded violently.

"Check. And second—if it doesn't hurt your feelings, Tommy —you're afraid this girl you're in love with has—er—at least a streak of—felinity—in her—and so she's drawn to him?"

"Oh, Lord, Billy, if I only knew!"

"Well—er—suppose she really is, too, you know—would you still be keen on her?"

"I'd marry her if she turned into a dragon every Wednesday!" said Tommy, fervently.

Billy smiled. "H'm," he said, "then the obvious thing to do is to get rid of this M. Tibault. Lemme think."

He thought about two pipes full, while Tommy sat on pins and needles. Then, finally, he burst out laughing.

"What's so darn funny?" said Tommy, aggrievedly.

"Nothing, Tommy, only I've just thought of a stunt—something so blooming crazy—but if he is—h'm—what you think he is—it *might* work——" And, going to the bookcase, he took down a book.

"If you think you're going to quiet my nerves by reading me a bedtime story——"

"Shut up, Tommy, and listen to this—if you really want to get rid of your feline friend."

"What is it?"

"Book of Agnes Repplier's. About cats. Listen.

" 'There is also a Scandinavian version of the ever famous story which Sir Walter Scott told to Washington Irving, which Monk Lewis told to Shelley and which, in one form or another, we find embodied in the folklore of every land'—now, Tommy, pay attention—'the story of the traveller who saw within a ruined abbey, a procession of cats, lowering into a grave a little coffin with a crown upon it. Filled with horror, he hastened from the spot; but when he had reached his destination, he could not forbear relating to a friend the wonder he had seen. Scarcely had the tale been told when his friend's cat, who lay curled up tranquilly by the fire, sprang to its feet, cried out, "Then I am the King of the Cats!" and disappeared in a flash up the chimney.'

"Well?" said Billy, shutting the book.

"By gum!" said Tommy, staring. "By gum! Do you think there's a chance?"

"*I* think we're both in the booby-hatch. But if you want to try it——"

"Try it! I'll spring it on him the next time I see him. But— listen—I can't make it a ruined abbey——"

"Oh, use your imagination! Make it Central Park—anywhere. Tell it as if it happened to you—seeing the funeral procession and all that. You can lead into it somehow—let's see—some general line—oh, yes—'Strange, isn't it, how fact so often copies fiction. Why, only yesterday——' See?"

"Strange, isn't it, how fact so often copies fiction," repeated Tommy dutifully. "Why, only yesterday——"

"I happened to be strolling through Central Park when I saw something very odd."

"I happened to be strolling through—here, gimme that book!" said Tommy. "I want to learn the rest of it by heart!"

Mrs. Dingle's farewell dinner to the famous Monsieur Tibault, on the occasion of his departure for his Western tour, was looked forward to with the greatest expectations. Not only would everybody be there, including the Princess Vivrakanarda, but Mrs. Dingle, a hinter if there ever was one, had let it be known that at this dinner an announcement of very unusual interest to Society might be made. So everyone, for once, was almost on time, except for Tommy. He was at least fifteen minutes early, for he wanted to have speech with his aunt alone. Unfortunately, however, he had hardly taken off his overcoat when she was whispering some news in his ear so rapidly that he found it difficult to understand a word of it.

"And you mustn't breathe it to a soul!" she ended, beaming. "That is, not before the announcement—I think we'll have *that* with the salad—people never pay very much attention to salad——"

"Breathe what, Aunt Emily?" said Tommy, confused.

"The Princess, darling—the dear Princess and Monsieur

Tibault—they just got engaged this afternoon, dear things! Isn't it *fascinating?*"

"Yeah," said Tommy, and started to walk blindly through the nearest door. His aunt restrained him.

"Not there, dear—not in the library. You can congratulate them later. They're just having a sweet little moment alone there now——" And she turned away to harry the butler, leaving Tommy stunned.

But his chin came up after a moment. He wasn't beaten yet.

"Strange, isn't it, how often fact copies fiction?" he repeated to himself in dull mnemonics, and, as he did so, he shook his fist at the library door.

Mrs. Dingle was wrong, as usual. The Princess and M. Tibault were not in the library—they were in the conservatory, as Tommy discovered when he wandered aimlessly past the glass doors.

He didn't mean to look, and after a second he turned away. But that second was enough.

Tibault was seated in a chair and she was crouched on a stool at his side, while his hand, softly, smoothly, stroked her brown hair. Black cat and Siamese kitten. Her face was hidden from Tommy, but he could see Tibault's face. And he could hear.

They were not talking, but there was a sound between them. A warm and contented sound like the murmur of giant bees in a hollow tree—a golden, musical rumble, deep-throated, that came from Tibault's lips and was answered by hers—a golden purr.

Tommy found himself back in the drawing-room, shaking hands with Mrs. Culverin, who said, frankly, that she had seldom seen him look so pale.

The first two courses of the dinner passed Tommy like dreams, but Mrs. Dingle's cellar was notable, and by the middle of the meat course, he began to come to himself. He had only one re-solve now.

For the next few moments he tried desperately to break into the conversation, but Mrs. Dingle was talking, and even Gabriel will have a time interrupting Mrs. Dingle. At last, though, she paused for breath and Tommy saw his chance.

"Speaking of that," said Tommy, piercingly, without knowing in the least what he was referring to, "Speaking of that——"

"As I was saying," said Professor Tatto. But Tommy would not yield. The plates were being taken away. It was time for salad.

"Speaking of that," he said again, so loudly and strangely that Mrs. Culverin jumped and an awkward hush fell over the table. "Strange, isn't it, how often fact copies fiction?" There, he was started. His voice rose even higher. "Why, only to-day I was strolling through——" and, word for word, he repeated his lesson. He could see Tibault's eyes glowing at him, as he described the funeral. He could see the Princess, tense.

He could not have said what he had expected might happen when he came to the end; but it was not bored silence, everywhere, to be followed by Mrs. Dingle's acrid, "Well, Tommy, is that *quite* all?"

He slumped back in his chair, sick at heart. He was a fool and his last resource had failed. Dimly he heard his aunt's voice, saying, "Well, then——" and realized that she was about to make the fatal announcement.

But just then Monsieur Tibault spoke.

"One moment, Mrs. Dingle," he said, with extreme politeness, and she was silent. He turned to Tommy.

"You are—positive, I suppose, of what you saw this afternoon, Brooks?" he said, in tones of light mockery.

"Absolutely," said Tommy sullenly. "Do you think I'd——"

"Oh, no, no, no," Monsieur Tibault waved the implication aside, "but—such an interesting story—one likes to be sure of the details—and, of course, you *are* sure—*quite* sure—that the kind of crown you describe was on the coffin?"

"Of course," said Tommy, wondering, "but——"

"Then I'm the King of the Cats!" cried Monsieur Tibault in a voice of thunder, and, even as he cried it, the house-lights blinked —there was the soft thud of an explosion that seemed muffled in cotton-wool from the minstrel gallery—and the scene was lit for a second by an obliterating and painful burst of light that vanished in an instant and was succeeded by heavy, blinding clouds of white, pungent smoke.

"Oh, those *horrid* photographers," came Mrs. Dingle's voice in a melodious wail. "I *told* them not to take the flashlight picture till dinner was over, and now they've taken it *just* as I was nibbling lettuce!"

Someone tittered a little nervously. Someone coughed. Then, gradually the veils of smoke dislimned and the green-and-black spots in front of Tommy's eyes died away.

They were blinking at each other like people who have just come out of a cave into brilliant sun. Even yet their eyes stung with the fierceness of that abrupt illumination and Tommy found it hard to make out the faces across the table from him.

Mrs. Dingle took command of the half-blinded company with her accustomed poise. She rose, glass in hand. "And now, dear friends," she said in a clear voice, "I'm sure all of us are very happy to——" Then she stopped, open-mouthed, an expression of incredulous horror on her features. The lifted glass began to spill its contents on the tablecloth in a little stream of amber. As she spoke, she had turned directly to Monsieur Tibault's place at the table—and Monsieur Tibault was no longer there.

Some say there was a bursting flash of fire that disappeared up the chimney—some say it was a giant cat that leaped through the window at a bound, without breaking the glass. Professor Tatto puts it down to a mysterious chemical disturbance operating only over M. Tibault's chair. The butler, who is pious, believes the devil in person flew away with him, and Mrs. Dingle hesitates between witchcraft and a malicious ectoplasm dematerializing on the wrong cosmic plane. But be that as it may, one thing is certain—in the instant of fictive darkness which followed the glare of the flashlight, Monsieur Tibault, the great conductor, disappeared forever from mortal sight, tail and all.

Mrs. Culverin swears he was an international burglar and that she was just about to unmask him, when he slipped away under cover of the flashlight smoke, but no one else who sat at that historic dinner-table believes her. No, there are no sound explanations, but Tommy thinks he knows, and he will never be able to pass a cat again without wondering.

Mrs. Tommy is quite of her husband's mind regarding cats—she was Gretchen Woolwine, of Chicago—for Tommy told her his whole story, and while she doesn't believe a great deal of it, there is no doubt in her heart that one person concerned in the affair was a *perfect* cat. Doubtless it would have been more romantic to relate how Tommy's daring finally won him his Princess—but, unfortunately, it would not be veracious. For the Princess Vivrakanarda, also, is with us no longer. Her nerves, shattered by the spectacular denouement of Mrs. Dingle's dinner, required a sea-voyage, and from that voyage she has never returned to America.

Of course, there are the usual stories—one hears of her, a nun in a Siamese convent, or a masked dancer at Le Jardin de ma Soeur—one hears that she has been murdered in Patagonia or married in Trebizond—but, as far as can be ascertained, not one of these gaudy fables has the slightest basis of fact. I believe that Tommy, in his heart of hearts, is quite convinced that the sea-voyage was only a pretext, and that by some unheard-of means, she has managed to rejoin the formidable Monsieur Tibault, wherever in the world of the visible or the invisible he may be—in fact, that in some ruined city or subterranean palace they reign together now, King and Queen of all the mysterious Kingdom of Cats. But that, of course, is quite impossible.

Slime

JOSEPH PAYNE BRENNAN

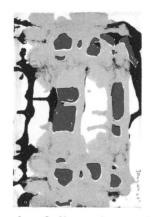

It was a great gray-black hood of horror moving over the floor of the sea. It slid through the soft ooze like a monstrous mantle of slime obscenely animated with questing life. It was by turns viscid and fluid. At times it flattened out and flowed through the carpet of mud like an inky pool; occasionally it paused, seeming to shrink in upon itself, and reared up out of the ooze until it resembled an irregular cone or a gigantic hood. Although it possessed no eyes, it had a marvelously developed sense of touch, and it possessed a sensitivity to minute vibrations which was almost akin to telepathy. It was plastic, essentially shapeless. It could shoot out long tentacles, until it bore a resemblance to a nightmare squid or a huge starfish; it could retract itself into a round flattened disk, or squeeze into an irregular hunched shape so that it looked like a black boulder sunk on the bottom of the sea.

It had prowled the black water endlessly. It had been formed when the earth and the seas were young; it was almost as old as the ocean itself. It moved through a night which had no beginning and no dissolution. The black sea basin where it lurked had been dark since the world began—an environment only a little less inimical than the stupendous gulfs of interplanetary space.

It was animated by a single, unceasing, never-satisfied drive: a voracious, insatiable hunger. It could survive for months without food, but minutes after eating it was as ravenous as ever. Its appetite was appalling and incalculable.

On the icy ink-black floor of the sea the battle for survival was savage, hideous—and usually brief. But for the shape of moving slime there was no battle. It ate whatever came its way, regardless of size, shape or disposition. It absorbed microscopic plankton and giant squid with equal assurance. Had its surface been less fluid, it might have retained the circular scars left by the grappling suckers of the wildly threshing deep-water squid, or the jagged toothmarks of the anachronistic frillshark, but as it was, neither left any evidence of its absorption. When the lifting curtain of living slime swayed out of the mud and closed upon them, their fiercest death throes came to nothing.

The horror did not know fear. There was nothing to be afraid of. It ate whatever moved, or tried not to move, and it had never encountered anything which could in turn eat it. If a squid's sucker, or a shark's tooth, tore into the mass of its viscosity, the rent flowed in upon itself and immediately closed. If a segment was detached, it could be retrieved and absorbed back into the whole.

The black mantle reigned supreme in its savage world of slime and silence. It groped greedily and endlessly through the mud, eating and never sleeping, never resting. If it lay still, it was only to trap food which might otherwise be lost. If it rushed with terrifying speed across the slimy bottom, it was never to escape an enemy, but always to flop its hideous fluidity upon its sole and inevitable quarry—food.

It had evolved out of the muck and slime of the primitive sea floor, and it was as alien to ordinary terrestrial life as the weird denizens of some wild planet in a distant galaxy. It was an anachronistic experiment of nature compared to which the saber-toothed tiger, the woolly mammoth and even Tyrannosaurus, the slashing, murderous king of the great earth reptiles, were as tame, weak entities.

Had it not been for a vast volcanic upheaval on the bottom of the ocean basin, the black horror would have crept out its entire existence on the silent sea ooze without ever manifesting its hideous powers to mankind.

Fate, in the form of a violent subterranean explosion, covering huge areas of the ocean's floor, hurled it out of its black slime world and sent it spinning toward the surface.

Had it been an ordinary deep-water fish, it never would have survived the experience. The explosion itself, or the drastic lessening of water pressure as it shot toward the surface, would have destroyed it. But it was no ordinary fish. Its viscosity, or plasticity, or whatever it was that constituted its essentially amoebic structure, permitted it to survive.

It reached the surface slightly stunned and flopped on the surging waters like a great blob of black blubber. Immense waves stirred up by the subterranean explosion swept it swiftly toward shore, and because it was somewhat stunned it did not try to resist the roaring mountains of water.

Along with scattered ash, pumice and the puffed bodies of dead fish, the black horror was hurled toward a beach. The huge waves carried it more than a mile inland, far beyond the strip of sandy shore, and deposited it in the midst of a deep brackish swamp area.

As luck would have it, the submarine explosion and subsequent tidal wave took place at night, and therefore the slime horror was not immediately subjected to a new and hateful experience —light.

Although the midnight darkness of the storm-lashed swamp did not begin to compare with the stygian blackness of the sea bottom where even violet rays of the spectrum could not penetrate, the marsh darkness was nevertheless deep and intense.

As the water of the great wave receded, sluicing through the thorn jungle and back out to sea, the black horror clung to a mud bank surrounded by a rank growth of cattails. It was aware of the sudden, startling change in its environment and for some time it lay motionless, concentrating its attention on obscure internal readjustment which the absence of crushing pressure and a surrounding cloak of frigid sea water demanded. Its adaptability was incredible and horrifying. It achieved in a few hours what an ordinary creature could have attained only through a process of gradual evolution. Three hours after the titanic wave flopped it onto the mud bank, it had undergone swift organic changes which left it relatively at ease in its new environment.

In fact, it felt lighter and more mobile than it ever had before in its sea basin existence.

As it flung out feelers and attuned itself to the minutest vibrations and emanations of the swamp area, its pristine hunger drive reasserted itself with overwhelming urgency. And the tale which its sensory apparatus returned to the monstrous something which served it as a brain, excited it tremendously. It sensed at once that the swamp was filled with luscious tidbits of quivering food —more food, and food of a greater variety than it had ever encountered on the cold floor of the sea.

Its savage, incessant hunger seemed unbearable. Its slimy mass was swept by a shuddering wave of anticipation.

Sliding off the mud bank, it slithered over the cattails into an adjacent area consisting of deep black pools interspersed with water-logged tussocks. Weed stalks stuck up out of the water and the decayed trunks of fallen trees floated half-submerged in the larger pools.

Ravenous with hunger, it sloshed into the bog area, flicking its fluid tentacles about. Within minutes it had snatched up several fat frogs and a number of small fish. These, however, merely titillated its appetite. Its hunger turned into a kind of ecstatic fury. It commenced a systematic hunt, plunging to the bottom of each pool and quickly but carefully exploring every inch of its oozy bottom. The first creature of any size which it encountered was a muskrat. An immense curtain of adhesive slime suddenly swept out of the darkness, closed upon it—and squeezed.

Heartened and whetted by its find, the hood of horror rum-

maged the rank pools with renewed zeal. When it surfaced, it carefully probed the tussocks for anything that might have escaped it in the water. Once it snatched up a small bird nesting in some swamp grass. Occasionally it slithered up the crisscrossed trunks of fallen trees, bearing them down with its unspeakable slimy bulk, and hung briefly suspended like a great dripping curtain of black marsh mud.

It was approaching a somewhat less swampy and more deeply wooded area when it gradually became aware of a subtle change in its new environment. It paused, hesitating, and remained half in and half out of a small pond near the edge of the nearest trees.

Although it had absorbed twenty-five or thirty pounds of food in the form of frogs, fish, water snakes, the muskrat and a few smaller creatures, its fierce hunger had not left it. Its monstrous appetite urged it on, and yet something held it anchored in the pond.

What it sensed, but could not literally see, was the rising sun spreading a gray light over the swamp. The horror had never encountered any illumination except that generated by the grotesque phosphorescent appendages of various deep-sea fishes. Natural light was totally unknown to it.

As the dawn light strengthened, breaking through the scattering storm clouds, the black slime monster fresh from the inky floor of the sea sensed that something utterly unknown was flooding in upon it. Light was hateful to it. It cast out quick feelers, hoping to catch and crush the light. But the more frenzied its efforts became, the more intense became the abhorred aura surrounding it.

At length, as the sun rose visibly above the trees, the horror, in baffled rage rather than in fear, grudgingly slid back into the pond and burrowed into the soft ooze of its bottom. There it remained while the sun shone and the small creatures of the swamp ventured forth on furtive errands.

A few miles away from Wharton's Swamp, in the small town of Clinton Center, Henry Hossing sleepily crawled out of the improvised alley shack which had afforded him a degree of shelter for the night and stumbled into the street. Passing a hand across his rheumy eyes, he scratched the stubble on his cheek and blinked listlessly at the rising sun. He had not slept well; the storm of the night before had kept him awake. Besides he had gone to bed hungry, and that never agreed with him.

Glancing furtively along the street, he walked slouched forward, with his head bent down, and most of the time he kept his eyes on the walk or on the gutter in the hopes of spotting a chance coin.

Clinton Center had not been kind to him. The handouts were sparse, and only yesterday he had been warned out of town by one of the local policemen.

Grumbling to himself, he reached the end of the street and started to cross. Suddenly he stooped quickly and snatched up something from the edge of the pavement.

It was a crumpled green bill, and as he frantically unfolded it, a look of stupefied rapture spread across his bristly face. Ten dollars! More money than he had possessed at any one time in months!

Stowing it carefully in the one good pocket of his seedy gray jacket, he crossed the street with a swift stride. Instead of sweeping the sidewalks, his eyes now darted along the rows of stores and restaurants.

He paused at one restaurant, hesitated, and finally went on until he found another less pretentious one a few blocks away.

When he sat down, the counterman shook his head. "Get goin', bud. No free coffee today."

With a wide grin, the hobo produced his ten-dollar bill and spread it on the counter. "That covers a good breakfast here, pardner?"

The counterman seemed irritated. "O.K. O.K. What'll you have?" He eyed the bill suspiciously.

Henry Hossing ordered orange juice, toast, ham and eggs, oatmeal, melon and coffee.

When it appeared, he ate every bit of it, ordered three additional cups of coffee, paid the check as if two-dollar breakfasts were customary with him, and then sauntered back to the street.

Shortly after noon, after his three-dollar lunch, he saw the liquor store. For a few minutes he stood across the street from it, fingering his five-dollar bill. Finally he crossed with an abstracted smile, entered and bought a quart of rye.

He hesitated on the sidewalk, debating whether or not he should return to the little shack in the side alley. After a minute or two of indecision, he decided against it and struck out instead for Wharton's Swamp. The local police were far less likely to disturb him there, and since the skies were clearing and the weather mild, there was little immediate need of shelter.

Angling off the highway which skirted the swamp several miles from town, he crossed a marshy meadow, pushed through a fringe of brush and sat down under a sweet-gum tree which bordered a deeply wooded area.

By late afternoon he had achieved a quite cheerful glow, and he had little inclination to return to Clinton Center. Rousing himself from reverie, he stumbled about collecting enough wood for a small fire and went back to his sylvan seat under the sweet-gum.

He slept briefly as dusk descended, but finally bestirred himself again to build a fire, as deeper shadows fell over the swamp. Then he returned to his swiftly diminishing bottle. He was suspended in a warm net of inflamed fantasy when something abruptly broke the spell and brought him back to earth.

The flickering flames of his fire had dwindled down until now only a dim eerie glow illuminated the immediate area under the sweet-gum. He saw nothing and at the moment heard nothing and yet he was filled with a sudden and profound sense of lurking menace.

He stood up, staggering, leaned back against the sweet-gum and peered fearfully into the shadows. In the deep darkness beyond the waning arc of firelight he could distinguish nothing which had any discernible form or color.

Then he detected the stench and shuddered. In spite of the

reek of cheap whiskey which clung around him, the smell was overpowering. It was a fulsome fetidness, alien and utterly repellent. It was vaguely fishlike, but otherwise beyond any known comparison.

As he stood trembling under the sweet-gum, Henry Hossing thought of something dead which had lain for long ages at the bottom of the sea.

Filled with mounting alarm, he looked around for some wood which he might add to the dying fire. All he could find nearby however were a few twigs. He threw these on and the flames licked up briefly and subsided.

He listened and heard—or imagined he heard—an odd sort of slithering sound in the nearby bushes. It seemed to retreat slightly as the flames shot up.

Genuine terror took possession of him. He knew that he was in no condition to flee—and now he came to the horrifying conclusion that whatever unspeakable menace waited in the surrounding darkness was temporarily held at bay only by the failing gleam of his little fire.

Frantically he looked around for more wood. But there was none. None, that is, within the faint glow of firelight. And he dared not venture beyond.

He began to tremble uncontrollably. He tried to scream but no sound came out of his tightened throat.

The ghastly stench became stronger, and now he was sure that he could hear a strange sliding, slithering sound in the black shadows beyond the remaining spark of firelight.

He stood frozen in absolute helpless panic as the tiny fire smouldered down into darkness.

At the last instant a charred bit of wood broke apart, sending up a few sparks, and in that flicker of final light he glimpsed the horror.

It had already glided out of the bushes and now it rushed across the small clearing with nightmare speed. It was a final incarnation of all the fears, shuddering apprehensions and bad dreams which Henry Hossing had ever known in his life. It was a fiend from the pit of Hell come to claim him at last.

A terrible ringing scream burst from his throat, but it was smothered before it was finished as the black shape of slime fastened upon him with irresistible force.

Giles Gowse—"Old Man" Gowse—got out of bed after eight hours of fitful tossing and intermittent nightmares and grouchily brewed coffee in the kitchen of his dilapidated farmhouse on the edge of Wharton's Swamp. Half the night, it seemed, the stench of stale sea-water had permeated the house. His interrupted sleep had been full of foreboding, full of shadowy and evil portents.

Muttering to himself, he finished breakfast, took a milk pail from the pantry and started for the barn where he kept his single cow.

As he approached the barn, the strange offensive odor which had plagued him during the night assailed his nostrils anew.

"Wharton's Swamp! That's what it is!" he told himself. And he shook his fist at it.

When he entered the barn the stench was stronger than ever. Scowling, he strode toward the rickety stall where he kept the cow, Sarey.

Then he stood still and stared. Sarey was gone. The stall was empty.

He re-entered the barnyard. "Sarey!" he called.

Rushing back into the barn, he inspected the stall. The rancid reek of the sea was strong here and now he noticed a kind of shine on the floor. Bending closer, he saw that it was a slick coat of glistening slime, as if some unspeakable creature covered with ooze had crept in and out of the stall.

This discovery, coupled with the weird disappearance of Sarey, was too much for his jangled nerves. With a wild yell he ran out of the barn and started for Clinton Center, two miles away.

His reception in the town enraged him. When he tried to tell people about the disappearance of his cow, Sarey, about the reek of sea and ooze in his barn the night before, they laughed at him. The more impolite ones, that is. Most of the others patiently heard him out—and then winked and touched their heads significantly when he was out of sight.

One man, the druggist, Jim Jelinson, seemed mildly interested. He said that as he was coming through his backyard from the garage late the previous evening, he had heard a fearful shriek somewhere in the distant darkness. It might, he averred, have come from the direction of Wharton's Swamp. But it had not been repeated and eventually he had dismissed it from his mind.

When Old Man Gowse started for home late in the afternoon he was filled with sullen, resentful bitterness. They thought he was crazy, eh? Well, Sarey *was* gone; they couldn't explain *that* away, could they? They explained the smell by saying it was dead fish cast up by the big wave which had washed into the swamp during the storm. Well—maybe. And the slime on his barn floor they said was snails. *Snails!* As if any he'd ever seen could cause that much slime!

As he was nearing home, he met Rupert Barnaby, his nearest neighbor. Rupert was carrying a rifle and he was accompanied by Jibbe, his hound.

Although there had been an element of bad blood between the two bachelor neighbors for some time, Old Man Gowse, much to Barnaby's surprise, nodded and stopped.

"Evenin' hunt, neighbor?"

Barnaby nodded. "Thought Jibbe might start up a coon. Moon later, likely."

"My cow's gone," Old Man Gowse said abruptly. "If you should see her—" He paused. "But I don't think you will. . . ."

Barnaby, bewildered, stared at him. "What you gettin' at?"

Old Man Gowse repeated what he had been telling all day in Clinton Center.

He shook his head when he finished, adding, "I wouldn't go huntin' in that swamp tonight fur—ten thousand dollars!"

Rupert Barnaby threw back his head and laughed. He was a big man, muscular, resourceful and levelheaded—little given to even mild flights of the imagination.

"Gowse," he laughed, "no use you givin' me those spook stories! Your cow just got loose and wandered off. Why, I ain't even seen a bobcat in that swamp for over a year!"

Old Man Gowse set his lips in a grim line. "Maybe," he said, as he turned away, "you'll see suthin' worse than a wildcat in that swamp tonight!"

Shaking his head, Barnaby took after his impatient hound. Old Man Gowse was getting queer all right. One of these days he'd probably go off altogether and have to be locked up.

Jibbe ran ahead, sniffing, darting from one ditch to another. As twilight closed in, Barnaby angled off the main road onto a twisting path which led into Wharton's Swamp.

He loved hunting. He would rather tramp through the brush than sit home in an easy chair. And even if an evening's foray turned up nothing, he didn't particularly mind. Actually he made out quite well; at least half his meat supply consisted of the rabbits, racoons and occasional deer which he brought down in Wharton's Swamp.

When the moon rose, he was deep in the swamp. Twice Jibbe started off after rabbits, but both times he returned quickly, looking somewhat sheepish.

Something about his actions began to puzzle Barnaby. The dog seemed reluctant to move ahead; he hung directly in front of the hunter. Once Barnaby tripped over him and nearly fell headlong.

The hunter paused finally, frowning, and looked ahead. The swamp appeared no different than usual. True, a rather offensive stench hung over it, but that was merely the result of the big waves which had splashed far inland during the recent storm. Probably an accumulation of seaweed and the decaying bodies of some dead fish lay rotting in the stagnant pools of the swamp.

Barnaby spoke sharply to the dog. "What ails you, boy? Git now! You trip me again, you'll get a boot!"

The dog started ahead some distance, but with an air of reluctance. He sniffed the clumps of marsh grass in a perfunctory manner and seemed to have lost interest in the hunt.

Barnaby grew exasperated. Even when they discovered the fresh track of a racoon in the soft mud near a little pool, Jibbe manifested only slight interest.

He did run on ahead a little further however, and Barnaby began to hope that, as they closed in, he would regain his customary enthusiasm.

In this he was mistaken. As they approached a thickly wooded area, latticed with tree thorns and covered with a heavy growth of cattails, the dog suddenly crouched in the shadows and refused to budge.

Barnaby was sure that the racoon had taken refuge in the nearby thickets. The dog's unheard of conduct infuriated him.

After a number of sharp cuffs, Jibbe arose stiffly and moved ahead, the hair on his neck bristled up like a lion's mane.

Swearing to himself, Barnaby pushed into the darkened thickets after him.

It was quite black under the trees, in spite of the moonlight, and he moved cautiously in order to avoid stepping into a pool.

Suddenly, with a frantic yelp of terror, Jibbe literally darted between his legs and shot out of the thickets. He ran on, howling weirdly as he went.

For the first time that evening Barnaby experienced a thrill of fear. In all his previous experience, Jibbe had never turned tail. On one occasion he had even plunged in after a sizeable bear.

Scowling into the deep darkness, Barnaby could see nothing. There were no baleful eyes glaring at him.

As his own eyes tried to penetrate the surrounding blackness, he recalled Old Man Gowse's warning with a bitter grimace. If the old fool happened to spot Jibbe streaking out of the swamp, Barnaby would never hear the end of it.

The thought of this angered him. He pushed ahead now with a feeling of sullen rage for whatever had terrified the dog. A good rifle shot would solve the mystery.

All at once he stopped and listened. From the darkness immediately ahead, he detected an odd sound, as if a large bulk were being dragged over the cattails.

He hesitated, unable to see anything, stoutly resisting an idiotic impulse to flee. The black darkness and the slimy stench of stagnant pools here in the thickets seemed to be suffocating him.

His heart began to pound as the slithering noise came closer. Every instinct told him to turn and run, but a kind of desperate stubbornness held him rooted to the spot.

The sound grew louder and suddenly he was positive that something deadly and formidable was rushing toward him through the thickets with accelerated speed.

Throwing up his rifle, he pointed at the direction of the sound and fired.

In the brief flash of the rifle he saw something black and enormous and glistening, like a great flapping hood, break through the final thicket. It seemed to be *rolling* toward him, and it was moving with nightmare swiftness.

He wanted to scream and run, but even as the horror rushed forward, he understood that flight at this point would be futile. Even though the blood seemed to have congealed in his veins, he held the rifle pointed up and kept on firing.

The shots had no more visible effect than so many pebbles launched from a slingshot. At the last instant his nerve broke and he tried to escape, but the monstrous hood lunged upon him, flapped over him and squeezed, and his attempt at a scream turned into a tiny gurgle in his throat.

Old Man Gowse got up early, after another uneasy night, and walked out to inspect the barnyard area. Nothing further seemed amiss, but there was still no sign of Sarey. And that detestable odor arose from the direction of Wharton's Swamp when the wind was right.

After breakfast, Gowse set out for Rupert Barnaby's place, a mile or so distant along the road. He wasn't sure himself what he expected to find.

When he reached Barnaby's small but neat frame house, all was quiet. Too quiet. Usually Barnaby was up and about soon after sunrise.

On a sudden impulse, Gowse walked up the path and rapped on the front door. He waited and there was no reply. He knocked again, and after another pause, stepped off the porch.

Jibbe, Barnaby's hound, slunk around the side of the house. Ordinarily he would bound about and bark. But today he stood motionless—or nearly so—he was trembling—and stared at Gowse. The dog had a cowed, frightened, guilty air which was entirely alien to him.

"Where's Rup?" Gowse called to him. "Go get Rup!"

Instead of starting off, the dog threw back his head and emitted an eerie, long-drawn howl.

Gowse shivered. With a backward glance at the silent house, he started off down the road.

Now maybe they'd listen to him, he thought grimly. The day before they had laughed about the disappearance of Sarey. Maybe they wouldn't laugh so easily when he told them that Rupert Barnaby had gone into Wharton's Swamp with his dog— and that the dog had come back alone!

When Police Chief Miles Underbeck saw Old Man Gowse come into headquarters in Clinton Center, he sat back and sighed heavily. He was busy this morning and undoubtedly Old Man Gowse was coming in to inquire about the infernal cow of his that had wandered off.

The old eccentric had a new and startling report, however. He claimed that Rupert Barnaby was missing. He'd gone into the swamp the night before, Gowse insisted, and had not returned.

When Chief Underbeck questioned him closely, Gowse admitted that he wasn't *positive* Barnaby hadn't returned. It was barely possible that he had returned home very early in the morning and then left again before Gowse arrived.

But Gowse fixed his flashing eyes on the Chief and shook his head. "He never came out, I tell ye! That dog of his knows! Howled, he did, like a dog howls for the dead! Whatever come took Sarey—got Barnaby in the swamp last night!"

Chief Underbeck was not an excitable man. Gowse's burst of melodrama irritated him and left him unimpressed.

Somewhat gruffly he promised to look into the matter if Barnaby had not turned up by evening. Barnaby, he pointed out, knew the swamp better than anyone else in the county. And he was perfectly capable of taking care of himself. Probably, the Chief suggested, he had sent the dog home and gone elsewhere after finishing his hunt the evening before. The chances were he'd be back by suppertime.

Old Man Gowse shook his head with a kind of fatalistic skepticism. Vouching that events would soon prove his fears well founded, he shambled grouchily out of the station.

The day passed and there was no sign of Rupert Barnaby. At six o'clock, Old Man Gowse grimly marched into the Crown, Clinton Center's second-rate hotel, and registered for a room. At seven o'clock Chief Underbeck dispatched a prowl car to Barnaby's place. He waited impatiently for its return, drumming on the desk, disinterestedly shuffling through a sheaf of reports which had accumulated during the day.

The prowl car returned shortly before eight. Sergeant Grimes made his report. "Nobody there, sir. Place locked up tight. Searched the grounds. All we saw was Barnaby's dog. Howled and ran off as if the devil were on his tail!"

Chief Underbeck was troubled. If Barnaby *was* missing, a search should be started at once. But it was already getting dark, and portions of Wharton's Swamp were very nearly impassable even during the day. Besides, there was no proof that Barnaby had not gone off for a visit, perhaps to nearby Stantonville, for instance, to call on a crony and stay overnight.

By nine o'clock he had decided to postpone any action till morning. A search now would probably be futile in any case. The swamp offered too many obstacles. If Barnaby had not turned up by morning, and there was no report that he had been seen elsewhere, a systematic search of the marsh could begin.

Not long after he had arrived at this decision, and as he was somewhat wearily preparing to leave Headquarters and go home, a new and genuinely alarming interruption took place.

Shortly before nine-thirty, a car braked to a sudden stop outside Headquarters. An elderly man hurried in, supporting by the arm a sobbing, hysterical young girl. Her skirt and stockings were torn and there were a number of scratches on her face.

After assisting her to a chair, the man turned to Chief Underbeck and the other officers who gathered around.

"Picked her up on the highway out near Wharton's Swamp. Screaming at the top of her lungs!" He wiped his forehead. "She ran right in front of my car. Missed her by a miracle. She was so crazy with fear I couldn't make sense out of what she said. Seems like something grabbed her boy friend in the bushes out there. Anyway, I got her in the car without much trouble and I guess I broke a speed law getting here."

Chief Underbeck surveyed the man keenly. He was obviously shaken himself, and since he did not appear to be concealing anything, the Chief turned to the girl.

He spoke soothingly, doing his best to reassure her, and at length she composed herself sufficiently to tell her story.

Her name was Dolores Rell and she lived in nearby Stantonville. Earlier in the evening she had gone riding with her fiance, Jason Bukmeist of Clinton Center. As Jason was driving along the highway adjacent to Wharton's Swamp, she had remarked that the early evening moonlight looked very romantic over the marsh. Jason had stopped the car, and after they had surveyed the scene for some minutes, he suggested that since the evening was warm, a brief "stroll in the moonlight" might be fun.

Dolores had been reluctant to leave the car, but at length had been persuaded to take a short walk along the edge of the marsh where the terrain was relatively firm.

As the couple were walking along under the trees, perhaps twenty yards or so from the car, Dolores became aware of an unpleasant odor and wanted to turn back. Jason, however, told her she only imagined it and insisted on going further. As the trees grew closer together, they walked Indian file, Jason taking the lead.

Suddenly, she said, they both heard something swishing through the brush toward them. Jason told her not to be frightened, that it was probably someone's cow. As it came closer, however, it seemed to be moving with incredible speed. And it didn't seem to be making the kind of noise a cow would make.

At the last second Jason whirled with a cry of fear and told her to run. Before she could move, she saw a monstrous something rushing under the trees in the dim moonlight. For an instant she stood rooted with horror; then she turned and ran. She thought she heard Jason running behind her. She couldn't be sure. But immediately after she heard him scream.

In spite of her terror, she turned and looked behind her.

At this point in her story she became hysterical again and several minutes passed before she could go on.

She could not describe exactly what she had seen as she looked over her shoulder. The thing which she had glimpsed rushing under the trees had caught up with Jason. It almost completely covered him. All she could see of him was his agonized face and part of one arm, low near the ground, as if the thing were squatting astride him. She could not say what it was. It was black, formless, bestial and yet not bestial. It was the dark gliding kind of indescribable horror which she had shuddered at when she was a little girl alone in the nursery at night.

She shuddered now and covered her eyes as she tried to picture what she had seen. "O God—*the darkness came alive! The darkness came alive!*"

Somehow, she went on presently, she had stumbled through the trees into the road. She was so terrified she hardly noticed the approaching car.

There could be no doubt that Dolores Rell was in the grip of genuine terror. Chief Underbeck acted with alacrity. After the white-faced girl had been driven to a nearby hospital for treatment of her scratches and the administration of a sedative, Underbeck rounded up all available men on the force, equipped them with shotguns, rifles and flashlights, hurried them into four prowl cars and started off for Wharton's Swamp.

Jason Bukmeist's car was found where he had parked it. It had not been disturbed. A search of the nearby swamp area, conducted in the glare of flashlights, proved fruitless. Whatever had attacked Bukmeist had apparently carried him off into the farthest recesses of the sprawling swamp.

After two futile hours of brush breaking and marsh sloshing, Chief Underbeck wearily rounded up his men and called off the hunt until morning.

As the first faint streaks of dawn appeared in the sky over Wharton's Swamp, the search began again. Reinforcements, including civilian volunteers from Clinton Center, had arrived, and a systematic combing of the entire swamp commenced.

By noon, the search had proved fruitless—or nearly so. One of the searchers brought in a battered hat and a rye whiskey bottle which he had discovered on the edge of the marsh under a sweet-gum tree. The shapeless felt hat was old and worn, but it was dry. It had, therefore, apparently been discarded in the swamp since the storm of a few days ago. The whiskey bottle looked new; in fact, a few drops of rye remained in it. The searcher reported that the remains of a small campfire were also found under the sweet-gum.

In the hope that this evidence might have some bearing on the disappearance of Jason Bukmeist, Chief Underbeck ordered a canvass of every liquor store in Clinton Center in an attempt to learn the names of everyone who had recently purchased a bottle of the particular brand of rye found under the tree.

The search went on, and mid-afternoon brought another, more ominous discovery. A diligent searcher, investigating a trampled area in a large growth of cattails, picked a rifle out of the mud.

After the slime and dirt had been wiped away, two of the searchers vouched that it belonged to Rupert Barnaby. One of them had hunted with him and remembered a bit of scrollwork on the rifle stock.

While Chief Underbeck was weighing this unpalatable bit of evidence, a report of the liquor store canvass in Clinton Center arrived. Every recent purchaser of a quart bottle of the particular brand in question had been investigated. Only one could not be located—a tramp who had hung around the town for several days and had been ordered out.

By evening most of the exhausted searching party were convinced that the tramp, probably in a state of homicidal viciousness brought on by drink, had murdered both Rupert Barnaby and Jason and secreted their bodies in one of the deep pools of the swamp. The chances were the murderer was still sleeping off the effects of drink somewhere in the tangled thickets of the marsh.

Most of the searchers regarded Dolores Rell's melodramatic story with a great deal of skepticism. In the dim moonlight, they pointed out, a frenzied, wild-eyed tramp bent on imminent murder might very well have resembled some kind of monster. And the girl's hysteria had probably magnified what she had seen.

As night closed over the dismal morass, Chief Underbeck reluctantly suspended the hunt. In view of the fact that the murderer probably still lurked in the woods, however, he decided to establish a system of night-long patrols along the highway which paralleled the swamp. If the quarry lay hidden in the treacherous tangle of trees and brush, he would not be able to escape onto the highway without running into one of the patrols. The only other means of egress from the swamp lay miles across the mire where the open sea washed against a reedy beach. And it was quite unlikely that the fugitive would even attempt escape in that direction.

The patrols were established in three-hour shifts, two men to a patrol, both heavily armed and both equipped with powerful searchlights. They were ordered to investigate every sound or movement which they detected in the brush bordering the highway. After a single command to halt, they were to shoot to kill. Any curious motorists who stopped to inquire about the hunt were to be swiftly waved on their way, after being warned not to give rides to anyone and to report all hitchhikers.

Fred Storr and Luke Matson, on the midnight to three o'clock patrol, passed an uneventful two hours on their particular stretch of the highway. Matson finally sat down on a fallen tree stump a few yards from the edge of the road.

"Legs givin' out," he commented wryly, resting his rifle on the stump. "Might as well sit a few minutes."

Fred Storr lingered nearby. "Guess so, Luke. Don't look like—" Suddenly he scowled into the black fringes of the swamp. "You hear something, Luke?"

Luke listened, twisting around on the stump. "Well, maybe," he said finally, "kind of a little scratchy sound like."

He got up, retrieving his rifle.

"Let's take a look," Fred suggested in a low voice. He stepped over the stump and Luke followed him toward the tangle of brush which marked the border of the swamp jungle.

Several yards further along they stopped again. The sound became more audible. It was a kind of slithering, scraping sound, such as might be produced by a heavy body dragging itself over uneven ground.

"Sounds like—a snake," Luke ventured. "A damn big snake!"

"We'll get a little closer," Fred whispered. "You be ready with that gun when I switch on my light!"

They moved ahead a few more yards. Then a powerful yellow ray stabbed into the thickets ahead as Fred switched on his flashlight. The ray searched the darkness, probing in one direction and then another.

Luke lowered his rifle a little, frowning. "Don't see a thing," he said. "Nothing but a big pool of black scum up ahead there."

Before Fred had time to reply, the pool of black scum reared up into horrible life. In one hideous second it hunched itself into an unspeakable glistening hood and rolled forward with fearful speed.

Luke Matson screamed and fired simultaneously as the monstrous scarf of slime shot forward. A moment later it swayed above him. He fired again and the thing fell upon him.

In avoiding the initial rush of the horror, Fred Storr lost his footing. He fell headlong—and turned just in time to witness a sight which slowed the blood in his veins.

The monster had pounced upon Luke Matson. Now, as Fred watched, literally paralyzed with horror, it spread itself over and around the form of Luke until he was completely enveloped. The faint writhing of his limbs could still be seen. Then the thing squeezed, swelling into a hood and flattening itself again, and the writhing ceased.

As soon as the thing lifted and swung forward in his direction, Fred Storr, goaded by frantic fear, overcame the paralysis of horror which had frozen him.

Grabbing the rifle which had fallen beside him, he aimed it at the shape of living slime and started firing. Pure terror possessed him as he saw that the shots were having no effect. The thing lunged toward him, to all visible appearances entirely oblivious to the rifle slugs tearing into its loathsome viscid mass.

Acting out of some instinct which he himself could not have named, Fred Storr dropped the rifle and seized his flashlight, playing its powerful beam directly upon the onrushing horror.

The thing stopped, scant feet away, and appeared to hesitate. It slid quickly aside at an angle, but he followed it immediately with the cone of light. It backed up finally and flattened out, as if trying by that means to avoid the light, but he trained the beam on it steadily, sensing with every primitive fiber which he possessed that the yellow shaft of light was the one thing which held off hideous death.

Now there were shouts in the nearby darkness and other lights began stabbing the shadows. Members of the adjacent patrols, alarmed by the sound of rifle fire, had come running to investigate.

Suddenly the nameless horror squirmed quickly out of the flashlight's beam and rushed away in the darkness.

In the leaden light of early dawn Chief Underbeck climbed into a police car waiting on the highway near Wharton's Swamp and headed back for Clinton Center. He had made a decision and he was grimly determined to act on it at once.

When he reached Headquarters, he made two telephone calls in quick succession, one to the governor of the state and the other to the commander of the nearby Camp Evans Military Reservation.

The horror in Wharton's Swamp—he had decided—could not be coped with by the limited men and resources at his command.

Rupert Barnaby, Jason Bukmeist and Luke Matson had without any doubt perished in the swamp. The anonymous tramp, it now began to appear, far from being the murderer, had been only one more victim. And Fred Storr—well, he hadn't disappeared. But the other patrol members had found him sitting on the ground near the edge of the swamp in the clutches of a mind-warping fear which had, temporarily at least, reduced him to near idiocy. Even after he had been taken home and put to bed, he had refused to loosen his grip on a flashlight which he squeezed in one hand. When they switched the flashlight off, he screamed, and they had to switch it on again. His story was so wildly melodramatic it could scarcely be accepted by rational minds. And yet—they had said as much about Dolores Rell's hysterical account. And Fred Storr was no excitable young girl; he had a reputation for levelheadedness, stolidity and verbal honesty which was touched with understatement rather than exaggeration. As Chief Underbeck arose and walked out to his car in order to start back to Wharton's Swamp, he noticed Old Man Gowse coming down the block.

With a sudden thrill of horror he remembered the eccentric's missing cow. Before the old man came abreast, he slammed the car door and issued crisp directions to the waiting driver. As the car sped away, he glanced in the rear-view mirror.

Old Man Gowse stood grimly motionless on the walk in front of Police Headquarters.

"Old Man Cassandra," Chief Underbeck muttered. The driver shot a swift glance at him and stepped on the gas.

Less than two hours after Chief Underbeck arrived back at Wharton's Swamp, the adjacent highway was crowded with cars —state police patrol cars, cars of the local curious and Army trucks from Camp Evans.

Promptly at nine o'clock over three hundred soldiers, police and citizen volunteers, all armed, swung into the swamp to begin a careful search.

Shortly before dusk most of them had arrived at the sea on the far side of the swamp. Their exhaustive efforts had netted nothing. One soldier, noticing fierce eyes glaring out of a tree, had bagged an owl, and one of the state policemen had flushed a young bobcat. Someone else had stepped on a copperhead and been treated for snakebite. But there was no sign of a monster, a murderous tramp, nor any of the missing men.

In the face of mounting skepticism, Chief Underbeck stood firm. Pointing out that so far as they knew to date, the murderer prowled only at night, he ordered that after a four-hour rest and meal period the search should continue.

A number of helicopters which had hovered over the area during the afternoon landed on the strip of shore, bringing food and supplies. At Chief Underbeck's insistence, barriers were set up on the beach. Guards were stationed along the entire length of the highway; powerful searchlights were brought up. Another truck from Camp Evans arrived with a portable machine-gun and several flame-throwers.

By eleven o'clock that night the stage was set. The beach barriers were in place, guards were at station, and huge searchlights, erected near the highway, swept the dismal marsh with probing cones of light.

At eleven-fifteen the night patrols, each consisting of ten strongly-armed men, struck into the swamp again.

Ravenous with hunger, the hood of horror reared out of the mud at the bottom of a rancid pool and rose toward the surface. Flopping ashore in the darkness, it slid quickly away over the clumps of scattered swamp grass. It was impelled, as always, by a savage and enormous hunger.

Although hunting in its new environment had been good, its immense appetite knew no appeasement. The more food it consumed, the more it seemed to require.

As it rushed off, alert to the minute vibrations which indicated food, it became aware of various disturbing emanations. Although it was the time of darkness in this strange world, the darkness at this usual hunting period was oddly pierced by the monster's hated enemy—light. The food vibrations were stronger than the shape of slime had ever experienced. They were on all sides, powerful, purposeful, moving in many directions all through the lower layers of puzzling, light-riven darkness.

Lifting out of the ooze, the hood of horror flowed up a lattice-work of gnarled swamp snags and hung motionless, while drops of muddy water rolled off its glistening surface and dripped below. The thing's sensory apparatus told it that the maddening streaks of lack of darkness were everywhere.

Even as it hung suspended on the snags like a great filthy carpet coated with slime, a terrible touch of light slashed through the surrounding darkness and burned against it.

It immediately loosened its hold on the snags and fell back into the ooze with a mighty *plop*. Nearby, the vibrations suddenly increased in intensity. The maddening streamers of light shot through the darkness on all sides.

Baffled and savage, the thing plunged into the ooze and propelled itself in the opposite direction.

But this proved to be only a temporary respite. The vibrations redoubled in intensity. The darkness almost disappeared, riven and pierced by bolts and rivers of light.

For the first time in its incalculable existence, the thing experienced something vaguely akin to fear. The light could not be snatched up and squeezed and smothered to death. It was an alien enemy against which the hood of horror had learned only one defense—flight, hiding.

And now as its world of darkness was torn apart by sudden floods and streamers of light, the monster instinctively sought the refuge afforded by that vast black cradle from which it had climbed.

Flinging itself through the swamp, it headed back for sea.

The guard patrols stationed along the beach, roused by the sound of gunfire and urgent shouts of warning from the interior of the swamp, stood or knelt with ready weapons as the clamor swiftly approached the sea.

The dismal reedy beach lay fully exposed in the harsh glare of searchlights. Waves rolled in toward shore, splashing white crests of foam far up the sands. In the searchlights' illumination the dark waters glistened with an oily iridescence.

The shrill cries increased. The watchers tensed, waiting. And suddenly across the long dreary flats clotted with weed stalks and sunken drifts there burst into view a nightmare shape which froze the shore patrols in their tracks.

A thing of slimy blackness, a thing which had no essential shape, no discernible earthly features, rushed through the thorn thickets and onto the flats. It was a shape of utter darkness, one second a great flapping hood, the next a black viscid pool of living ooze which flowed upon itself, sliding forward with incredible speed.

Some of the guards remained rooted where they stood, too overcome with horror to pull the triggers of their weapons. Others broke the spell of terror and began firing. Bullets from half a dozen rifles tore into the black monster speeding across the mud flats.

As the thing neared the end of the flats and approached the first sand dunes of the open beach, the patrol guards who had flushed it from the swamp broke into the open.

One of them paused, bellowing at the beach guards. "It's heading for sea! For God's sake don't let it escape!"

The beach guards redoubled their firing, suddenly realizing with a kind of sick horror that the monster was apparently unaffected by the rifle slugs. Without a single pause, it rolled through the last fringe of cattails and flopped onto the sands.

As in a hideous nightmare, the guards saw it flap over the nearest sand dune and slide toward the sea. A moment later however, they remembered the barbed wire beach barrier which Chief Underbeck had stubbornly insisted on their erecting.

Gaining heart, they closed in, running over the dunes toward the spot where the black horror would strike the wire.

Someone in the lead yelled in sudden triumph. "It's caught! It's stuck on the wire!"

The searchlights concentrated swaths of light on the barrier.

The thing had reached the barbed wire fence and apparently flung itself against the twisted strands. Now it appeared to be hopelessly caught; it twisted and flopped and squirmed like some unspeakable giant jellyfish snared in a fisherman's net.

The guards ran forward, sure of their victory. All at once however, the guard in the lead screamed a wild warning. "It's squeezing through! It's getting away!"

In the glare of light they saw with consternation that the monster appeared to be *flowing* through the wire, like a blob of liquescent ooze.

Ahead lay a few yards of downward slanting beach and, beyond that, rolling breakers of the open sea.

There was a collective gasp of horrified dismay as the monster, with a quick forward lurch, squeezed through the barrier. It tilted there briefly, twisting, as if a few last threads of itself might still be entangled in the wire.

As it moved to disengage itself and rush down the wet sands into the black sea, one of the guards hurled himself forward until he was almost abreast of the barrier. Sliding to his knees, he aimed at the escaping hood of horror.

A second later a great searing spout of flame shot from his weapon and burst in a smoky red blossom against the thing on the opposite side of the wire.

Black oily smoke billowed into the night. A ghastly stench flowed over the beach. The guards saw a flaming mass of horror grope away from the barrier. The soldier who aimed the flame-thrower held it remorselessly steady.

There was a hideous bubbling, hissing sound. Vast gouts of thick, greasy smoke swirled into the night air. The indescribable stench became almost unbearable.

When the soldier finally shut off the flame-thrower, there was nothing in sight except the white-hot glowing wires of the barrier and a big patch of blackened sand.

With good reason the mantle of slime had hated light, for the ultimate source of light is fire—the final unknown enemy that even the black hood could not drag down and devour.

The Man Who Sold Rope to the Gnoles

IDRIS SEABRIGHT

The gnoles had a bad reputation, and Mortensen was quite aware of this. But he reasoned, correctly enough, that cordage must be something for which the gnoles had a long unsatisfied want, and he saw no reason why he should not be the one to sell it to them. What a triumph such a sale would be! The district sales manager might single out Mortensen for special mention at the annual sales-force dinner. It would help his sales quota enormously. And, after all, it was none of his business what the gnoles used cordage for.

Mortensen decided to call on the gnoles on Thursday morning. On Wednesday night he went through his *Manual of Modern Salesmanship,* underscoring things.

"The mental states through which the mind passes in making a purchase," he read, "have been catalogued as: 1) arousal of interest 2) increase of knowledge 3) adjustment to needs . . ." There were seven mental states listed, and Mortensen underscored all of them. Then he went back and double-scored No. 1, arousal of interest, No. 4, appreciation of suitability, and No. 7, decision to purchase. He turned the page.

"Two qualities are of exceptional importance to a salesman," he read. "They are adaptability and knowledge of merchandise." Mortensen underlined the qualities. "Other highly desirable attributes are physical fitness, a high ethical standard, charm of manner, a dogged persistence, and unfailing courtesy." Mortensen underlined these too. But he read on to the end of the paragraph without underscoring anything more, and it may be that his failure to put "tact and keen power of observation" on a footing with the other attributes of a salesman was responsible for what happened to him.

The gnoles live on the very edge of Terra Cognita, on the far side of a wood which all authorities unite in describing as dubious. Their house is narrow and high, in architecture a blend of Victorian Gothic and Swiss chalet. Though the house needs paint, it is kept in good repair. Thither on Thursday morning, sample case in hand, Mortensen took his way.

No path leads to the house of the gnoles, and it is always dark in that dubious wood. But Mortensen, remembering what he had learned at his mother's knee concerning the odor of gnoles, found the house quite easily. For a moment he stood hesitating before it. His lips moved as he repeated, "Good morning, I have come to supply your cordage requirements," to himself. The words were the beginning of his sales talk. Then he went up and rapped on the door.

The gnoles were watching him through holes they had bored in the trunks of trees; it is an artful custom of theirs to which the prime authority on gnoles attests. Mortensen's knock almost threw them into confusion, it was so long since anyone had knocked at their door. Then the senior gnole, the one who never leaves the house, went flitting up from the cellars and opened it.

The senior gnole is a little like a Jerusalem artichoke made of India rubber, and he has small red eyes which are faceted in the same way that gemstones are. Mortensen had been expecting something unusual, and when the gnole opened the door he bowed politely, took off his hat, and smiled. He had got past the sentence about cordage requirements and into an enumeration of the different types of cordage his firm manufactured when the gnole, by turning his head to the side, showed him that he had no ears. Nor was there anything on his head which could take their place in the conduction of sound. Then the gnole opened his little fanged mouth and let Mortensen look at his narrow, ribbony tongue. As a tongue it was no more fit for human speech than was a serpent's. Judging from his appearance, the gnole could not safely be assigned to any of the four

physio-characterological types mentioned in the *Manual;* and for the first time Mortensen felt a definite qualm.

Nonetheless, he followed the gnole unhesitatingly when the creature motioned him within. Adaptability, he told himself, adaptability must be his watchword. Enough adaptability, and his knees might even lose their tendency to shakiness.

It was the parlor the gnole led him to. Mortensen's eyes widened as he looked around it. There were whatnots in the corners, and cabinets of curiosities, and on the fretwork table an album with gilded hasps; who knows whose pictures were in it? All around the walls in brackets, where in lesser houses the people display ornamental plates, were emeralds as big as your head. The gnoles set great store by their emeralds. All the light in the dim room came from them.

Mortensen went through the phrases of his sales talk mentally. It distressed him that that was the only way he could go through them. Still, adaptability! The gnole's interest was already aroused, or he would never have asked Mortensen into the parlor; and as soon as the gnole saw the various cordages the sample case contained he would no doubt proceed of his own accord through "appreciation of suitability" to "desire to possess."

Mortensen sat down in the chair the gnole indicated and opened his sample case. He got out henequen cable-laid rope, an assortment of ply and yarn goods, and some superlative slender abaca fiber rope. He even showed the gnole a few soft yarns and twines made of cotton and jute.

On the back of an envelope he wrote prices for hanks and cheeses of the twines, and for fifty- and hundred-foot lengths of the ropes. Laboriously he added details about the strength, durability, and resistance to climatic conditions of each sort of cord. The senior gnole watched him intently, putting his little feet on the top rung of his chair and poking at the facets of his left eye now and then with a tentacle. In the cellars from time to time someone would scream.

Mortensen began to demonstrate his wares. He showed the gnole the slip and resilience of one rope, the tenacity and stubborn strength of another. He cut a tarred hemp rope in two and laid a five foot piece on the parlor floor to show the gnole how absolutely "neutral" it was, with no tendency to untwist of its own accord. He even showed the gnole how nicely some of the cotton twines made up in square knotwork.

They settled at last on two ropes of abaca fiber, $\frac{3}{16}$ and $\frac{5}{8}$ inch in diameter. The gnole wanted an enormous quantity. Mortensen's comment on those ropes, "unlimited strength and durability," seemed to have attracted him.

Soberly Mortensen wrote the particulars down in his order book, but ambition was setting his brain on fire. The gnoles, it seemed, would be regular customers; and after the gnoles, why should he not try the Gibbelins? They too must have a need for rope.

Mortensen closed his order book. On the back of the same envelope he wrote, for the gnole to see, that delivery would be made within ten days. Terms were 30 per cent with order, balance upon receipt of goods.

The senior gnole hesitated. Shyly he looked at Mortensen with his little red eyes. Then he got down the smallest of the emeralds from the wall and handed it to him.

The sales representative stood weighing it in his hands. It was the smallest of the gnoles' emeralds, but it was as clear as water, as green as grass. In the outside world it would have ransomed a Rockefeller or a whole family of Guggenheims; a legitimate profit from a transaction was one thing, but this was another; "a high ethical standard"—any kind of ethical standard—would forbid Mortensen to keep it. He weighed it a moment longer. Then with a deep, deep sigh he gave the emerald back.

He cast a glance around the room to see if he could find something which would be more negotiable. And in an evil moment he fixed on the senior gnole's auxiliary eyes.

The senior gnole keeps his extra pair of optics on the third shelf of the curiosity cabinet with the glass doors. They look like fine dark emeralds about the size of the end of your thumb. And if the gnoles in general set store by their gems, it is nothing at

all compared to the senior gnole's emotions about his extra eyes.
The concern good Christian folk should feel for their soul's welfare is a shadow, a figment, a nothing, compared to what the
thoroughly heathen gnole feels for those eyes. He would rather,
I think, choose to be a mere miserable human being than that
some vandal should lay hands upon them.

If Mortensen had not been elated by his success to the point
of anaesthesia, he would have seen the gnole stiffen, he would
have heard him hiss, when he went over to the cabinet. All innocent, Mortensen opened the glass door, took the twin eyes out,
and juggled them sacrilegiously in his hand; the gnole could feel
them clink. Smiling to evince the charm of manner advised in
the *Manual,* and raising his brows as one who says, "Thank
you, these will do nicely," Mortensen dropped the eyes into his
pocket.

The gnole growled.

The growl awoke Mortensen from his trance of euphoria. It
was a growl whose meaning no one could mistake. This was
clearly no time to be doggedly persistent. Mortensen made a
break for the door.

The senior gnole was there before him, his network of tentacles
outstretched. He caught Mortensen in them easily and wound
them, flat as bandages, around his ankles and his hands. The
best abaca fiber is no stronger than those tentacles; though the
gnoles would find rope a convenience, they get along very well
without it. Would you, dear reader, go naked if zippers should
cease to be made? Growling indignantly, the gnole fished his
ravished eyes from Mortensen's pockets, and then carried him
down to the cellar to the fattening pens.

But great are the virtues of legitimate commerce. Though they
fattened Mortensen sedulously, and, later, roasted and sauced
him and ate him with real appetite, the gnoles slaughtered him
in quite a humane manner and never once thought of torturing
him. That is unusual, for gnoles. And they ornamented the plank
on which they served him with a beautiful border of fancy knotwork made of cotton cord from his own sample case.

Henry Martindale, Great Dane

MIRIAM ALLEN deFORD

What woke Lida was being hit on the nose with a pajama button. She opened her eyes abruptly. It was just barely light. She turned sleepily, took one look at the other side of the double bed and let out a screech. The thing lying there opened its eyes—Henry's eyes—and said—in Henry's voice, "What's the matter, honey?"

It wasn't Henry, though. It was a Great Dane in Henry's pajamas, with the top buttons popped off by its barrel chest.

Lida shot out of bed. She got as far as the door before it occurred to her that she might be the one who had gone crazy. Trembling, she inched back and took another look.

It was a Great Dane, all right.

"I—I—you look like a dog!" she managed to gasp.

Henry—or whatever was there—took it calmly. Henry always took everything calmly.

"Are you just calling me a so-and-so in a nice way, or is something wrong with your eyes?"

Lida made a tremendous effort and pulled herself together. Ordinarily she was almost as calm as Henry.

"It isn't my eyes," she breathed. "Either I've lost my mind or something awful has happened to you. Look at yourself—uh-Henry, and tell me which it is."

Henry's myopic blue eyes inspected his arm—his foreleg—well, his upper limb.

"Can't see a thing without my glasses. Give them to me, honey. Something does feel funny. Bring me your hand-mirror, too."

The glasses wouldn't go on Henry's new broad nose. Lida held them with one shaking hand and passed over the mirror with the other. There was a long silence.

"You're not crazy, Lida," Henry said at last. "Something's happened."

Lida was speechless. Even Henry was shaken. He didn't drop the mirror, but he laid it down with a distinct thump. Perhaps that was because he had been holding it in the crook of his—limb. He no longer had an opposable thumb with which to grasp it. Unquestionably, what he now had was a large dog's paw.

"Shades of Kafka!" he said in an awed tone. "Thank God I didn't turn into a giant cockroach!"

"B-but what——"

"How do I know? Things do happen. I've been trying for years to get you to take Charles Fort seriously. He has records of stranger things than this."

Lida burst into tears.

"Now don't cry, honey." He put out a comforting paw, but she shrank from it involuntarily. Fortunately for his feelings, Henry didn't see that. His glasses had fallen off as soon as she let go of them.

"We'll have to figure things out and use our common sense," he said in the reasonable tone she had been listening to for eight years.

"C-common sense! What has common sense to do with this unbelievable, horrible——"

"Hysteria won't help. Horrible maybe, but not unbelievable because it has happened—and when a thing is real, we have to believe it."

He climbed laboriously out from under the bedclothes, hesitated a moment, his hind paws hovering over his slippers, then stood solidly on all fours. The pajama pants fell down. Solemnly he peered at himself in Lida's full-length pier glass.

"I can't get a good look this way. Find some adhesive tape and fasten my glasses on for me, will you, Lida? And take this pajama top off me. It's—it's inappropriate."

In a waking nightmare, Lida did as she was told. Henry took a long look.

"A Great Dane!" he murmured. "I wonder why. I never cared for them particularly. They cost too much to feed. Well, let's get down to cases."

He glanced helplessly at the pad and pencil which always stood on the night table on his side of the bed. Until this morning, Henry Martindale had been a reasonably prosperous radio and television script writer.

"I can't think without notes, Lida," he sighed. "Write down what I tell you and I'll try to reason this thing out. But put on your dressing-gown first, dear, or you'll freeze."

This evidence of husbandly concern transformed Lida's horror into passionate loyalty and love. Somewhere within this canine shape, her own Henry lived intact. Suppose it had happened to her instead? Suppose she had awakened to find herself a Pekinese or a Siamese cat or a parakeet? Could she doubt that Henry would have stood by her?

She reached for her dressing-gown, wrapped herself in it and took up the pad and pencil.

At his dictation, she began to write the first considered reflections of Henry Martindale, Great Dane.

"One," he began, "this is either temporary or permanent. If it is temporary, I may wake up as myself tomorrow morning. In any event, I can manage to wait for a week—with your cooperation, Lida——" She nodded and even contrived to smile. "For a week, without arousing suspicion. Call up everybody we had engagements with and tell them I have the flu. Tell Mrs. Whoozis the same thing when she comes to clean and keep her out of this room. I have a deadline on that story for Channel Twenty, but I can dictate it as usual and you can deliver it. You'd better do all the phoning, too. I could talk, but I doubt if I could hold the phone."

Lida hid her shudder. Henry went on dictating.

"Two—if this condition is permanent, if it isn't gone in a week or so, then it may mean that I must face my remaining life-span as a Great Dane. Question—have I now the life expectancy of a human being or of a dog?

"I must then make a major decision: where and how can I live? I have earned my living for fifteen years now as a writer. I could continue to dictate my stories, of course, but it would be utterly impossible to conceal my—my present appearance. It would be still more impossible to explain it, even to such hardened sophisticates as the script editors and agency men for whom I write. As for the family—my brother and Aunt Agatha and your mother, Lida, and the rest of your relatives—I could, perhaps, brazen it out and make advantageous connections with a television program."

"I won't have that!" Lida burst out hotly. "I won't have you displaying yourself as a—as a freak!"

"An intelligent talking dog might be worth big money to the right sponsor," Henry said reasonably.

"No. They'd investigate first and—you couldn't get away with it anyway, Henry. Your eyes—they're still yours and people would wonder. And your voice—you've talked too often in public and on the air."

"Perhaps you're right—it might be too risky—even though it would have been rather fun. Well, then, if I'm stuck for an indefinite period with this—this phenomenon, there will be only one thing I can do. We must go somewhere where we know nobody, where you can be a widow who lives alone with only her dog for company." He paused. "Wait a moment, Lida. No, don't write this down. Maybe I'm assuming too much. I'm taking it for granted that you'll be with me. No, let me finish. If you feel you can't stand it—if you want to go away, I'll understand—I'd never blame you. And, Lida, I beg of you, don't stick by me out of a sense of duty, just because a dog without an owner—even a dog that can think and talk—is a lost dog. Just because . . ."

He had to stop. His throat had tightened too much for him to go on.

Lida's last vestige of horror left her. "Don't be a fool, darling," she said brusquely. "I married you, not your looks. *You're* still here. If we have to go to the ends of the earth—if I have to pretend forever that you're my pet Great Dane . . ." She gulped down a sob. "Just so we're together . . ."

"Bless you, dearest," Henry said quietly. He had recovered his usual calm. "Go on taking this down now. We won't have to go to the ends of the earth. We can find some secluded place in the country, perhaps not more than a hundred miles from here. We'll have to think of ways to fend off our families and friends. But I can dictate my stories to you and we can handle all my business contacts by mail. There will be difficulties, of course. How can I sign letters or endorse checks, for instance?"

"I can forge your signature. I've done it before on letters, when you were deep in a story and didn't want to be disturbed."

"Yes, that would work. And we'll find means to solve the other problems as they come up. All we need face now is a week of waiting to see if this—transformation is permanent."

A thought occurred to Lida. "About food, Henry," she suggested nervously. "Do you want to eat as usual or—or should I buy some Canine Delight?"

"Hm—that's a point." Henry let his mind dwell on ham and eggs, then on Canine Delight. "I'm sorry, dear," he said apologetically, "but I'm afraid you'd better lay in a supply of dog food."

"It's eight o'clock. The grocery at the corner will be open. I'll dress and go out to get some—some breakfast for you. And here —I'll fasten your glasses on firmly so you can read the paper while I'm gone."

Already, she discovered gratefully, she was becoming accustomed to the new Henry. Her hands were steady as she adjusted the tape. She restrained an impulse to stroke the tawny head.

Henry watched her leave, his large myopic blue eyes moist. He had not mentioned the fear that gnawed at him, a fear worse than the bite of hunger. Suppose this were an intermediate stage—suppose he should gradually become more dog and less man, lose his power of speech, his power of human thought?

Time enough to face that if it began to happen. Time, probably, to run away alone into the unknown before she could stop him. Fortunately, all they possessed was in their joint names and ultimately Lida would have to let him be declared dead and cash in on his sizable insurance.

He gazed unseeingly at the paper most of the time while she was gone. Nothing in it was as strange as what had happened to Henry Martindale.

The week went by somehow. Every night Henry went to sleep a Great Dane—he admitted he was more comfortable sleeping on a rug beside the bed—and every morning he woke up a Great Dane again. He ate Canine Delight and one night when Lida broiled two chops for herself, he enjoyed the juicy bones. But he felt no impulse to wag his tail or to bark. Inside, he was still completely Henry.

They devised a strap to hold his spectacles on, to avoid the pulling of hair that accompanied removing the adhesive tape. Physically, he was comfortable, though he began to long for exercise and fresh air. He could stand anything for a week—even Aunt Agatha's insistence that she must come to help nurse the poor boy, plus her resentment of Lida's firm refusal. Once there was a scare when the woman who came twice a week to clean insisted that she could vacuum the bedroom without bothering the invalid—but Lida won that round.

At the end of the week, it became obvious that the metamorphosis was either permanent or would be of indefinite duration. Henry had met his deadline and dictated the beginning of an-

other story in his television series, but he felt distracted and uninterested.

"I guess this is it, Lida," he conceded on the eighth day. "We have to plan."

They pored over maps and made a list of upstate villages to be inspected.

"I can make the trips and come back and report to you," said Lida dubiously. "But I hate to leave you here all alone day after day. You could let the phone ring, but suppose Aunt Agatha came or Bill Goodlett or the Harrisons? Or a telegram or a special delivery letter?"

"I'll go with you," Henry decided promptly. "Call up all the likely people and tell them I'm better, but you're taking me to the country to recuperate. We'll write everybody later, when we've found a place, that we're going to stay for a while. But first you'd better buy me a dog collar and a leash, and then take me downtown and get a license for me."

"Oh, *darling!*"

"I know—it's grim. But we must be practical. I'll have to have a name, too. What do you want to call your Great Dane? Anything but Hamlet will suit me."

"Why can't you still be Henry?" asked Lida faintly.

"Well, I guess it wouldn't matter—where we're going, wherever that is, they wouldn't get the point. All right, register me as Henry. I'll sit in the back of the car, as a dog should. Thank goodness you can drive, honey. I'd hate to travel in a baggage car!"

So Lida, her huge dog in the back seat, began visiting rural real estate offices to inquire about secluded cottages for rent. There was no sense in tying up their capital by buying a house, when at any moment—as they still assured each other—this calamity might end and Henry be himself again.

All they got was turndowns. There was nothing, simply nothing, to be had. Villagers, they learned, don't rent their homes.

They had reached a state of dull despair when, almost the last on their hopeful list, they drove to Farmington.

Yes, said Mr. Bullis, there *was* one place—the old Gassingham house. It was in kinda bad shape, needed some work done and it was three miles from the highway. But Liz Gassingham—she was all that was left—she lived in town now and she refused to sell. She'd never said she'd rent, but she might.

Lida almost said she would take it sight unseen, but stopped herself in time.

"There is only one thing, Mrs. Martindale. That dog of yours . . ." He cast an unfriendly eye on Henry, lying peaceably on the floor of the real estate office.

"You mean Miss Gassingham wouldn't let me keep a pet?"

"Pet, yes—but pets to Liz is cats. She mightn't like the idea of a tenant with a dog—a monster dog like that, especially."

"But, Mr. Bullis, I told you—I'm all alone since my husband —went . . ." Lida's voice shook. "The doctor said I must go to the country to get back my strength. But I'd be afraid to live so far from people without Henry to protect me."

"That his name, Henry?"

Henry laid a warning paw on her foot. They had agreed that they must keep their own name because of the mail and she was remembering that most of the letters would be addressed to Henry.

"It's silly—perhaps you'll think it's crazy—but that was my husband's name. I—it makes me feel less lonely to call the dog Henry, too. He—went so suddenly."

"Um." Mr. Bullis sounded disapproving. "Well, let's go see Liz. Put the mutt in your car. You might talk her over, but not if she saw him first. Funny-looking dog at that, if you don't mind my saying so—awful funny-looking eyes. Will he make a row if you leave him?"

"Oh, no, Henry never—Great Danes don't bark much."

"Better lock him in. If the kids spot him, they'll be all over him and you don't want him jumping out."

Henry settled down philosophically in the car and took a nap.

Lida came back triumphant.

"I told her you were a settled old dog, Henry, too lazy to do any damage," she announced. "And that you were clean and never had fleas and just loved cats."

"Good gosh!" said Mr. Bullis, staring. "You talk to that mutt just like he was human!"

Lida tried to smile it off. "That's what being alone does to people, Mr. Bullis."

The house was pretty dreadful. It was big and water-tight, but that was about all that could be said for it. Their modern furniture would look weird in it. The only lighting was by kerosene lamps. The water came from an outdoor pump—Henry wondered dismally if he could learn to pump with his mouth. The sanitary arrangements consisted of an outhouse in the back yard, and the cooking had to be done on a wood stove, with a fireplace for central heating.

But they had to have it and they could get along somehow. At least, Mr. Bullis said, Lida could hire Ed Monahan to chop wood and do the heaviest chores and there was old Mrs. Sharp —she sometimes took in washing for the summer people and she might be willing to do Mrs. Martindale's household laundry. He looked disparagingly at Lida's city-bred slenderness.

A month later, all the lies had been told, all the arrangements had been made and Lida and Henry were residents of Farmington.

It was pretty rugged. Henry had to be careful—and make sure his spectacles were off—whenever anyone came to the house. But they managed. His mind had never been working better and he dictated scripts like mad, till he had a good backlog in several agency inventories. Smith, of D.D.B. & I., wrote him that if rusticating for their health would add the same touch of originality and conviction to other writers' stuff, he'd recommend it to all his regulars. Henry twitched his ears irascibly when he read that one.

In a way, it was Lida who unwittingly brought on the inevitable crisis.

It was an evening in early November. She was sitting by the fireplace, knitting a sweater for Henry, who was lying contentedly at her feet. Henry had become almost reconciled to being a dog. It was nice not having to wear clothes, for instance, though when the really cold weather came, he would probably want the sweater. He wished he could help Lida more with the housework, but there aren't many household tasks that can be done without hands.

Suddenly Lida said, "Henry, I've been thinking."

"So I've noticed. What about?" he countered.

"I've been thinking about—it."

"It" was what they had tacitly agreed to call Henry's transmogrification.

"What's the use of thinking about it?"

"That's just what I mean. You're just taking it lying down."

Henry rose to his feet and looked at her apologetically.

"Don't be silly," she said impatiently. "I don't mean that way. I mean you've—you've just accepted it. You haven't tried to— oh, to think how or why it happened or whether there's any way to undo it."

"Did the swan that was found in Central Park try to figure out how it could become Dorothy Arnold again?" Henry inquired sententiously.

"I don't know what you're talking about."

"Fort—I'm a Fortean phenomenon. He never said anything about the possibility of reversal."

"That doesn't mean it couldn't happen."

"Perhaps not. My guess is it would have to be spontaneous. But if it will make you any happier, Lida, I'll try anything you suggest."

"Henry, don't you *want* to be human again?"

"Because *you're* human, yes. But selfishly, I confess, so long as I have the mind and the power of speech of a human being . . ."

"That's one of the things I've been wondering about. A dog's throat and mouth aren't formed for human speech, yet you can talk clearly with your own voice."

"I know. I've been puzzled about that, too. And my sight— dogs haven't very good sight, anyway, so that might fit. But they're supposed to be color-blind and I'm not any more than I ever was. I know very well that sweater you're knitting is beige and maroon."

"What about your other senses?"

"Well, I always had good hearing and I still have. But I certainly don't have the sense of smell of a dog—of other dogs, I mean."

"Don't say that!"

"I'm sorry. I get sort of confused sometimes. And there are other—disadvantages, of course. But, Lida, there's no use in going into all that. I don't know how to change it."

"Tell me, can you remember anything special about that night —the night before it happened?"

"I've tried. I remember I was working late on a script. It was nearly two when I went to bed and you were sound asleep. The last thing I recall was thinking, 'I'm dog-tired.' And then you woke me and it was morning and I was—like this."

"Dog-tired. Do you think . . ."

"Nonsense—pure coincidence. Or maybe . . ."

Henry felt sudden excitement thrill through him from head to tail. All his calm acceptance dropped from him as his pajamas once had done.

"Lida, I've just remembered! The story I was working on that night was the one about a werewolf who evolved from a primitive wolf-like creature instead of from apes, like us."

Lida stared at him. "You mean . . ."

"Could be. Perhaps that story wasn't just imaginary—perhaps I happened on actual facts and got transformed as a warning, maybe, or maybe that's how people turn into werewolves."

"Then there might be a way for you to change back again!"

"I don't see how. I didn't engineer it and I wouldn't know how to engineer the reversal. I'd have to get in touch somehow with a real werewolf. Hey, here's an idea! Let's get to work on another story about werewolves. It might be like—like tuning them in, if they really exist. And perhaps my transformer would get on my beam again. He might be glad to straighten me out."

"But suppose he isn't. *You're* not altogether sorry about being a dog—you just told me so. Suppose he decides you *like* being a pet, with no responsibilities."

"That's not fair, honey." Henry's tone was aggrieved. "Don't I work just as hard as I ever did?"

"Oh, darling. I didn't mean you—just him!"

"In that case, he won't want to change me back and everything will stay the way it is now. What else could he do to me?"

Henry began dictating the new werewolf script the next morning. It went fast and smoothly, as if something in him knew beforehand what to say.

Yet neither of them felt comfortable. He said nothing to Lida, but under the flow of words he was conscious of an inner struggle, as though something or somebody were trying vainly to impede them. And she, though the original incitement had been her own, grew increasingly nervous and apprehensive.

At the end of three hours, the script was half done and both of them were exhausted.

"Let's knock off for the rest of the day," Henry suggested. "We can go on with it tomorrow. We both need exercise. I'd like to explore those thick woods—the ones we've never gone into."

Nothing could have been more trim, tame and civilized than Farmington. Yet not five miles from the village, in the back country, lay the last remnants of what was once virgin forest. Its trees were of no value as timber and it had a bad reputation. There were said to be wildcats there, even bears. Parts of it belonged to landowners who never bothered with it, parts were still in the public domain. Local stories made it the hideout of robbers in the past and children were disciplined by threats of taking them there and leaving them.

Lida took Henry's spectacles off him and put on his collar and leash. Passing through the village in the car, they encountered Liz Gassingham, who scarcely returned Lida's greeting and snorted at sight of Henry.

"Great, horrible thing!" she muttered, glaring. "If she ever lets it loose to hurt my kitties, I'll throw her out, lease or no lease!"

They parked the car at the end of the road and walked half a mile over fields to the edge of the wood. Once inside, Lida shrank back a little.

"Henry," she said, "do you think there really are wild animals here? Let's not go too far."

Henry couldn't smile any more, but he laid a protecting paw on her hand. "The Great Dane," he said soothingly, "was originally a boarhound. I can handle anything we're likely to meet. And we won't get lost—don't forget I have the canine sense of direction. I can't explain it, Lida, but all day I've felt impelled toward these woods," he added.

"Maybe something *is* going to happen here," said Lida hopefully. "Oh, darling, if it only would! You do want it, too, don't you?"

"I want us to be alike again, dearest."

They walked for an hour among the old trees and Henry ran eagerly from tree to tree, sniffing. They startled woodchucks and squirrels, but nothing larger appeared. It was very quiet and peaceful and not too cold, even with the trees bare and patches of early snow left here and there on the ground from the first fall of the season. After a while, they found themselves climbing until the level floor of the woods had become a hill.

Suddenly Henry darted through some underbrush toward a depression in the hillside, behind the bulk of a huge uprooted tree.

"You know," he called back in a voice that shook a little, "this could be dug out to make a good snug cave. I could do it myself with my paws."

"What of it? You don't want to live in a cave, do you?"

"I suppose not." The excitement deserted him. "I'm all confused. There was something very important I was thinking about and now I seem to have forgotten it completely."

"Poor Henry, you're tired. Let's go back. I'm tired, too."

"I guess it was all nonsense about werewolves, after all," said Henry in the car. "Well, it's a pretty good story, anyway. The agency ought to eat it up. You know, darling, I just remembered

—vampires turn people they bite into their own kind. Why not werewolves?"

"But you're a weredog," said Lida absently. Then, sharply, "Henry, you wouldn't!"

"Just one little nip, darling—after we get home, of course."

When rent day came around, Lida didn't turn up at Liz Gassingham's house.

Mrs. Sharp had a whole washing ready that Lida never called for.

Ed Monahan went out to chop wood, but found nobody home.

Mail piled up in the post office and the postmistress noted, as so often before, that most of it was addressed to the deceased Mr. Martindale. Why, she wondered loudly, didn't the woman tell his friends he had passed away—or deserted her, more likely? Something funny there!

But nobody moves fast in Farmington and over a week passed before a delegation, led by Mr. Bullis, went out to investigate.

The door was unlocked and the house was empty.

Everything was in order, with the table laid for breakfast and the stove stuffed with wood and paper, ready to light.

The bed had been slept in and at its foot, where apparently that dog slept on a rug, lay a white flannel nightgown frivolously printed with sprigs of roses. All its buttons were off.

The rest of Lida's usual house attire lay over the back of a chair. Her shoes were beneath it, a pair of pink bedroom slippers beside the bed.

In the living room, they found a partly knitted maroon-and-beige sweater, evidently intended for the dog, and beside the typewriter a pile of manuscript.

Nobody ever saw Lida Martindale again.

It was a year from the following summer that two adventurous boys from the village, egging each other on, raided the big woods. They came back, pale and frightened, to report that they had seen the dog that used to belong to Mrs. Martindale. It had emerged from the thick underbrush, they said, where the slope of the ground began to climb the hill. It had gone back to the wild, the boys claimed, and they had been lucky to get away without harm.

"You might have been killed. Somebody ought to go out there and shoot the thing," Mr. Bullis asserted.

"Aw," said the older of the two, aged fifteen, looking a bit sick, "it wasn't doing nobody no hurt. Nobody hardly ever goes there anyhow. I know I ain't going no more."

"There was a she-dog too, just like him, and some puppies," the younger boy blurted out.

"Shut up!" growled the older. "You want folks to think you're crazy? Jim was so scared, he got to seeing things, Mr. Bullis. There wasn't nothing there 'cept that big mutt of Mrs. Martindale's."

"I wasn't scared," Jim retorted. He caught his friend's eye and added hastily, "But I could of made a mistake."

"You must have, my boy," said Mr. Bullis kindly. "That dog was a Great Dane and there's never been another anywhere around here that I ever heard of."

"You idiot!" The fifteen-year-old scolded when the two boys were alone again. "Don't you ever open your yap about that again. They'd put us both in the booby-hatch."

They kept far away from the woods after that and gradually they became convinced that they must have been out of their heads for a while. How *could* a dog have yelled, "Scram, you kids, or do you want me to bite?"

The Microscopic Giants

PAUL ERNST

It happened toward the end of the Great War, which was an indirect cause. You'll find mention of it in the official records filed at Washington. Curious reading, some of those records! Among them are accounts of incidents so bizarre—freak accidents and odd discoveries fringing war activities—that the filing clerks must have raised their eyebrows skeptically before they buried them in steel cabinets, to remain unread for the rest of time.

But this particular one will never be buried in oblivion for me. Because I was on the spot when it happened, and I was the one who sent in the report.

Copper!

A war-worn world was famished for it. The thunder of guns, from the Arctic to the Antarctic and from the Pacific to the Atlantic and back again, drummed for it. Equipment behind the lines demanded it. Statesmen lied for it and national bankers ran up bills that would never be paid to get it.

Copper, copper, copper!

Every obscure mine in the world was worked to capacity. Men risked their lives to salvage fragments from battlefields a thousand miles long. And still not enough copper was available.

Up in the Lake Superior region we had gone down thirty-one thousand feet for it. Then, in answer to the enormous prices being paid for copper, we sank a shaft to forty thousand five hundred feet, where we struck a vein of almost pure ore. And it was shortly after this that my assistant, a young mining engineer named Belmont, came into my office, his eyes afire with the light of discovery.

"We've uncovered the greatest archaeological find since the days of the Rosetta Stone!" he announced bluntly. "Down in the new low level. I want to phone the Smithsonian Institution at once. There may be a war on, but the professors will forget all about war when they see this!"

Jim Belmont was apt to be over-enthusiastic. Under thirty, a tall, good-looking chap with light blue eyes looking lighter than they really were in a tanned, lean face, he sometimes overshot his mark by leaping before he looked.

"Wait a minute!" I said. "What have you found? Prehistoric bones? Some new kind of fossil monster?"

"Not bones," said Belmont, fidgeting toward the control board that dialed our private number to Washington on the radio telephone. "Footprints, Frayter. Fossil footsteps."

"You mean men's footprints?" I demanded, frowning. The rock formation at the forty-thousand-foot level was age-old. The Pleistocene era had not occurred when those rocks were formed. "Impossible."

"But I tell you they're down there! Footprints preserved in the solid rock. Men's footprints! They antedate anything ever thought of in the age of Man."

Belmont drew a deep breath.

"And more than that," he almost whispered. "They are prints of shod men, Frank! The men who made those prints, millions of years ago, wore shoes. We've stumbled on traces of a civilization that existed long, long before man was supposed to have evolved on this earth at all!"

His whisper reverberated like a shout, such was its great import. But I still couldn't believe it. Prints of men—at the forty-thousand-foot level—and prints of shod feet at that!

"If they're prints of feet with shoes on them," I said, "they might be simply prints of our own workmen's boots. If the Smithsonian men got up here and found that, a laugh would go up that would ruin us."

"No, no," said Belmont. "That's impossible. You see, these prints are those of *little* men. I hadn't told you before, had I? I guess I'm pretty excited. The men who made these prints were small—hardly more than two feet high, if the size of their feet can be taken as a true gauge. The prints are hardly more than three inches long."

"Where did you happen to see them?" I asked.

"Near the concrete we poured to fill in the rift we uncovered at the far end of the level."

"Some of the workmen may have been playing a trick."

"Your confounded skepticism!" Belmont cried. "Tricks! Perhaps they're prints of our own men! Didn't I tell you the prints were preserved in *solid rock?* Do you think a workman would take the trouble to carve, most artistically, a dozen footprints three inches long in solid rock? Or that—if we had any men with feet that small—their feet would sink into the rock for a half inch or more? I tell you these are fossil prints, made millions of years ago when that rock was mud and preserved when the rock hardened."

"And I tell you," I replied a little hotly, "that it's all impossible. Because I supervised the pouring of that concrete, and I would have noticed if there were prints."

"Suppose you come down and look," said Belmont. "After all, that's the one sure way of finding out if what I say is true."

I reached for my hat. Seeing for myself was the one way of finding out if Belmont had gone off half-cocked again.

It takes a long time to go down forty thousand feet. We hadn't attempted to speed up the drop too much; at such great depths there are abnormalities of pressure and temperature to which the human machine takes time to become accustomed.

By the time we'd reached the new low level I'd persuaded myself that Belmont must surely be mad. But having come this far I went through with it, of course.

Fossil prints of men who could not have been more than two feet high, shod in civilized fashion, preserved in rock at the forty-thousand-foot level! It was ridiculous.

We got near the concrete fill at the end of the tunnel, and I pushed the problem of prints out of my mind for a moment while I examined its blank face. Rearing that slanting concrete wall had presented some peculiar problems.

As we had bored in, ever farther under the thick skin of Mother Earth, we had come to a rock formation that had no right to exist there at all. It was a layer of soft, mushy stuff, with gaping cracks in it, slanting down somewhere toward the bowels of the earth. Like a soft strip of marrow in hard bone, it lay between dense, compressed masses of solid rock. And we had put ten feet of concrete over its face to avoid cave-ins.

Concrete is funny stuff. It acts differently in different pressures and temperatures. The concrete we'd poured here, where atmospheric pressure made a man gasp and the temperature was above a hundred and eighteen in spite of cooling systems, hadn't acted at all like any I'd ever seen before. It hadn't seemed to harden as well as it should, and it still rayed out perceptible, self-generated heat in the pressure surrounding it. But it seemed to be serving its purpose, all right, though it was as soft as cheese compared to the rock around it.

"Here!" said Belmont, pointing down in the bright light of the raw electric bulbs stringing along the level. "Look!"

I looked—and got a shock that I can still feel. A half inch or so deep in the rock floor of the level at the base of the concrete retaining wall, there were footprints. The oddest, tiniest things imaginable!

Jim Belmont had said they were three inches long. If anything he had overstated their size. I don't think some of them were more than two and a half inches long! And they were the prints of shod feet, undeniably. Perfect soles and heels, much like those of shoes we wear, were perceptible.

I stared at the prints with disbelief for a moment, even though my own eyes gave proof of their presence. And I felt an icy finger trace its way up my spine.

I had spent hours at this very spot while the concrete fill was made over the face of the down-slanting rift of mush rock. And I hadn't seen the little prints then. Yet here they were, a dozen of them made by feet of at least three varying sizes. How had I missed seeing them before?

"Prints made millions of years ago," Belmont whispered ecstatically. "Preserved when the mud hardened to rock—to be discovered here! Proof of a civilization on earth before man was thought to have been born . . . For Heaven's sake! Look at that concrete!"

I stared along the line of his pointing finger, and saw another queer thing. Queer? It was impossible!

The concrete retaining wall seemed slightly milky, and not quite opaque! Like a great block of frosted glass, into which the eye could see for a few inches before vision was lost.

And then, again, the icy finger touched my spine. This time so plainly that I shuddered a little in spite of the heat.

For a moment I had thought to see movement in the concrete! A vague, luminous swirl that was gone before I had fairly seen it. Or had I seen it! Was imagination, plus the presence of these eerie footprints, working overtime?

"Transparent concrete," said Belmont. "There's one for the book. Silicon in greater than normal amounts in the sand we used? Some trick of pressure? But it doesn't matter. The prints are more important. Shall we phone the Smithsonian, Frank?"

For a moment I didn't answer. I was observing one more odd thing:

The footprints went in only two directions. They led out from the concrete wall, and led back to it again. And I could still swear they hadn't been there up to three days before, when I had examined the concrete fill most recently.

But of course they must have been there—for a million years or more!

"Let's wait a while on it," I heard myself say. "The prints won't vanish. They're in solid rock."

"But why wait?"

I stared at Belmont, and I saw his eyes widen at something in my face.

"There's something more than peculiar about those prints!" I said. "Fossil footsteps of men two feet high are fantastic enough. But there's something more fantastic than that! See the way they point from the concrete, and then back to it again? As if whatever made them had come out of the concrete, and had looked around for a few minutes, and then had gone back into the concrete again!"

It was Belmont's turn to look at me as if suspecting a lack of sanity. Then he laughed.

"The prints were here a long, long time before the concrete was ever poured, Frank. They just happened to be pointing in the directions they do. All right, we'll wait on the Smithsonian Institution notifications." He stopped and exclaimed aloud, gazing on the rock floor.

"What's the matter?" I asked.

"An illustration of how you could have overlooked the prints when you were supervising the fill," he said, grinning. "When I was down here last, a few hours ago, I counted an even twelve prints. Now, over here where I'd have sworn there were no prints, I see four more, made by still another pair of feet back before the dawn of history. It's funny how unobservant the eye can be."

"Yes," I said slowly. "It's very—funny."

For the rest of the day the drive to get more ore out of the ground, ever more copper for the guns and war instruments, drove the thought of the prints to the back of my mind. But back there the thought persisted.

Tiny men, wearing civilized-looking boots, existing long, long ago! What could they have looked like? The prints, marvelously like those of our own shod feet, suggested that they must have been perfect little humans, like our midgets. What business could they have been about when they left those traces of their existence in mud marshes millions of years ago. . . .

Yes, of course, millions of years ago! Several times I had to rein in vague and impossible impressions with those words. But some deep instinct refused to be reined.

And then Carson, my foreman, came to me when the last of the men had emerged from the shafts.

Carson was old; all the young men save highly trained ones like Belmont and myself, who were more valuable in peace zones, were at the various war fronts. He was nearly seventy, and cool and level-headed. It was unusual to see a frown on his face such as was there when he walked up to me.

"Mr. Frayter," he said, "I'm afraid we'll have trouble with the men."

"Higher wages?" I said. "What they need is more patriotism."

"They're not kicking about wages," Carson said. "It's a lot different than that. Steve Boland, he started it."

He spat tobacco juice at a nailhead.

"Steve works on the new low level, you know. Near the concrete fill. And he's been passing crazy talk among the men. He says he can see into the concrete a little way——"

"That's right," I interrupted him. "I was down this afternoon, and for some curious reason the stuff is a little transparent. Doubtless we could investigate and find out what causes the phenomenon. But it isn't worth taking the time for."

"Maybe it would be worth it," replied Carson quietly. "If it would stop Steve's talk, it might save a shutdown."

"What is Steve saying?"

"He says he saw a man in the concrete, two hours ago. A little man."

I stared at Carson.

"I know he's crazy," the old man went on. "But he's got the rest halfway believing it. He says he saw a man about a foot and a half high, looking at him out of the concrete. The man was dressed in strips of some shiny stuff that made him look like he had a metal shell on. He looked at Steve for maybe a minute, then turned and walked back through the concrete, like it was

nothing but thick air. Steve followed him for a foot or so and then was unable to see him any more."

I smiled at Carson while sweat suddenly formed under my arms and trickled down my sides.

"Send Steve to me," I said. "I'll let him tell me the story too. Meanwhile, kill the story among the men."

Carson sighed.

"It's going to be pretty hard to kill, Mr. Frayter. You see, there's footprints down there. Little footprints that might be made by what Steve claimed he saw."

"You think a man eighteen inches high could sink into solid rock for half an inch——" I began. Then I stopped. But it was already too late.

"Oh, you've seen them too!" said Carson, with the glint of something besides worry in his eyes.

Then I told him of how and when the prints had been made.

"I'll send Steve to you," was all he said, avoiding my eyes.

Steve Boland was a hulking, powerful man of fifty. He was not one of my best men, but as far as I knew he had no record of being either unduly superstitious or a liar.

He repeated to me the story Carson had quoted him as telling. I tried to kill the fear I saw peering out of his eyes.

"You saw those prints, made long ago, and then you imagined you saw what had made them," I argued. "Use your head, man. Do you think anything could live and move around in concrete?"

"I don't think nothing about nothing, Mr. Frayter," he said doggedly. "I saw what I saw. A little man, dressed in some shiny stuff, in the concrete. And those footprints weren't made a long time ago. They were made in the last few days!"

I couldn't do anything with him. He was terrified, under his laborious show of self-control.

"I'm leaving, Mr. Frayter. Unless you let me work in an upper level. I won't go down there any more."

After he had left my office shack, I sent for Belmont.

"This may get serious," I told him, after revealing what I'd heard. "We've got to stop this story right now."

He laughed. "Of all the crazy stuff! But you're right. We ought to stop it. What would be the best way?"

"We'll pull the night shift out of there," I said, "and we'll spend the night watching the concrete. Tell all the men in advance. Then when we come up in the morning, we can see if they'll accept our word of honor that nothing happened." Belmont grinned and nodded.

"Take a gun," I added, staring at a spot over his head.

"What on earth for?"

"Why not?" I evaded. "They don't weigh much. We might as well carry one apiece in our belts."

His laugh stung me as he went to give orders to the crew usually working at night in the forty-thousand-foot level.

We started on the long trip down, alone.

There is no day or night underground. Yet somehow, as Belmont and I crouched in the low level, we could know that it was not day. We could sense that deep night held the world outside; midnight darkness in which nothing was abroad save the faint wind rattling the leaves of the trees.

We sat on the rock fragments, with our backs against the wall, staring at the concrete fill till our eyes ached in the raw electric light. We felt like fools, and said so to each other. And yet——

"Steve has some circumstantial evidence to make his insane yarn sound credible," I said. "The way we overlooked those footprints in the rock till recently makes it look as if they'd been freshly formed. You observed a few more this afternoon than you'd noticed before. And this ridiculous concrete is a shade transparent, as though some action or movement within it had changed its character slightly."

Belmont grimaced toward the concrete.

"If I'd known the report about the footprints was going to turn us all into crazy men," he grumbled, "I'd have kept my mouth shut——"

His voice cracked off abruptly. I saw the grin freeze on his lips; saw him swallow convulsively.

"Look!" he whispered, pointing toward the center of the eight-by-thirty-foot wall.

I stared, but could see nothing unusual about the wall. That is, nothing but the fact we'd observed before; you could look into the thing for a few inches before vision was lost.

"What is it?" I snapped, stirred by the expression on his face.

He sighed, and shook his head.

"Nothing, I guess. I thought for a minute I saw something in the wall. A sort of moving bright spot. But I guess it's only another example of the kind of imagination that got Steve Boland ———"

Again he stopped abruptly. And this time he got unsteadily to his feet.

"No, it's not imagination! Look, Frank! If you can't see it, then I'm going crazy!"

I stared again. And this time I could swear I saw something too.

Deep in the ten-foot-thick retaining wall, a dim, luminous spot seemed to be growing. As though some phosphorescent growth were slowly mushrooming in there.

"You see it too?" he breathed.

"I see it too," I whispered.

"Thank God for that! Then I'm sane or we're both mad. What's happening inside that stuff? It's getting brighter, and larger———" His fingers clamped over my arm. "Look! Look!"

But there was no need for him to tell me to look. I was staring already with starting eyes, while my heart began to hammer in my chest like a sledge.

As the faint, luminous spot in the concrete grew larger it also took recognizable form. And the form that appeared in the depths of the stuff was that of a human!

Human? Well, yes, if you can think of a thing no bigger than an eighteen-inch doll as being human.

A mannikin a foot and a half high, embedded in the concrete! But not embedded—for it was moving! Toward us!

In astounded silence, Belmont and I stared. It didn't occur to us then to be afraid. Nothing occurred to us save indescribable wonder at the impossible vision we saw.

I can close my eyes and see the thing now: a manlike little figure walking toward us through solid concrete. It bent forward as
though shouldering a way against a sluggish tide, or a heavy
wind; it moved as a deep-sea diver might move in clogging
water. But that was all the resistance the concrete seemed to
offer to it, that sluggish impediment to its forward movement.

Behind it there was a faint swirl of luminosity, like phosphorescent water moving in the trail of a tiny boat. And the luminosity surrounded the thing like an aura.

And now we could see its face and I heard Belmont's whispered exclamation. For the face was as human as ours, with a
straight nose, a firm, well-shaped mouth, and eyes glinting with
intelligence.

With intelligence—and something else!

There was something deadly about those eyes peering at us
through the misty concrete. Something that would have sent our
hands leaping for our guns had not the thing been so little. You
can't physically fear a doll only a foot and a half high.

"What on earth is it—and how can it move through solid concrete?" breathed Belmont.

I couldn't even guess the answer. But I had a theory that
sprang full grown into my mind at the first sight of the little figure. It was all I had to offer in the way of explanation later, and
I gave it to Belmont for what it was worth at the time.

"We must be looking at a hitherto unsuspected freak of evolution," I said, instinctively talking in a whisper. "It must be that
millions of years ago the human race split. Some of it stayed on
top of the ground; some of it went into deep caves for shelter.
As thousands of years passed, the under-earth beings went ever
deeper as new rifts leading downward were discovered. But far
down in the earth is terrific pressure, and heat. Through the ages
their bodies adapted themselves. They compacted—perhaps in
their very atomic structure.

"Now the density of their substance, and its altered atomic
character, allows them to move through stuff that is solid to us.

Like the concrete and the mush rock behind it, which is softer than the terrifically compressed stone around it."

"But the thing has eyes," murmured Belmont. "Anything living for generations underground would be blind."

"Animals, yes. But this is human; at least it has human intelligence. It has undoubtedly carried light with it."

The little mannikin was within a few inches of the surface of the wall now. It stood there, staring out at us as intently as we stared in at it. And I could see that Steve Boland had added no imaginative detail in his description of what he had seen.

The tiny thing was dressed in some sort of shiny stuff, like metal, that crisscrossed it in strips. It reminded me of something, and finally I got it. Our early airmen, trying for altitude records high in the stratosphere, had laced their bodies with heavy canvas strips to keep them from disrupting outward in the lessened pressure of the heights. The metallic-looking strips lacing this little body looked like those.

"It must be that the thing comes from depths that make this forty-thousand-foot level seem high and rarefied," I whispered to Belmont. "Hundreds of thousands of feet, perhaps. They've heard us working at the ore, and have come far up here to see what was happening."

"But to go through solid concrete——" muttered Belmont, dazed.

"That would be due to the way the atoms of their substance have been compressed and altered. They might be like the stuff on Sirius' companion, where substance weighs a ton to the cubic inch. That would allow the atoms of their bodies to slide through far-spaced atoms of ordinary stuff, as lead shot could pour through a wide-meshed screen. . . ."

Belmont was so silent that I stared at him. He was paying no attention to me, probably hadn't even heard me. His eyes were wild and wide.

"There's another of them. And another! Frank—we're mad. We must be."

Two more luminous swirls had appeared in the depths of the

concrete. Two more tiny little human figures slowly appeared as, breasting forward like deep-sea divers against solid water, they plodded toward the face of the wall.

And now three mannikins, laced in with silvery-looking metal strips, stared at us through several inches of the milky appearing concrete. Belmont clutched my arm again.

"Their eyes!" he whispered. "They certainly don't like us, Frank! I'm glad they're like things you see under a low powered microscope instead of man-sized or bigger!"

Their eyes were most impressive—and threatening. They were like human eyes, and yet unlike them. There was a lack of something in them. Perhaps of the thing we call, for want of a more definite term, Soul. But they were as expressive as the eyes of intelligent children.

I read curiosity in them as intense as that which filled Belmont and me. But over and above the curiosity there was—menace.

Cold anger shone from the soulless eyes. Chill outrage, such as might shine from the eyes of a man whose home has been invaded. The little men palpably considered us trespassers in these depths, and were glacially infuriated by our presence.

And then both Belmont and I gasped aloud. For one of the little men had thrust his hands forward, and hands and arms had protruded from the wall, like the hands of a person groping a way out of a thick mist. Then the tiny body followed it. And as if at a signal, the other two little men moved forward out of the wall too.

The three metal-laced mannikins stood in the open air of the tunnel, with their backs to the wall that had offered no more resistance to their bodies than cheese offers to sharp steel. And behind them there were no holes where they had stepped from. The face of the concrete was unbroken.

The atomic theory must be correct, I thought. The compacted atoms of which they were composed slid through the stellar spaces between ordinary atoms, leaving them undisturbed.

But only a small part of my mind concerned itself with this.

Nine-tenths of it was absorbed by a growing, indefinable fear. For now the three little men were walking slowly toward us. And in every line of their tiny bodies was a threat.

Belmont looked at me. Our hands went uncertainly toward our revolvers. But we did not draw them. You don't shoot at children, and the diminutive size of the three figures still made us consider them much as harmless children, though in the back of my mind, at least, if not in Belmont's, the indefinable fear was spreading.

The three stopped about a yard from us. Belmont was standing, and I was still seated, almost in a paralysis of wonder, on my rock fragment. They looked far up at Belmont and almost as far up at me. Three little things that didn't even come up to our knees!

And then Belmont uttered a hoarse cry and dragged out his gun at last. For one of the three slid his tiny hand into the metal lacing of his body and brought it out with a sort of rod in it about the size of a thick pin, half an inch long. And there was something about the look in the mannikin's eyes that brought a rush of frank fear to our hearts at last, though we couldn't even guess at the nature of the infinitesimal weapon he held.

The mannikin pointed the tiny rod at Belmont, and Belmont shot. I didn't blame him. I had my own gun out and trained on the other two. After all, we knew nothing of the nature of these fantastic creatures who had come up from unguessable depths below. We couldn't even approximate the amount of harm they might do, but their eyes told us they'd do whatever they could to hurt us.

An exclamation ripped from my lips as the roar of the shot thundered down the tunnel.

The bullet had hit the little figure. It couldn't have helped but hit it; Belmont's gun was within a yard of it, and he'd aimed point-blank.

But not a mark appeared on the mannikin, and he stood there apparently unhurt!

Belmont fired again, and to his shot I added my own. The

bullets did the little men no damage at all.

"The slugs are going right through the things!" yelled Belmont, pointing.

Behind the mannikins, long scars in the rock floor told where the lead had ricocheted. But I shook my head in a more profound wonder than that of Belmont's.

"The bullets aren't going through them! They're going through the bullets. The stuff they're made of is denser than lead!"

The little man with the tiny rod took one more step forward. And then I saw something that had been lost for the time being in the face of things even more startling. I saw how the tiny tracks had been made.

As the mannikin stepped forward, I saw his advancing foot sink into the rock of the floor till the soles of his metallic-looking shoes were buried!

That small figure weighed so much that it sank into stone as a man would sink into ooze!

And now the microscopic rod flamed a little at the tip. And I heard Belmont scream—just once.

He fell, and I looked at him with a shock too great for comprehension, so that I simply stood there stupidly and saw without really feeling any emotion.

The entire right half of Belmont's chest was gone. It was only a crater—a crater that gaped out, as holes gape over spots where shells bury themselves deep and explode up and out.

There had been no sound, and no flash other than the minute speck of flame tipping the mannikin's rod. At one moment Belmont had been whole. At the next he was dead, with half his chest gone. That was all.

I heard myself screaming, and felt my gun buck in my hand as I emptied it. Then the infinitesimal rod turned my way, and I felt a slight shock and stared at my right wrist where a hand and a gun had once been.

I heard my own yells as from a great distance. I felt no pain; there are nerve shocks too great for pain-sensation. I felt only crazed, stupefied rage.

I leaped at the three little figures. With all my strength I swung my heavily booted foot at the one with the rod. There was death in that swing. I wanted to kill these three. I was berserk, with no thought in mind other than to rend and tear and smash. That kick would have killed an ox, I think.

It caught the little man in the middle of the back. And I screamed again and sank to the floor with the white-hot pain of broken small bones spiking my brain. That agony, less than the shock of losing a hand, I could feel all right. And in a blind haze of it I saw the little man smile bleakly and reach out his tiny hand toward Belmont, disregarding me as utterly as though I no longer existed.

And then through the fog of my agony I saw yet another wonder. The little man lifted Belmont's dead body.

With the one hand, and apparently with no more effort than I would have made to pick up a pebble, he swung the body two inches off the floor, and started toward the concrete wall with it.

I tried to follow, crawling on my knees, but one of the other little men dashed his fist against my thigh. It sank in my flesh till his arm was buried to the shoulder, and the mannikin staggered off-balance with the lack of resistance. He withdrew his arm. There was no mark in the fabric of my clothing and I could feel no puncture in my thigh.

The little man stared perplexedly at me, and then at his fist. Then he joined the other two. They were at the face of the concrete wall again.

I saw that they were beginning to look as though in distress. They were panting, and the one with the rod was pressing his hand against his chest. They looked at each other and I thought a message was passed among them.

A message of haste? I think so. For the one picked up Belmont again, and all three stepped into the concrete. I saw them forge slowly ahead through it. And I saw Belmont, at arm's length of the little man who dragged him, flattened against the smooth side of the stuff.

I think I went a little mad, then, as I understood at last just what had happened.

The little men had killed Belmont as a specimen, just as a man might kill a rare insect. They wanted to take him back to their own deep realms and study him. And they were trying to drag him through the solid concrete. It offered only normal resistance to their own compacted tons of weight, and it didn't occur to them what it would do to Belmont's body.

I flung myself at the wall and clawed at it with my left hand. The body of my friend was suspended there, flattened against it as the little man within tried to make solid matter go through solid matter, ignorant of the limitation of the laws of physics as we on earth's surface know them.

They were in extreme distress now. Even in my pain and madness I could see that. Their mouths were open like the mouths of fish gasping in air. I saw one clutch the leader's arm and point urgently downward.

The leader raised his tiny rod. Once more I saw the infinitesimal flash at its tip. Then I saw a six-foot hole yawn in the concrete around Belmont's body. What was their ammunition? Tiny pellets of gas, so compressed at the depths they inhabited that it was a solid, and then expanded enormously when released at these pressures? No one will ever know—I hope!

In one last effort, the leader dragged the body of my friend into the hole in the concrete. Then, when it stubbornly refused to follow into the substance through which they could force their own bodies, they gave up. One of the three staggered and fell, sinking in the concrete as an overcome diver might sink through water to the ocean's bed. The other two picked him up and carried him. Down and away.

Down and away—down from the floor of the forty-thousand-foot level, and away from the surface of the concrete wall.

I saw the luminous trails they left in the concrete fade into indistinct swirls, and finally die. I saw my friend's form sag back from the hole in the concrete, to sink to the floor.

And then I saw nothing but the still form, and the ragged six-foot crater that had been blown soundlessly into the solid concrete by some mysterious explosive that had come from a thing no larger than a thick pin, and less than half an inch long. . . .

They found me an hour later—men who had come down to see why neither Belmont nor I answered the ring of the radio phone connecting the low level with the surface.

They found me raving beside Belmont's body, and they held my arms with straps as they led me to the shaft.

They tried me for murder and sabotage. For, next day, I got away from the men long enough to sink explosive into the forty-thousand-foot level and blow it up so that none could work there again. But the verdict was not guilty in both cases.

Belmont had died and I had lost my right hand in an explosion the cause of which was unknown, the military court decided. And I had been insane from shock when I destroyed the low level, which, even with the world famished for copper, was almost too far down to be commercially profitable anyway.

They freed me, and I wrote in my report, and some filing clerk had, no doubt, shrugged at its impossibility and put it in a steel cabinet where it will be forever ignored.

But there is one thing that cannot be ignored. That is, those mannikins, those microscopic giants, if ever they decide to return by slow stages of pressure-acclimation to the earth's surface!

Myriads of them, tiny things weighing incredible tons, forging through labyrinths composed of soft veins of rock like little deep-sea divers plodding laboriously but normally through impeding water! Beings as civilized as ourselves, if not more so, with infinitely deadly weapons, and practically invulnerable to any weapons we might try to turn against them!

Will they tunnel upward some day and decide calmly and leisurely to take possession of a world that is green and fair, instead of black and buried?

If they do, I hope it will not be in my lifetime!

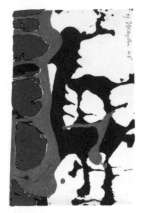

The Young One

JEROME BIXBY

Old Buster was suddenly crouched on stiff legs, right up out of a sound sleep, and his ears were laid back flat against his head, and he was letting out the deep, wet-sounding growl he always used on rattlers.

Young Johnny Stevens looked up in surprise.

The new kid was standing out in the middle of the road, about ten feet away. He'd come up so silently Johnny hadn't even known he was there—until old Buster let out that growl.

Johnny stopped whittling. He sat there on the damp, tree-shaded grass in front of the Stevens farmhouse, his big silver-mounted hunting knife in one hand, the shaved stick in the other, and stared at old Buster.

The dog's head was down, his eyes were up and slitted on the new kid. His lips were curled back tight against his teeth.

Johnny started to reach for Buster's scruff, afraid he was getting set to attack. But Buster gave him a mean, panicky, sideways glance, and Johnny pulled back his hand, because he knew his dog. Then Buster whined. His tail went between his legs and he started to walk backward, one slow step after another. He emerged from the shade of the big elm, where he'd been sleeping at Johnny's feet ever since lunch, and kept going backward until he was about twenty feet up the lawn toward the house. Then he stopped and threw back his head as if to howl—but he didn't. He held the pose for a second, his eyes glaring on the new kid down along the sides of his muzzle, and then he turned and ran around the corner of the house.

114

Buster had never even run from bear. Johnny had once had to drag him off the scent of one.

Johnny turned to look at the new kid, mad clear through and curious as heck at the same time.

The kid looked friendly, curious—and kind of lost. He was dark and thin, with big eyes. His short, stiff, black hair fit his long skull like a cap. His voice had a funny accent, and it was kind of hesitant, almost like he was afraid to talk.

"Hello," he said.

Johnny Stevens stood up. Woodshavings spilled off his lap onto the grass.

"What'd you do to Buster?" he demanded.

"I—I don't know. Dogs just don't like me. I'm sorry I frightened him."

Johnny scowled. "You didn't frighten him," he denied formally. "He musta seen something across the road."

"It was me," said the new kid softly.

Johnny turned to look at the corner of the house. Buster was poking his head around, low down, ears still back. The new kid looked over that way too, and Buster ducked out of sight like he was yanked. A second later Johnny heard the dog's claws gallop across the cellar door along the side of the house, and knew Buster must be heading for the field out back, where he went and hid whenever he was punished.

Johnny scowled harder. "Who're you?"

"Kovacs. Hello."

Johnny didn't answer—just stared suspiciously.

"What are you making?" Kovacs asked, after a minute.

"I dunno," Johnny said. Then, because that didn't sound smart, he added, "A cane, maybe. Or a fishing rod. Kovacs what?"

"Bela."

"That's a funny name."

"What is yours?"

"Johnny Stevens."

"Hello, Johnny," Kovacs Bela said again, hopefully.

"Hello," Johnny said sourly.

Kovacs Bela came to the edge of the road, where it gave onto a slope of rock and root-studded dirt that rose a few feet to the Stevens lawn. There he stopped, his thin shadow lying up the slope in front of him, as if he were waiting to be invited.

Johnny sat down again, still scowling. He didn't say anything.

Kovacs half-turned, looking down the road over his shoulder, as if sorry he'd stopped.

They watched a couple of robins chase each other through the sun-bleached rails of the fence across the road. Summer heat danced along the waving tips of wheat in the field beyond, and shimmered up the green-brown sides of the low hillocks that lined the old creek-bed.

Johnny started whittling again.

"You from that new family who bought the old Burman place?" he asked.

"Yes."

"Moved in last week, din'cha? I heard about it."

"Yes."

The robins tired of darting through the fence-rails and set off across the wheatfield, wings blurring, bodies almost brushing the carpet of tips.

"We played around there a lot," Johnny grunted. "The Burman place. Guess we can't now . . . 'cause you moved in."

Kovacs Bela was silent.

"We used the silo for a robber hideout," Johnny said accusingly.

"Silo . . . ?"

"Don't you know what that is?"

Kovacs shook his dark head.

"It's the big round building, like a tin can. You're kinda dumb."

Kovacs bit his lip and stood silently, his big, dark eyes unhappy. "Do you want me to go away?" he asked.

"Sure," said Johnny, still feeling mean.

Kovacs started to turn away, with that aimless look to his

movements that means one is going no place in particular—just leaving.

Johnny relented a little. "I was just kiddin' . . . c'mon and sit down."

Kovacs Bela stood for a moment, then smiled hesitantly and came up the dirt slope into the shade of the trees. He sank to the grass and curled his legs under him with an oddly graceful motion. "Thank you," he said.

Johnny peeled a long sliver of bark off the stick with his big, razor-sharp knife. "I wanna know what you did to Buster. How'd you make him act that way?"

"Animals just don't like me."

"Why?"

"My father once said it is the way we smell—" Kovacs' voice trailed off. "I don't know. They don't like us."

"Us? You mean your whole family?"

"I—yes."

"You're a funny guy. Where you from, they don't have silos? You talk funny too."

"I am from Hungary."

Johnny looked closely at Kovacs Bela, taking in the dark features, the big eyes, the soft mouth. There was something about the face that disturbed him, but he couldn't pin it down.

"Oh . . . a foreigner. I guess Buster never saw a foreigner before."

The two robins, or another pair, came hedgehopping back over the wheatfield, arced up over the fence, over the road and into the uppermost branches of the tree directly overhead. They set up a loud chirping, and commenced flitting from branch to branch.

"Where are you from?" Kovacs Bela asked.

"Right here. Michigan." Johnny thought for a second, balancing his big knife on one finger, the heavy blade on one side, the silver-mounted handle on the other. "There's Bela Lugosi in the movies. He's always a monster or something. But Bela's his *first* name."

"It is my first name too. In Hungary, the first name comes last. I should have said my name is Bela Kovacs . . . that is the way you would say it here."

Johnny shook his head, as if wondering at the crazy things foreigners did—and the crazy way they must smell, to wake old Buster up and send him kiting the way Bela had.

Without being obvious about it, he tried to get a whiff of Bela Kovacs—but he couldn't smell a thing. Well, dogs could smell lots more than people. Old Buster sure must have.

Bela Kovacs had noticed the headshake. He said a little defensively, "I talk English well, don't I?"

Johnny started to deprecate; but he said instead, honestly, "Yeah. I gotta admit, you talk pretty good."

"We have been in America for almost a year. In New York. And my father taught English to me and my mother before we came."

Johnny was working up considerable interest in his first foreigner. "You mean your father's English?"

"He is Hungarian. He had to teach himself first. It took him a long time. But he said we had to move, and America was the best place for us to go. We brought over some paintings, and my father sold them to buy the farm."

"Your father paints pitchers?"

"My grandfather painted them. He was a famous artist in Hungary."

"What d'you mean, you *had* to move?"

"We . . . we just had to. We had to move to a new country. That's what Father said." Bela Kovacs looked around at the blue summer sky, the heat-shimmering hillocks, the groves of trees that lay along the landscape like clean green cushions, the dusty road that wound through low hills to Harrisville thirty miles to the east. "I am glad we finally moved out here. I did not like New York. In Hungary, we lived in the country."

The two robins had been hopping lower and lower in the tree overhead, and now they dropped side by side from the bottom branches to the lawn, where they began searching the thick grass for insects.

One hopped to within a few feet of Bela Kovacs, who still sat with his legs curled under him in that relaxed yet curiously steel-spring position.

Suddenly the robin froze—cocked its head—regarded the boy with a startled beady eye.

Then it chirped a thin note, and both birds streaked away across the lawn as fast as they could go.

Johnny stared after them.

"I like birds," Bela Kovacs said wistfully. "I would not hurt them. I wish they liked me. I wish animals did not hate us."

Johnny began to work up even more interest in his first foreigner—because maybe it wasn't the way he smelled after all.

Because birds could hardly smell anything.

Then he noticed something funny. Bela Kovacs was still looking at the place where the robins had vanished, and Johnny saw what it was that had disturbed him about Bela's face ever since he'd first seen it.

"You have funny eyebrows," he said. "They're awful thick, and they meet in the middle. They grow all the way across."

Bela didn't look at him. The remark seemed to have brought back his shyness. He lowered his head and raised one slender hand to the side of his face, as if wanting to conceal the eyebrows.

After a second, Johnny was sorry he'd said anything.

"Heck, that's okay," he said. "Look—I haven't got any end on this finger." He held up the pinkie he'd caught in the wheel on the well two years ago.

Bela Kovacs stared at the smooth pink end and his straight bar of brows rose at the outsides.

"We're all different," Johnny said—and realized that, curiously, where he had before been teasing this new kid, he was now trying almost to console him. And he wondered more than ever what could be wrong with Bela Kovacs, to make him act so funny. Guilty, almost—like he was ashamed of something—something he was maybe afraid people would find out.

Bela was sitting in the same position, but somehow he seemed smaller than before, like he was huddled into himself. His hand was still up to his face.

"We're all different," Johnny said again. "My dad always tells me that . . . and he says it doesn't matter. He says for me never to care where anybody comes from, or how funny they look, or anything like that. That's why I don't mind you being a foreigner. I'm sorry Buster acted the way he did."

Bela Kovacs said muffledly, "I'm *so* different."

"Naw."

"I am." Bela looked at Johnny's finger. "I was *born* different."

"Naw," Johnny said again, because he couldn't think of anything else to say. Heck, he knew Bela Kovacs *was* different—anybody could see that. And he was itching to know what the mystery was all about.

He said uncomfortably, "Want to hike or something?"

"Hike?"

"Go walking." Johnny stood up and shoved the hunting knife in his belt. "C'mon, Bela. There's lots of swell places to play—I'll show 'em to you. There's the hollow tree, and the injun fort, and—"

"A real Indian fort?" Bela said, looking up finally, dark eyes wide.

"Naw. We built it outa rocks. And there's the caves, back in the hills . . . miles of 'em. You go in through a little chink that don't look like nothin' at all, and then you flash your light around and there's walls that look like waving cloth, all pink and green and blue, and secret passages and stalatites and stagmites and holes where you can't even see the bottom they're so deep."

"That sounds wonderful," Bela Kovacs said. "Will you take me there, Johnny?"

"Sure. C'mon, I'll pick up my flashlight." Johnny started up the lawn toward the house.

Bela rose gracefully to his feet, as if the steel-spring had suddenly uncoiled, and walked a few steps after Johnny. Then he stopped and looked up at the high summer sun.

"What is the time?" he asked.

"Oh . . . 'bout three o'clock, I guess."

"Is it far—to the caves?"

"Two, three miles."

Bela looked at the grass at his feet. "I have to be home by seven o'clock."

"We can make it easy. C'mon." Johnny started off again.

Bela fell into step. "Johnny—"

"Yeah?"

"I *have* to be home by seven."

"Why?"

"I—I just have to. My parents will be terribly angry if I'm not. We will not get lost, or go too far away, will we?"

"Heck, no. I know the caves better'n anybody." Johnny glanced sideways at Bela. "Won't your parents let you play at night? *Mine* do."

"It's—only on certain days that I can't go out at night. Certain times of the month."

"Why?"

"I can't tell you. But I have to be home by seven."

Johnny was intrigued by this new addition to the mystery. "Don't worry," he said. "Nothing'll happen."

They reached the front porch.

"Wait here," said Johnny.

He went into the house and into the kitchen, where Mom was already working on supper, because the Youngs were coming over for bridge tonight and supper was always something special for guests.

Johnny got his flashlight from under the sink.

Mom looked up from the chicken she was stuffing. "What are you doing, dear?"

"Goin' to the caves."

Mom frowned. "I wish you'd stay away from that place, Johnny. I wish your father would do something to make you. It's so dangerous . . . they go on for miles. Suppose you got lost sometime?"

"I won't get lost," Johnny said contemptuously. "I know every inch."

"Suppose the flashlight failed?"

"Aw, Mom, don't worry . . . I'm just going to show the new kid around."

"The new kid?"

"Bela Kovacs . . . his family bought the old Burman place."

Mom looked surprised, and a little pleased. "So they have a little boy! Now you'll have a new playmate. Is he a nice boy?"

Johnny juggled the flashlight. "Well, he's kinda funny. He's a foreigner from Hungary. That's in Europe. I guess he's all right."

"I'd like to meet him."

"He's right outside waitin' . . . c'mon, I'll interduce you."

Johnny started through the house toward the porch where he'd left Bela. Mom smiled and wiped her hands on a towel and followed.

They were just passing through the front room when they heard old Buster barking and snarling like he'd gone crazy.

Buster had Bela Kovacs backed against the porch steps, and was snaking back and forth in front of the boy as if he wanted to attack worse than anything else in the world, but was afraid to.

Bela's dark face had gone bone-colored, and he was half-crouched in an almost animal position, looking ready to move instantly in any direction, including straight up.

Johnny Stevens dropped over the porch-rail and lit beside Bela and shouted, "Buster! Cut it out! *Stop* it!"

Old Buster looked at him with the red-lamp eyes of a mad dog. Watery froth dripped from his stretched lips. His tail was curled so hard between his legs that it pressed up along his belly. He trembled so hard he could hardly stand—but Johnny knew that scared or not, Buster was set to attack any second.

Johnny hissed and clapped his hands in front of him, hard and fast. That meant Buster had better git, or end up with a sore rump.

Buster took a prowling, back-high, head-low step forward. His lips were so curled that his head seemed half teeth.

Mom screamed from the porch, "Johnny, come away!" and Johnny turned his head frantically to look at her, and Buster chose that moment to charge Bela Kovacs.

Then everything happened almost too fast to see.

Johnny felt a tug at his belt, where he'd stuck the hunting knife, and saw Bela Kovacs swing the heavy blade at Buster's head.

Old Buster lost heart, and turned and ran again, howling his heart out.

Bela Kovacs screamed, "*Silver* . . . the knife is *silver!*" and he dropped the knife and ran off across the lawn, crying and flapping the hand he'd grabbed the knife handle with. He turned and ran down the road, faster than Johnny had ever seen a kid run.

Johnny's mother was off the porch and on her knees, frantically examining Johnny to see if he'd been bitten; and Johnny's father drove up just then in the station-wagon, craned his neck after Bela Kovacs, and asked what in heck was going on.

After supper, the grownups sat around and talked about the new family before starting to play bridge.

Everybody who had met either Mr. or Mrs. Kovacs seemed to like them all right—that was the consensus. Mrs. Young said that McIntyre, the grocer, who was generally looked up to as a pretty good judge of character, had let it be known yesterday that Mr. Kovacs had impressed him favorably. Mr. Kovacs had come in to stock up on food and some implements and McIntyre had tried to pump him, and Mr. Kovacs had answered the right questions and resisted the rest pleasantly, and McIntyre had liked that.

And Mrs. Kovacs had waited outside the store in the Kovacs' old Dodge, and three ladies had said she seemed like a nice woman, even if a little foreign-looking.

And Junior Murdock, at the gas-station, said that the Kovacs Dodge was in very good shape for its age, and showed signs of recent careful overhauling—and Murdock liked people who cared for their cars, particularly old cars that someone else might lose pride in. He thought it told a lot about them.

Nobody thought them too strange, it seemed—just foreign.

Mrs. Young and Johnny's Mom decided, on the basis of the evidence, to suggest at the next meeting of the Ladies' Club that Mrs. Kovacs be invited to join.

Then the talk got around to what had happened this afternoon.

Old Buster had come back around five o'clock, sneaking out of his hideaway in the field and looking around each time before he put his paw down for a step.

While Mom and Johnny had stayed inside and watched through the front window, and Johnny had blinked back tears of worry, Dad had gone out with his pistol in one hand and coaxed Buster over to him and, with the gun to the animal's head, examined him carefully. Dad knew a lot about animals.

Old Buster wagged his tail and took a couple of laps out of the pan of water Dad carried in his other hand.

Dad came back and said, "He's okay. I don't know what got into him. There are some people animals just hate, and I guess the Kovacs boy is one of them. It's nothing against him . . . from what Johnny says, he likes animals himself. They just don't like *him*."

"He tried to kill Buster," Johnny said. He'd been mad about that all afternoon. "He took my knife and tried to kill Buster."

Dad said, "You shouldn't be angry about that, Johnny. It was an instinctive thing to do . . . the kid was probably scared silly. Buster was out for blood, God knows why, and Bela grabbed the knife and took a swipe in self-defense. He's probably sorry he did it."

"I don't care," Johnny said sullenly. "He tried to kill him."

Dad sighed. "It's just lucky that Buster saw the knife and lit out—and that Bela missed with the knife. Bela didn't get bitten, and Buster's all right."

"It wasn't the knife," Johnny said. "Buster ain't scared of my knife. He was scared of *Bela* . . . he ran before he even saw the knife."

"Well," Dad said, "maybe. Anyway, everything's all right now. Nothing really bad happened." He paused. "You know, I feel a little sorry for the kid . . . animals hating him like that. No wonder he acts a little strange. A kid ought to be able to have a pet. Maybe he feels a little inferior to kids who can."

But Johnny was still mad. After Dad finished talking to him, he was less mad than before—but he still resented anyone taking a knife to his dog. No matter what the provocation. And *his* knife to boot.

"I wonder why he dropped the knife and ran," Mom mused. "He yelled that it was silver, and acted like it burned his hand."

"Oh," Dad said, "he probably said 'sliver.' Maybe he got a sliver from the knife handle."

Johnny started to object, but let it go. His knife handle was of smooth, worn, hard wood and silver strips—he knew darned well there weren't any slivers on it. But still, he let it go. He'd settle the whole thing in his own way.

When Dad suggested that he go over the next day and apologize to Bela Kovacs for Buster's behavior, and show the new boy that nobody held his actions against him, Johnny said all right.

Because, though he knew Dad was absolutely right and it hadn't been Bela's fault, he still wanted to get back at Bela for trying to kill Buster—and he had a good idea of how to do it.

He'd scare the living daylights out of the kid—and maybe find out what the mysterious reason was why Bela had to be home every night by that time at certain times of the month.

The grownups finally started their bridge game, and Johnny went outside and sat on the porch with Buster and looked up at the big, yellow full moon that rode the night sky like a spotlight.

Buster had spent the last two hours prowling around the lawn, smelling everyplace where Bela Kovacs had walked, growling deep in his throat and every so often letting out a scared-sounding howl.

Now Johnny scratched Buster's ears, and thought about tomorrow.

It was a good idea. He'd scare Bela spitless—and then tell him why he'd done it and make friends with him again. Because Bela really wasn't a bad guy . . . he was just a little strange.

The next day Johnny took his flashlight and went over to the old Burman place around three o'clock. He went cross-country instead of down the road, and as he came out of the weed-grown cornfield that old Burman had once tended so lovingly, he saw Bela Kovacs playing in the yard by the windmill.

When Bela saw him, he stood stock-still, dark eyes wide, again with that animal look to him, as if he were ready to run.

Johnny said, "I came over to say I'm sorry Buster tried to bite you."

"Oh." Bela blinked. He had his hands cupped in front of him, about belt-level.

Johnny waited for Bela to say something else, but he didn't. Johnny looked curiously at Bela's cupped hands. "What you got?" he asked.

Bela's mouth twisted. He lifted the top hand, and Johnny saw that he held a mouse. It was curled into a ball, and its mouth hung wide open—but Johnny noticed it wasn't trying to bite its way loose. Tiny black eyes glittered up in terror.

"I caught it," Bela said. "In the barn."

"What d'you want to catch a *mouse* for?" Johnny said disgustedly. "Why not get a cat?"

Bela blinked again, and Johnny suddenly wondered if Bela hadn't been just about to cry or something, before Johnny showed up, and if he wasn't holding it back now.

"I wanted to make friends with it," Bela said softly. "But it is no different in America. All the animals hate me—fear me."

"Heck, any mouse'd be scared, caught and held that way."

"Not this frightened." Bela knelt and gently placed the mouse on the ground. For a second it stayed there, a huddled gray ball —then legs erupted and it bounded off so fast that halfway to the barn it tripped and rolled over twice, and when it reached a gap between two boards in the side of the barn, it bounced off hard because of bad aim. Then it vanished, hind legs scrabbling.

"See?" said Bela. "It runs in terror. So would a cat. I have never had a pet." He straightened and gave Johnny his shy, lonely smile. "I am sorry about yesterday too, Johnny. I am sorry I tried to hurt your dog. I did not mean—"

"Aw," Johnny said uncomfortably, remembering how Dad had felt sorry for Bela last night—and remembering what he planned to do today in the caves. "Aw . . . forget it."

Bela took Johnny into the farmhouse to meet his parents.

Mr. Kovacs was a big, handsome, middle-aged man who moved the same smooth way Bela did. And Mrs. Kovacs moved that way too—Johnny noticed it the instant he came through the front door into the living room, for Bela's parents had just been finishing their lunch, and when they saw Johnny come in, they rose from the table with Old World courtesy. And with that strange animal grace.

"Father and Mother," said Bela, "this is Johnny Stevens, the boy I met yesterday."

Mr. Kovacs took Johnny's hand and shook it firmly and gently —and Johnny could tell, from the size of Mr. Kovacs' hand and the hard feel of its palm against his own, that Mr. Kovacs was very, very strong.

And a funny thing—when Johnny took his hand away, the ends of his fingers rubbed against something sort of bristly in Mr. Kovacs' hard palm. It felt almost like Dad's cheek, just after he shaved—like short whisker stubble.

But that was silly. Nobody had hair on their palms. He'd probably just felt dried skin peeling away from work callouses.

Mrs. Kovacs, a slim, pretty woman, nodded pleasantly and said, with an accent much more pronounced than Bela's, "How do you do, Mr. Stevens."

Johnny swelled a little. It was the first time anyone had ever called him Mr. Stevens.

"I'm pleased to meet you," he said.

"Bela has told us what happened yesterday," Mr. Kovacs said. "Please, may we add our apologies to his? It is unfortunate— but animals just do not like us. It is a peculiarity of our family."

"Heck," Johnny said. "*I* came over to apologize. And to play with Bela."

Mrs. Kovacs smiled and said almost exactly what Johnny's mother had said the day before: "How nice . . . for Bela to have such a nice boy his own age to play with."

It was Johnny's turn to smile shyly. He looked away, and for the first time got a look at the inside of the Kovacs home.

The last time he'd been in this house, about three weeks ago, it had been bare walls and refuse-cluttered floors. Now there was furniture—mostly ordinary stuff. But there were some things— the round table in the middle of the room, for instance, and that big bookcase-desk against the wall—that were pretty foreign-looking. And the pictures—most of them were in fancier, heavier frames than any he'd ever seen, and a lot of them were of funny foreign buildings. And the tablecloth, and the candlesticks and lamps and the rug—oh, lots of the smaller things around the room had a foreign look. A sort of solid, warm, old look.

Mr. Kovacs, noting Johnny's interest, said in a deep bass voice. "We brought many of our things from Hungary."

"It looks nice," Johnny said.

"Thank you," said Mr. Kovacs gravely.

Mrs. Kovacs commenced to clear the table, and Johnny glanced casually at the plates . . . and when he saw what the lunch had consisted of, his jaw sagged and he looked again.

Raw meat. A roast of beef, it looked like—except it wasn't roasted. And nothing else. A big platter of red, blood-juicy beef in the middle of the table, three red-stained plates at the chair-places, glasses and a pitcher of water.

Again Mr. Kovacs noted Johnny's interest. Or his amazement.

"Raw meat," he said, a little heavily, "is good for the blood. We eat raw beefsteak once or twice a week, young man."

"Oh," said Johnny, trying not to stare so hard. "I guess I read about that someplace myself—'bout raw meat being good for you. But I don't think . . ." His voice trailed off.

"You do not think you would like it," Mrs. Kovacs smiled, picking up the plates. "But you are too polite to say so."

Johnny nodded uncomfortably.

"Now," said Mr. Kovacs, "come here, young man."

Johnny moved to stand before the man's chair. He didn't know exactly why—except that he felt somehow that Mr. Kovacs was a friendly man.

Mr. Kovacs looked appreciatively—almost critically—at Johnny's well-muscled arms and firm neck and clear eyes. "You are in good health," he said.

"I—I guess so."

"You will make a good playmate for our Bela," Mr. Kovacs said. "He is very active. Do you know the country here?"

"I've lived here all my life."

"Good. You will tell Bela of any dangers that exist, yes?"

"Sure."

"Good. Now, Bela, why don't you show your new friend around the house?"

Mrs. Kovacs began to remove the platter of raw beef. Mr. Kovacs reached out and took one of the remaining chunks and bit into it with teeth that, when he opened his mouth wide, were startlingly long and white and, from the way the meat tore, sharp.

He chewed and looked at Johnny again, a little reflectively. Johnny and Bela were over by the bookcase by the stairs—Bela was showing Johnny what Hungarian writing looked like.

Mrs. Kovacs looked too, and her large eyes—now they were almost luminous—traveled up and down Johnny's body, along the muscular arms and legs, dwelt on the tanned throat. She licked her lips.

"In the old country . . ." she murmured in Hungarian.

"Eva," said Mr. Kovacs, softly but warningly, also in Hungarian.

"Ah, *imadot* Ferenc, I am only thinking. But *look* at him . . ."

Mr. Kovacs smiled at the expression on her face. "Sh-h, now, Eva. We have left all that behind . . . it is best not even to think."

"*Sajnos* . . ." Mrs. Kovacs picked up a small piece of beef and bit into it with teeth as long and sharp as her husband's. She sighed again. "A new country, a new life . . . I know, my dear."

"You are unhappy, Eva?"

"Unhappy?" Eva Kovacs smiled down at him, and since her lower lip concealed the points of her teeth, it was quite a pleasant smile. "Only my belly suffers. I am happy that we are safe, Ferenc."

He took her hand and pressed it against his shoulder. "The old country, the old life . . . it is impossible to live that way any longer, Eva. We are known. Not you, perhaps, nor I, nor little Bela, but *we* . . . all of us . . . known by signs familiar to the smallest child. While here—here they do not know us, or even believe in us—and we must let it remain so. We must forsake the old ways."

"You are not disappointed in America, then."

He shook his massive head. "America is best, in every way. There is no tradition to expose us. The political situation is good. And living conditions, and opportunity. No, mamma, I am well content here—except—" he put his big hands palms up on the table before him and flexed them and then slowly made fists around the clean-shaven stubble on the palms—"except at this time of the month, when the moon turns her full face to us . . ."

"Yes," said Eva Kovacs softly. "Yes."

"But beef does not taste so bad, my dear. Not so bad, at least, as a silver bullet."

Mrs. Kovacs popped the last of the beef into her mouth, chewed powerfully, and swallowed. She seemed to be tasting it in her throat, feeling it, almost analyzing it as it went toward her stomach. "No," she said slowly. "Once you are used to it, it is not bad. But—"

"Do not think about it, Eva."

"We cannot even chase the cow," she said softly. "We must go and buy—"

"I know."

Mrs. Kovacs looked across the room again at Johnny Stevens, and her large eyes grew larger.

"Eva," Mr. Kovacs said, a little sharply. "You would not think of—"

"No, no," she said, and licked blood from fingers which seemed to have grown just a little hairier, and the nails a little longer. "Of course not, *imadot* Ferenc. It is just when I remember . . ."

"We must forget."

"And they are so *healthy* here . . ."

"We must never *change* again, Eva. Never."

"And Bela?"

Ferenc Kovacs sighed. "He is too young yet—too young to know. We must be sure that he is always with us when he *changes*. Soon he will be old enough to control the *change,* as we do—then we must worry no longer in our new home."

Bela had been showing Johnny his room, which held an old posterbed, a very old maple bureau, and a carved chest full of fascinating toys such as Johnny had never seen before.

Now the boys came back to the living room, and Bela said, "Mother, we are going out to play."

"All right, Bela. But remember—come home before seven o'clock."

"Yes, mamma."

"You know what time of the month this is, don't you?"

"Yes, mamma." Bela looked uncomfortably at Johnny. "I will be back."

"You *must,*" said Mr. Kovacs. "Just as you did in New York. You know why, Bela . . ." He turned to Johnny. "You will not keep our Bela out late, will you? You see—he is not well . . . that is why it is very important that he return home before nightfall."

"Oh," said Johnny. "I'll be careful. I mean, I'll—I won't—" And he looked away in confusion, thinking of what he planned to do in the cave.

Mr. Kovacs' big eyes were still on his face when he looked up, and Johnny felt they were looking right through his own eyes at the inside of his skull.

"I think," said Mr. Kovacs, "that you had better be."

Bela's parents came to the door and stood in the sunshine, and as Johnny and Bela turned to wave at them from the edge of the cornfield, Johnny noticed for the first time that their eyebrows were just like Bela's—straight, thick bars of hair that ran right across their foreheads.

The entrance to the caves was just a black chink in the rocks on the hillside. They climbed up toward it, leaping from one big boulder to the next under the afternoon sun.

They reached the black hole, and felt the coolness of it on their faces, even in the sunshine.

Bela hung back when Johnny started to go right in.

"Johnny . . ." he said.

"Yeah?"

"Don't forget . . . I *have* to be back before seven."

Johnny put his hands on his hips. "Well, f'gosh sakes, yes! I heard it enough. What's so awful that'll happen to you if you don't? D'you have to take medicine or something?"

Bela shook his head. "I can't tell you. But—you won't get lost or anything, will you?"

"No," said Johnny emphatically, crossing his fingers behind his back.

"You heard what my parents said . . . I have to be home before the moon rises."

"The *moon!* What's the moon got to do with it?"

Bela just looked nervously at the black hole in the hillside.

And Johnny didn't ask about it again. He just sniffed. "The moon, f'gosh sakes!" as if he were dismissing it as something else crazy that foreigners—especially Hungarians—worried about. Because he knew he had a better way of finding out.

"Johnny . . . perhaps I had better not go in. Not now."

Johnny put a jeer in his voice. "Scared?"

"Not for the reasons you think," Bela said, dark eyes flashing. "You do not understand."

"Well, come on, then . . . I promise—" the crossed fingers again—"I won't get lost."

Johnny started again into the black chink. Bela hesitated for a second, and then followed.

Actually, Johnny thought as they made their way through the narrow fissure into increasing darkness, the crossed fingers weren't necessary—because he wasn't planning to really get lost; only to *pretend* to get lost.

And he wasn't sure he was going to do even that, now—not if Bela was *sick*. That was different. Maybe it explained a lot— even old Buster's behavior. Dogs sometimes got funny around sick people.

But he wasn't sure that that *was* the explanation. It sounded a little fishy to him. Why all the mystery, if Bela was just sick? Or was it some awful-to-*gosh* disease? If so, why was Bela let out to play and maybe give the disease to someone else? And Mr. Kovacs had said that Bela was very active. That didn't sound like he was sick. And Bela sure didn't look sick.

Johnny decided he'd wait and decide what to do later.

The floor of the chink dipped down, and turned at a right angle, and they were inside the caves.

Johnny turned on his flashlight. And heard Bela gasp.

All around them were curtains and draperies and carpets and fountains of stone—gray, pink, blue, green, lavender, stretching from where they stood to a sharp sixty-foot downslope ahead of them, which led to the cave floor below and off into inky shadows that looked almost like solids.

Johnny played the beam of light around, giving Bela a good look at everything worth seeing here near the entrance. Then he said, "Let's start down."

They made their way across ripples of pastel-shaded stone to where the downslope began. The sounds they made started to echo, and the air was very dry and cool.

The beam of the flashlight was hard and bright, and the blackness pressed in on it as if trying to squash it down to pencil-thinness—but the beam moved like lightning, cutting like a knife, and wherever it opened the blackness it revealed wonders of color and shape.

"The waves in the slope make steps," Johnny said, pointing the light downward. "See? We can go down that way. How do you like it?"

"It is beautiful," Bela whispered.

They started down, Johnny keeping the light always on their footing and guiding their progress down the face of rock by familiar rippling formations and splashes of color.

At last they reached the bottom, and Johnny said, "This way."

As they started across the uneven floor of the cave, Bela asked, "Do you know the time, Johnny?"

" 'Bout four . . . you got lotsa time."

And soon the caves became so beautiful that Bela forgot entirely to worry about the time.

They passed fountains and sprays and mists and museums of stone, gleaming with colors purer and more delicate than any ever seen on Earth's surface. They passed marching stalagmites of green and blue and bright orange, here and there united with drooping stalactites to form arching passageways and gardens of pillars. They moved slowly beneath walls of rippled stone, as if blue or pink or purple lava had been frozen in midflow.

They passed lakes of blue-black water, so still and smooth that one had almost to touch them to be convinced that they weren't glass.

They moved up vast slopes of colored stone like insects up a giant Christmas tree ornament, and when they reached the top, Johnny would select this dark passage or that and lead them on into royal chambers of purple and white, and then up a curving crimson staircase to a balcony of coral pink and green where more passages offered further mysteries to be explored.

They moved along the edges of crevices so deep that a penny dropped made no sound—not even the whisper of an echo.

Once Johnny turned off his light and told Bela to stand still, and they listened to the silence which can not be qualified, the silence which is absolute—the silence that exists only underground.

They heard their own hearts beating.

At last Johnny was sure the time must be about six o'clock.

"We'd better get started back," he told Bela. "If you're going to get home by seven. This way."

And he led the way back to the place where they had entered the caves. And there he pretended to get lost.

It was easy. Bela was new to the caves. He probably wouldn't recognize the entrance even if Johnny flashed his light up the long slope right to the chink where they'd come in.

Johnny wasn't sure yet whether he wanted to keep up the pretense for more than a few minutes—maybe he'd just throw a short scare into Bela, and then take him on out of the caves so he could go home by seven. After all, if Bela was sick . . .

But he wasn't sure about that. It still sounded fishy. And he was more curious than ever to know what the mystery was all about—even if it *was* some kind of disease.

He said worriedly, "Bela . . . I—I'm not sure which way we go from here. I think maybe I'm lost . . ."

And he looked to see what effect it would have on the Hungarian boy.

Bela's eyes grew huge. "Oh, *no* . . . Johnny, you do not mean it! You *promised!*"

John pretended to be confused—even afraid. "I—I'm sorry," he stammered. "I just lost the way. I was so interested showing you around. Gosh, Bela—"

"But, Johnny, I *have* to get out. I have to get home before . . ."

"Come on," Johnny said, making his voice worried. "Maybe—maybe it's this way."

And he led Bela in a huge circle through the pillars and passages and hanging stone curtains that surrounded the entrance. It took about half an hour, and then they were right back where they'd started from—within a hundred feet of the entrance.

Johnny said, "I just don't know where we *are!*"

"What time do you think it is?" Bela asked, his voice terrified.

"Six thirty, about."

Bela shuddered and looked at Johnny, his eyes shining enormously in the light. "Johnny, I have to get *out* . . ."

Johnny put panic in his voice. "Well, what can *I* do? I'm sorry! I'm scared too! Maybe we'll *never* get out!"

"Try," Bela begged. "Try, Johnny . . . can't you remember the way?

Looking at Bela in the light, at the big dark eyes and smooth brown skin and white straight teeth and lithe body, Johnny decided abruptly that the story about Bela's being sick must be phony. It was something *else* . . . there was some other reason why Bela was so frantic about being home by seven, and why his parents were so emphatic on the same point. Some real strange, funny reason—and Johnny wanted to know what.

He decided to do as he'd originally planned—keep Bela down here and watch to see what happened.

He turned around as if in indecision. "I think—I think maybe it's off this way. Come on!"

And he led Bela in a circle the other way around, by a slightly different route, and they ended up by the entrance again.

Johnny knew it must be nearly seven by now. He kept a sharp eye on Bela while pretending to search for the entrance chink that was really right up the slope over their heads.

Would Bela know, somehow, when seven o'clock had arrived? And was it something that would happen to him right at seven that he was afraid of? But how could he know the time? . . . and what could happen down here in the caves? Or was it something his parents would do to him later, as punishment for not getting home by that time?

"Johnny!" Bela said suddenly, close by Johnny in the blackness, a quaver in his voice.

Johnny stopped his pretense of searching, and put the beam of light on Bela. "Yeah?"

Bela was trembling all over, and he was looking up at the roof of the cave. As Johnny watched, he hunched his shoulders a little—sort of cringed—and his face got even tighter, as if he saw something horrible coming at him right down through the blackness, the solid rock.

"It is almost seven . . . Johnny . . . *do something* . . . it is going to *happen!*"

"What's going to happen? *What* can I do?"

"I do not know," Bela cried, and echoes came back, *I do not know, do not know* . . .

"You don't know what I can do?"

"I do not know . . ." . . . *do notknow, notknow, know, know* . . .

"You don't know what's going to happen?"

"I do not know! I am frightened . . . it never happened to me away from home before . . . Johnny, you *promised* . . . ah, mamma, mamma, *mamma*—" and Bela began to cry. He sank to a heap on the colored stone floor, and tears rolled down his cheeks and splashed on the stone and made the colors deeper, and he wailed things in Hungarian until he could hardly talk any more but just cried.

"You don't know what's going to happen?" Johnny asked, amazed.

Bela choked trying to talk, and coughed hard, and the echoes came back like footsteps across his frantic voice. "Yes, I know— but I do not know what it is, or why, it just *happens* . . . ah, mamma, *mamma* . . ."

Suddenly his back stiffened, and his hands clawed out in front of him. His streaming eyes rolled up to Johnny's face. He whined like an animal. "Johnny . . . it is seven . . . the moon is rising . . . I can feel it . . ."

"Feel the moon? Down *here?* How can—"

"It does not matter where . . . I can *feel* it . . . I can feel . . . mamma, mamma—ah, ah, *ah!*"

And Bela's face twisted into an expression of such terror and agony that Johnny was suddenly chilled—and he decided that his joke had gone far enough. In fact, all of a sudden he was pretty darned scared—he hadn't expected anything like this! Golly, if Bela really *was* sick . . .

He bent over the huddled figure on the cave floor and pointed his flashlight upward.

"Bela, look!" he said loudly. "Look up there . . . *there's* where we came in! Come on—let's go out!"

Bela didn't answer.

"Bela . . . *C'mon.*"

Bela moved, and his fingernails scratched the rock so hard it sounded like they'd tear off.

Johnny began to tremble. He looked down, the flashlight still pointing up.

Bela's eyes gleamed up at him from the floor—enormous, yellowish in the reflected light, glassy, fixed—somehow baleful.

As Johnny watched, they seemed to move closer together, and get yellower.

Johnny was so startled he dropped the flashlight. It thumped on the stone at his feet, and glass broke and the light went out.

In the blackness—the utter thick blackness—Johnny heard a scuffling sound near his feet, and a low, soft, animal snarl.

He yelled and leaped back. His foot struck the flashlight, and even as he went down he got one hand on it, and with the other hand he dragged his big hunting knife out of his belt. He hit hard on his side. He pressed the flashlight button and prayed that it would work.

It did.

Bela was gone.

Wide-eyed, Johnny rolled over. Kneeling there, he darted the light this way and that. Finally he found his voice.

"B-Bela . . ." he quavered.

Nothing happened.

He got to his feet and stood shaking. "Bela?"

There was a claws-on-stone sound from the blackness behind him.

He whirled, his neck stiff and cold, and lashed the beam of light across the shadows. He held his hunting knife hard, the point straight out, ready to stab or slice from almost any angle.

At first he saw nothing. Rocks. Curtains and pillars of colored stone. Black shadows that seemed to lean toward him.

Then a low shadow moved at the corner of his vision.

He swung the light that way.

Two yellow eyes, low against the stone floor, blazed back at him.

"B-Bela?" Johnny whispered, and lifted the light so that it shone directly on the possessor of the eyes.

The creature slitted the eyes and snarled to reveal sharp white fangs—and charged.

Mr. and Mrs. Kovacs were looking both furious and terrified at the same time. They stood by the big table in the living room, where they'd been sitting playing some kind of game with big colored cards when Johnny came bursting in to tell them what had happened in the caves.

"I'm sorry," Johnny said, for the dozenth time—and wiped a hand across his tear-stained cheeks.

"I didn't mean to do it . . . it was just a joke. Please, call Sheriff Morris and ask him to get a posse out . . . they'll find Bela, honest they will!"

Mr. Kovacs' large eyes were brilliant with anger—and his deep voice was almost a snarl. "*I* will go look for Bela, young man—and you had better go home. I do not think we want to see you any more!"

Johnny turned miserably toward the door.

There was a growl from the darkness right outside.

Mrs. Kovacs gasped, *"Bela . . ."*

The creature came panting through the open door and made a beeline for Johnny's leg.

Johnny said, "It isn't Bela . . . it's that darned wolf cub!" He dodged and dropped to one knee and cuffed the cub playfully on the side of the head.

It snarled like a lapdog and backed off and put its belly against the floor. Its tiny ears were flat against its head, just as old Buster's had been when he'd first seen Bela, and its yellow eyes gleamed hungrily on Johnny's throat.

It charged again, stubby legs pumping.

Johnny caught it neatly by the scruff of the neck and shook it gently. It snapped and snarled and waved its legs.

"I'll be darned," he said, forgetting for the moment that Mr. Kovacs had practically ordered him out of the house. "The little feller must've followed me here . . ."

"You saw the little wolf tonight?" Mr. Kovacs said sharply, eyes widening and glowing a little brighter.

"Sure. In the cave. Just after Bela ran off. It tried to bite me then too, and now it followed me all the way to your place." Johnny grinned feebly, looking from Mr. Kovacs' rather grim face to Mrs. Kovacs' somehow relieved one. "I guess it wants to eat me or something."

"I suppose," said Mr. Kovacs heavily, "it does."

"I'll take it outside and turn it loose again," Johnny said.

"Again?"

The cub swung from Johnny's grasp, rolling its yellow eyes hungrily at the nearest finger. Johnny nodded. "I carried it up out of the caves, after I gave up hollering for Bela. Figured it wasn't right to let it die down there. Maybe when it gets older, I'll shoot it if I see it . . . but now I figured to give it a chance, it's so young."

"Oh, give him to me, young man," said Mrs. Kovacs. "He's so cute!" And she took the wolf cub from Johnny's arms before Johnny could protest it was dangerous, and cuddled it in her own. It whined and looked up at her with its big yellow eyes, and didn't struggle at all to free itself.

Johnny was too unhappy to wonder at that, though, or even notice it.

"Now go home, young man," said Mr. Kovacs.

Johnny turned to the door again. "Will you turn it loose afterwards, Mr. Kovacs? You won't kill it, will you?"

"I will not kill it."

"And you better call the sheriff to help you look for Bela. I'll help too, if—if you want. I know the caves like—"

"Bela will be all right," Mr. Kovacs said.

"When you find him, will you please tell him I'm sorry for what I did?"

"Yes."

Johnny had reached the front door when Mrs. Kovacs said something soft in Hungarian, and Mr. Kovacs grunted and said,

"Young man."

Johnny turned. "Yes, sir?"

The wolf cub was on the table, and Mr. Kovacs was thoughtfully scratching the scruff of its neck.

"Young man," Mr. Kovacs said slowly. "I do not want to be harsh. I have thought it over. What you did was not very nice— but I think it is understandable. I think it may be forgiven. And you came to us immediately and told us about it—and now you have offered to help undo what you have done."

"Yes, sir?"

"You may come here as often as you wish, and play with our Bela."

Johnny brightened. "Yes, sir! Thank you!"

"Provided you never do anything like that again."

"Yes, sir. I mean, no, sir!"

"Now," said Mr. Kovacs a little intently. "I would like to make absolutely certain of what happened in the cave. It happened like this, yes? Our Bela became sick; you dropped your flashlight; when you turned the light on again, Bela was gone."

"That's right, sir."

"You did *not* see where Bela went."

"No, sir."

"And then you saw the little wolf."

"Uh, huh." Johnny grinned. "It was a dope to wander in there. Lucky I came along."

"M'm," said Mr. Kovacs. "Yes." His eyes, which had become a little larger as he questioned Johnny, lost some of their wary glow; and his fingers, which had become just a tiny bit hairier, relaxed. "Now, you had better go. I will—find Bela. Good night, young man."

"Good night, Mr. Kovacs. Good night, Mrs. Kovacs."

As Johnny turned to leave again, Mr. Kovacs said, "Another thing, young man."

Johnny paused.

"I was not entirely truthful with you. Our Bela is not really sick. It is just that at certain times of the month, he is expected to be home before nightfall because . . . well, I believe you might call it a custom. A Hungarian custom. An old family custom. It must be observed. Do you understand?"

"Yes, sir."

"We will not tell Bela what you did . . . if you will promise never to tell anyone what happened tonight."

"Yes, sir."

"We would not want to be thought queer by our neighbors. After all, young man, customs differ. We are all of us different."

"Yes, sir. My father taught me that."

"Did he teach you to keep promises?"

Johnny grinned. "He licks me when I don't."

"Do you promise, then?"

"Yes."

"You will make a good playmate for our Bela, as I said. Good night, young man."

Smiling, Johnny Stevens left. When he reached the edge of the cornfield, he began to whistle at the full moon overhead. He wondered if the moon always rose at seven in Hungary . . .

Naw. Maybe it was just a time set so Bela would always be home before it happened, and observe whatever the custom was. But, heck, lots of times the moon rose earlier than seven. Even the full moon, like tonight—it always rose when the sun set. Four o'clock sometimes, in winter.

Maybe—Johnny nodded, remembering something from school —maybe the Kovacs figured the time for Bela to be home by the seasons, by the months. Even by the—the—latitudes.

What a funny custom. Maybe someday Bela would tell him about it . . .

Mr. Kovacs looked thoughtfully at his son.

"We could have lost all," he told his wife, "but for a boy dropping a flashlight. Our new country is good to us. Now—the time has come when we must tell Bela what he is."

Doomsday Deferred

WILL F. JENKINS

If I were sensible, I'd say that somebody else told me this story, and then cast doubts on his veracity. But I saw it all. I was part of it. I have an invoice of a shipment I made from Brazil, with a notation on it, "José Ribiera's stuff." The shipment went through. The invoice, I noticed only today, has a mashed *soldado* ant sticking to the page. There is nothing unusual about it as a specimen. On the face of things, every element is irritatingly commonplace. But if I were sensible, I wouldn't tell it this way.

It began in Milhao, where José Ribiera came to me. Milhao is in Brazil, but from it the Andes can be seen against the sky at sunset. It is a town the jungle unfortunately did not finish burying when the rubber boom collapsed. It is so far up the Amazon basin that its principal contacts with the outer world are smugglers and fugitives from Peruvian justice who come across the mountains, and nobody at all goes there except for his sins. I don't know what took José Ribiera there. I went because one of the three known specimens of *Morpho andiensis* was captured nearby by Böhler in 1911, and a lunatic millionaire in Chicago was willing to pay for a try at a fourth for his collection.

I got there after a river steamer refused to go any further, and after four days more in a canoe with paddlers who had lived on or near river water all their lives without once taking a bath in it. When I got to Milhao, I wished myself back in the canoe. It's that sort of place.

But that's where José Ribiera was, and in back-country Brazil there is a remarkable superstition that *os Senhores Norteamericanos* are honest men. I do not explain it. I simply record it. And just as I was getting settled in a particularly noisome inn, José knocked on my door and came in. He was a small brown man, and he was scared all the way down deep inside. He tried to hide that. The thing I noticed first was that he was clean. He was barefoot, but his tattered duck garments were immaculate, and the rest of him had been washed, and recently. In a town like Milhao, that was startling.

"*Senhor,*" said José in a sort of apologetic desperation, "you are a *Senhor Norteamericano.* I—I beg your aid."

I grunted. Being an American is embarrassing, sometimes and in some places. José closed the door behind him and fumbled inside his garments. His eyes anxious, he pulled out a small cloth bundle. He opened it with shaking fingers. And I blinked. The lamplight glittered and glinted on the most amazing mass of tiny gold nuggets I'd ever seen. I hadn't a doubt it was gold, but even at first glance I wondered how on earth it had been gathered. There was no flour gold at all—that fine powder which is the largest part of any placer yield. Most of it was gravelly particles of pinhead size. There was no nugget larger than a half pea. There must have been five pounds of it altogether, though, and it was a rather remarkable spectacle.

"*Senhor,*" said José tensely, "I beg that you will help me turn this into cattle! It is a matter of life or death."

I hardened my expression. Of course, in thick jungle like that around Milhao, a cow or a bull would be as much out of place as an Eskimo, but that wasn't the point. I had business of my own in Milhao. If I started gold buying or cattle dealing out of amiability, my own affairs would suffer. So I said in polite regret, "I am not a businessman, *senhor*. I don't deal in gold or cattle either. To buy cattle, you should go down to São Pedro" —that was four days' paddle downstream, or considering the current perhaps three—"and take this gold to a banker. He will give you money for it if you can prove that it is yours. You can then buy cattle if you wish."

José looked at me desperately. Certainly half the population of Milhao—and positively the Peruvian-refugee half—would have cut his throat for a fraction of his hoard. He almost panted: "But, *senhor!* This would be enough to buy cattle in São Pedro and send them here, would it not?"

I agreed that at a guess it should buy all the cattle in São Pedro, twice over, and hire the town's wheezy steam launch to tow them upriver besides. José looked sick with relief. But, I said, one should buy his livestock himself, so he ought to go to São Pedro in person. And I could not see what good cattle would be in the jungle anyhow.

"Yet—it would buy cattle!" and José, gulping. "That is what I told—my friends. But I cannot go farther than Milhao, *senhor*. I cannot go to São Pedro. Yet I must—I need to buy cattle for— my friends! It is life and death! How can I do this, *senhor?*"

Naturally, I considered that he exaggerated the emergency.

"I am not a businessman," I repeated. "I would not be able to help you." Then at the terrified look in his eyes I explained, "I am here after butterflies."

He couldn't understand that. He began to stammer, pleading. So I explained.

"There is a rich man," I said wryly, "who wishes to possess a certain butterfly. I have pictures of it. I am sent to find it. I can pay one thousand milreis for one butterfly of a certain sort. But I have no authority to do other business, such as the purchase of gold or cattle."

José looked extraordinarily despairing. He looked numbed by the loss of hope. So, merely to say or do something, I showed him a color photograph of the specimen of *Morpho andiensis* which is in the Goriot collection in Paris. Bug collectors were in despair about it during the war. They were sure the Nazis would manage to seize it. Then José's eyes lighted hopefully.

"*Senhor!*" he said urgently. "Perhaps my—friends can find you such a butterfly! Will you pay for such a butterfly in cattle sent here from São Pedro, *senhor?*"

I said rather blankly that I would, but—Then I was talking to myself. José had bolted out of my room, leaving maybe five pounds of gravelly gold nuggets in my hands. That was not usual.

I went after him, but he'd disappeared. So I hid his small fortune in the bottom of my collection kit. A few drops of formaldehyde, spilled before closing up a kit of collection bottles and insects, is very effective in chasing away pilferers. I make use of it regularly.

Next morning I asked about José. My queries were greeted with shrugs. He was a very low person. He did not live in Milhao, but had a clearing, a homestead, some miles upstream, where he lived with his wife. They had one child. He was suspected of much evil. He had bought pigs, and taken them to his clearing and behold he had no pigs there! His wife was very pretty, and a Peruvian had gone swaggering to pay court to her, and he had never come back. It is notable, as I think of it, that up to this time no ant of any sort has come into my story. Butterflies, but no ants. Especially not *soldados*—army ants. It is queer.

I learned nothing useful about José, but I had come to Milhao on business, so I stated it publicly. I wished a certain butterfly, I said. I would pay one thousand milreis for a perfect specimen. I would show a picture of what I wanted to any interested person, and I would show how to make a butterfly net and how to use it, and how to handle butterflies without injuring them. But I wanted only one kind, and it must not be squashed.

The inhabitants of Milhao became happily convinced that I was insane, and that it might be profitable insanity for them. Each person leaped to the nearest butterfly and blandly brought it to me. I spent a whole day explaining to bright-eyed people that matching the picture of *Morpho andiensis* required more than that the number of legs and wings should be the same. But, I repeated, I would pay one thousand milreis for a butterfly exactly like the picture. I had plenty of margin for profit and loss, at that. The last time a *Morpho andiensis* was sold, it brought $25,000 at auction. I'd a lot rather have the money, myself.

José Ribiera came back. His expression was tense beyond belief. He plucked at my arm and said, *"Senhor,"* and I grabbed him and dragged him to my inn.

I hauled out his treasure. "Here!" I said angrily. "This is not mine! Take it!"

He paid no attention. He trembled. *"Senhor,"* he said, and swallowed. "My friends—my friends do not think they can catch the butterfly you seek. But if you will tell them—" He wrinkled his brows. *"Senhor,* before a butterfly is born, is it a little soft nut with a worm in it?"

That could pass for a description of a cocoon. José's friends— he was said not to have any—were close observers. I said so. José seemed to grasp at hope as at a straw.

"My—friends will find you the nut which produces the butterfly," he said urgently, "if you tell them which kind it is and what it looks like."

I blinked. Just three specimens of *Morpho andiensis* had ever been captured, so far as was known. All were adult insects. Of course nobody knew what the cocoon was like. For that matter, any naturalist can name a hundred species—and in the Amazon valley alone—of which only the adult forms have been named. But who would hunt for cocoons in jungle like that outside of Milhao?

"My friend," I said skeptically, "there are thousands of different such things. I will buy five of each different kind you can discover, and I will pay one milreis apiece. But only five of each kind, remember!"

I didn't think he'd even try, of course. I meant to insist that he take back his gold nuggets. But again he was gone before I could stop him. I had an uncomfortable impression that when I made my offer, his face lighted as if he'd been given a reprieve from a death sentence. In the light of later events, I think he had.

I angrily made up my mind to take his gold back to him next day. It was a responsibility. Besides, one gets interested in a man —especially of the half-breed class—who can unfeignedly ignore five pounds of gold. I arranged to be paddled up to his clearing next morning.

It was on the river, of course. There are no footpaths in Am-azon-basin jungle. The river flowing past Milhao is a broad deep stream perhaps two hundred yards wide. Its width seems less because of the jungle walls on either side. And the jungle is daunting. It is trees and vines and lianas as seen from the stream, but it is more than that. Smells come out, and you can't identify them. Sounds come out, and you can't interpret them. You cut your way into its mass, and you can see nothing. You come out, and you have learned nothing. You cannot affect it. It ignores you. It made me feel insignificant.

My paddlers would have taken me right on past José's clear-ing without seeing it, if he hadn't been on the river bank. He shouted. He'd been fishing, and now that I think, there were no fish near him, but there were some picked-clean fish skeletons. And I think the ground was very dark about him when we first saw him, and quite normal when we approached. I know he was sweating, but he looked terribly hopeful at the sight of me.

I left my two paddlers to smoke and slumber in the canoe. I followed José into the jungle. It was like walking in a tunnel of lucent green light. Everywhere there were tree trunks and vines and leaves, but green light overlay everything. I saw a purple butterfly with crimson wing tips, floating abstractedly in the jun-gle as if in an undersea grotto.

Then the path widened, and there was José's dwelling. It was a perfect proof that man does not need civilization to live in comfort. Save for cotton garments, an iron pot and a machete, there was literally nothing in the clearing or the house which was not of and from the jungle, to be replaced merely by stretching out one's hand. To a man who lives like this, gold has no value. While he keeps his wants at this level, he can have no temptations. My thoughts at the moment were almost sentimental.

I beamed politely at José's wife. She was a pretty young girl with beautifully regular features. But, disturbingly, her eyes were as panic-filled as José's. She spoke, but she seemed tremblingly absorbed in the contemplation of some crawling horror. The two of them seemed to live with terror. It was too odd to be quite believable. But their child—a brown-skinned three-year-old quite innocent of clothing—was unaffected. He stared at me, wide-eyed.

"Senhor," said José in a trembling voice, "here are the things you desire, the small nuts with worms in them."

His wife had woven a basket of flat green strands. He put it before me. And I looked into it tolerantly, expecting nothing. But I saw the sort of thing that simply does not happen. I saw a half bushel of cocoons!

José had acquired them somehow in less than twenty-four hours. Some were miniature capsules of silk which would yield little butterflies of wing spread no greater than a mosquito's. Some were sturdy fat cocoons of stout brown silk. There were cocoons which cunningly mimicked the look of bird droppings, and cocoons cleverly concealed in twisted leaves. Some were green—I swear it—and would pass for buds upon some unnamed vine. And——

It was simply, starkly impossible. I was stupefied. The Amazon basin has been collected, after a fashion, but the pupa and cocoon of any reasonably rare species is at least twenty times more rare than the adult insect. And these cocoons were fresh! They were alive! I could not believe it, but I could not doubt it. My hands shook as I turned them over.

I said, "This is excellent, José! I will pay for all of them at the rate agreed on—one milreis each. I will send them to São Pedro today, and their price will be spent for cattle and the bringing of the cattle here. I promise it!"

José did not relax. I saw him wipe sweat off his face.

"I—beg you to command haste, *Senhor,*" he said thinly.

I almost did not hear. I carried that basket of cocoons back to the riverbank. I practically crooned over it all the way back to Milhao. I forgot altogether about returning the gold pellets. And I began to work frenziedly at the inn.

I made sure, of course, that the men who would cart the parcel would know that it contained only valueless objects like cocoons. Then I slipped in the parcel of José's gold. I wrote a letter to the one man in São Pedro who, if God was good, might have sense enough to attend to the affair for me. And I was almost idiotically elated.

While I was making out the invoice that would carry my shipment by refrigerated air express from the nearest airport it could be got to, a large ant walked across my paper. One takes insects very casually in back-country Brazil. I mashed him, without noticing what he was. I went blissfully to start the parcel off. I had a shipment that would make history among bug collectors. It was something that simply could not be done!

The fact of the impossibility hit me after the canoe with the parcel started downstream. How the devil those cocoons had been gathered———

The problem loomed larger as I thought. In less than one day, José had collected a half bushel of cocoons, of at least one hundred different species of moths and butterflies. It could not be done! The information to make it possible did not exist! Yet it had happened. How?

The question would not down. I had to find out. I bought a pig for a present and had myself ferried up to the clearing again. My paddlers pulled me upstream with languid strokes. The pig made irritated noises in the bottom of the canoe. Now I am sorry about that pig. I would apologize to its ghost if opportunity offered. But I didn't know.

I landed on the narrow beach and shouted. Presently José came through the tunnel of foliage that led to his house. He thanked me, dry-throated, for the pig. I told him I had ordered cattle sent up from São Pedro. I told him humorously that every ounce of meat on the hoof the town contained would soon be on the way behind a wheezing steam launch. José swallowed and nodded numbly. He still looked like someone who contemplated pure horror.

We got the pig to the house. José's wife sat and rocked her child, her eyes sick with fear. I probably should have felt embarrassed in the presence of such tragedy, even if I could not guess at its cause. But instead, I thought about the questions I wanted to ask. José sat down dully beside me.

I was oblivious of the atmosphere of doom. I said blandly, "Your friends are capable naturalists, José. I am much pleased. Many of the 'little nuts' they gathered are quite new to me. I would like to meet such students of the ways of nature."

José's teeth clicked. His wife caught her breath. She looked at me with an oddly despairing irony. It puzzled me. I looked at José, sharply. And then the hair stood up on my head. My heart tried to stop. Because a large ant walked on José's shoulder, and I saw what kind of ant it was.

"My God!" I said shrilly. "*Soldados!* Army ants!"

I acted through pure instinct. I snatched up the baby from its mother's arms and raced for the river. One does not think at such times. The *soldado* ant, the army ant, the driver ant, is the absolute and undisputed monarch of all jungles everywhere. He travels by millions of millions, and nothing can stand against him. He is ravening ferocity and inexhaustible number. Even man abandons his settlements when the army ant marches in, and returns only after he has left—to find every bit of flesh devoured to the last morsel, from the earwigs in the thatch to a horse that may have been tethered too firmly to break away. The army ant on the march can and does kill anything alive, by tearing the flesh from it in tiny bites, regardless of defense. So— I grabbed the child and ran.

José Ribiera screamed at me, *"No! Senhor! No!"*

He sat still and he screamed. I'd never heard such undiluted horror in any man's voice.

I stopped. I don't know why. I was stunned to see José and his wife sitting frozen where I'd left them. I was more stunned, I think, to see the tiny clearing and the house unchanged. The army ant moves usually on a solid front. The ground is covered with a glistening, shifting horde. The air is filled with tiny clickings of limbs and mandibles. Ants swarm up every tree and shrub. Caterpillars, worms, bird nestlings, snakes, monkeys unable to flee—anything living becomes buried under a mass of ferociously rending small forms which tear off the living flesh in shreds until only white bones are left.

But José sat still, his throat working convulsively. I had seen *soldados* on him. But there were no *soldados*. After a moment José got to his feet and came stumbling toward me. He looked like a dead man. He could not speak.

"But look!" I cried. My voice was high-pitched. "I saw *soldado* ants! I saw them!"

José gulped by pure effort of will. I put down the child. He ran back to his mother.

"*S-si.* Yes," said José, as if his lips were very stiff and his throat without moisture. "But they are—special *soldados*. They are—pets. Yes. They are tame. They are my—friends. They—do tricks, *senhor*. I will show you!"

He held out his hand and made sucking noises with his mouth. What followed is not to be believed. An ant—a large ant, an inch or more long—walked calmly out of his sleeve and onto his outstretched hand. It perched there passively while the hand quivered like an aspen leaf.

"But yes!" said José hysterically. "He does tricks, *senhor!* Observe! He will stand on his head!"

Now, this I saw, but I do not believe it. The ant did something so that it seemed to stand on its head. Then it turned and crawled tranquilly over his hand and wrist and up his sleeve again.

There was silence, or as much silence as the jungle ever holds. My own throat went dry. And what I have said is insanity, but this is much worse. I felt Something waiting to see what I would do. It was, unquestionably, the most horrible sensation I had ever felt. I do not know how to describe it. What I felt was—not a personality, but a mind. I had a ghastly feeling that Something was looking at me from thousands of pairs of eyes, that it was all around me.

I shared, for an instant, what that Something saw and thought. I was surrounded by a mind which waited to see what I would do. It would act upon my action. But it was not a sophisticated mind. It was murderous, but innocent. It was merciless, but naïve.

That is what I felt. The feeling doubtless has a natural explanation which reduces it to nonsense, but at the moment I believed it. I acted on my belief. I am glad I did.

"Ah, I see!" I said in apparent amazement. "That is clever, José! It is remarkable to train an ant! I was absurd to be alarmed. But—your cattle will be on the way, José! They should get here very soon! There will be many of them!"

Then I felt that the mind would let me go. And I went.

My canoe was a quarter mile downstream when one of the paddlers lifted his blade from the water and held it there, listening. The other stopped and listened too. There was a noise in the jungle. It was mercifully far away, but it sounded like a pig. I have heard the squealing of pigs at slaughtering time, when instinct tells them of the deadly intent of men and they try punily to fight. This was not that sort of noise. It was worse; much worse.

I made a hopeless spectacle of myself in the canoe. Now, of course, I can see that, from this time on, my actions were not those of a reasoning human being. I did not think with proper scientific skepticism. It suddenly seemed to me that Norton's theory of mass consciousness among social insects was very plausible. Bees, says Norton, are not only units in an organization. They are units of an organism. The hive or the swarm is a creature— one creature—says Norton. Each insect is a body cell only, just as the corpuscles in our blood stream are individuals and yet only parts of us. We can destroy a part of our body if the welfare of the whole organism requires it, though we destroy many cells. The swarm or the hive can sacrifice its members for the hive's defense. Each bee is a mobile body cell. Its consciousness is a part of the whole intelligence, which is that of the group. The group is the actual creature. And ants, says Norton, show the fact more clearly still; the ability of the creature which is an ant colony to sacrifice a part of itself for the whole. . . . He gives illustrations of what he means. His book is not accepted by naturalists generally, but there in the canoe, going down-river from José's clearing, I believed it utterly.

I believed that an army-ant army was as much a single creature as a sponge. I believed that the Something in José's jungle clearing—its body cells were *soldado* ants—had discovered that other creatures perceived and thought as it did. Nothing more was needed to explain everything. An army-ant creature, without physical linkages, could know what its own members saw and knew and felt. It should need only to open its mind to perceive what other creatures saw and knew and felt.

The frightening thing was that when it could interpret such unantish sensations, it could find its prey with a terrible infallibility. It could flow through the jungle in a streaming, crawling tide of billions of tiny stridulating bodies. It could know the whereabouts and thoughts of every living thing around it. Nothing could avoid it, as nothing could withstand it. And if it came upon a man, it could know his thoughts too. It could perceive in his mind vast horizons beyond its former ken. It could know of food—animal food—in quantities never before imagined. It could, intelligently, try to arrange to secure that food.

It had.

But if so much was true, there was something else it could do. The thought made the blood seem to cake in my veins. I began frantically to thrust away the idea. The Something in José's clearing hadn't discovered it yet. But pure terror of the discovery had me drenched in sweat when I got back to Milhao.

All this, of course, was plainly delusion. It was at least a most unscientific attitude. But I'd stopped being scientific. I even stopped using good sense. Believing what I did, I should have got away from there as if all hell were after me. But the Something in José's clearing may already have been practicing its next logical step without knowing it. Maybe that's why I stayed.

Because I did stay in Milhao. I didn't leave the town again, even for José's clearing. I stayed about the inn, halfheartedly dealing with gentry who tried every known device, except seeking the *Morpho andiensis,* to extract a thousand milreis from me. Mostly they offered mangled corpses which would have been useless for my purpose even if they'd been the butterfly I was after. No argument would change their idea that I was insane, nor dash their happy hope of making money out of my hallucination that butterflies were worth money. But I was only halfhearted in these dealings, at best. I waited feverishly for the cattle from São Pedro. I was obsessed.

I couldn't sleep. By day I fought the thought that tried to come into my head. At night I lay in the abominable inn—in a hammock, because there are no beds in back-country Brazilian inns, and a man would be a fool to sleep in them if there were— and listened to the small, muted, unidentifiable noises from the jungle. *And* fought away the thought that kept trying to come into my mind. It was very bad.

I don't remember much about the time I spent waiting. It was purest nightmare. But several centuries after the shipment of the cocoons, the launch from São Pedro came puffing asthmatically up the reaches of the river. I was twitching all over, by that time, from the strain of not thinking about what the Something might discover next.

I didn't let the launch tie up to shore. I went out to meet it in a canoe, and I carried my collection kit with me, and an automatic pistol and an extra box of cartridges. I had a machete too. It was not normal commercial equipment for consummating a business deal, but I feverishly kept my mind on what I was going to do. The Something in José's clearing wouldn't be made suspicious by that. It was blessedly naïve.

The launch puffed loudly and wheezed horribly, going past Milhao between tall banks of jungle. It towed a flatboat on which were twenty head of cattle—poor, dispirited, tick-infested creatures. I had them tethered fast. My teeth chattered as I stepped on the flatboat. If the Something realized what it could do—— But my hands obeyed me. I shot a dull-eyed cow through the head. I assassinated an emaciated steer. I systematically murdered every one. I was probably wild-eyed and certainly fever-thin and positively lunatic in the eyes of the Brazilian launch crew. But to them *os Senhores Norteamericanos* are notoriously mad.

I was especially close to justifying their belief because of the thought that kept trying to invade my mind. It was, baldly, that if without physical linkage the Something knew what its separate body cells saw, then without physical linkage it also controlled what they did. And if it could know what deer and monkeys saw and knew, then by the same process it could control what *they* did. It held within itself, in its terrifying innocence, the power to cause animals to march docilely and blindly to it and into the tiny maws of its millions of millions of parts. As soon as it realized the perfectly inescapable fact, it could increase in number almost without limit by this fact alone. More, in the increase its intelligence should increase too. It should grow stronger, and be able to draw its prey from greater distances. The time should come when it could incorporate men into its organism by a mere act of will. They would report to it and be controlled by it. And of course they would march to it and drive their livestock to it so it could increase still more and grow wiser and more powerful still.

I grew hysterical, on the flatboat. The thought I'd fought so long wouldn't stay out of my mind any longer. I slashed the slain animals with the machete until the flatboat was more gruesome than any knacker's yard. I sprinkled everywhere a fine white powder from my collection kit—which did not stay white where it fell, but turned red—and pictured the Amazon basin taken over and filled with endlessly marching armies of *soldado* ants. I saw the cities emptied of humanity, and the jungle of all other life. And then, making whimpering noises to myself, I pictured all the people of all the world loading their ships with their cattle and then themselves—because that was what the Something would desire—and all the ships coming to bring food to the organism for which all earth would labor and die.

José Ribiera screamed from the edge of the jungle. The launch and the flatboat were about to pass his clearing. The reek of spilled blood had surrounded the flatboat with a haze of metallic-bodied insects. And José, so weakened by long terror and despair that he barely tottered, screamed at me from the shore line, and his wife added her voice pipingly to echo his cry.

Then I knew that the Something was impatient and eager and utterly satisfied, and I shouted commands to the launch, and I got into the canoe and paddled ashore. I let the bow of the canoe touch the sand. I think that, actually, everything was lost at that moment, and that the Something knew what I could no longer keep from thinking. It knew its power as I did. But there were thousands of flying things about the flatboat load of murdered cattle, and they smelled spilt blood, and the Something in the jungle picked their brains of pure ecstasy. Therefore, I think, it paid little heed to José or his wife or me. It was too eager. And it was naïve.

"José," I said with deep cunning, "get into the canoe with your wife and baby. We will watch our friends at their banquet."

There were bellowings from the launch. I had commanded that the flatboat be beached. The Brazilians obeyed, but they were upset. I looked like a thing of horror from the butchering I had done. I put José and his family on the launch, and I tried to thrust out my mind to the Something in the jungle. I imagined a jungle tree undermined—a little tree, I specified—to fall in the river.

The men of the launch had the flatboat grounded when a slender tree trunk quivered. It toppled slowly outward, delayed in its fall by lianas that had to break. But it fell on the flatboat and the carcasses of slaughtered cattle. The rest was automatic. Army ants swarmed out the thin tree trunk. The gory deck of the flatboat turned black with them. Cries of *"Soldados!"* arose in the launch. The towline was abandoned instantly.

I think José caused me to be hauled up into the launch, but I was responsible for all the rest. We paused at Milhao, going downstream, exactly long enough to tell that there were *soldados* in the jungle three miles upstream. I got my stuff from the inn. I paid. I hysterically brushed aside the final effort of a whiskery half-breed to sell me an unrecognizable paste of legs and wings as a *Morpho andiensis*. Then I fled.

After the first day or so I slept most of the time, twitching. At São Pedro I feverishly got fast passage on a steamer going downstream. I wanted to get out of Brazil, and nothing else; but I did take José and his family on board.

I didn't talk to him, though. I didn't want to. I don't even know where he elected to go ashore from the steamer, or where he is now. I didn't draw a single deep breath until I had boarded a plane at Belem and it was airborne and I was on the way home.

Which was unreasonable. I had ended all the danger from the Something in José's clearing. When I slaughtered the cattle and made that shambles on the flatboat's deck, I spread the contents of a three-pound, formerly airtight can of sodium arsenate over everything. It is wonderful stuff. No mite, fungus, mold or beetle will attack specimens preserved by it. I'd hoped to use a fraction of a milligram to preserve a *Morpho andiensis*. I didn't. I poisoned the carcasses of twenty cattle with it. The army ants which were the Something would consume those cattle to bare white bones. Not all would die of the sodium arsenate, though. Not at first.

But the Something was naïve. And always, among the army ants as among all other members of the ant family, dead and wounded members of the organism are consumed by the sound and living. It is like the way white corpuscles remove damaged red cells from our human blood stream. So the corpses of army ants—*soldados*—that died of sodium arsenate would be consumed by those that survived, and they would die, and their corpses in turn would be consumed by others that would die. . . .

Three pounds of sodium arsenate will kill a lot of ants anyhow, but in practice not one grain of it would go to waste.

Because no *soldado* corpse would be left for birds or beetles to feed on, so long as a single body cell of the naïve Something remained alive.

And that is that. There are times when I think the whole thing was a fever dream, because it is plainly unbelievable. If it is true— why, I saved a good part of South American civilization. Maybe I saved the human race, for that matter. Somehow, though, that doesn't seem likely. But I certainly did ship a half bushel of cocoons from Milhao, and I certainly did make some money out of the deal.

I didn't get a *Morpho andiensis* in Milhao, of course. But I made out. When those cocoons began to hatch, in Chicago, there were actually four beautiful *andiensis* in the crop. I anesthetized them with loving care. They were mounted under absolutely perfect conditions. But there's an ironic side light on that. When there were only three known specimens in the collections of the whole world, the last *andiensis* sold for $25,000. But with four new ones perfect and available, the price broke, and I got only $6800 apiece! I'd have got as much for one!

Which is the whole business. But if I were sensible I wouldn't tell about it this way. I'd say that somebody else told me this story, and then I'd cast doubts on his veracity.

Shadow, Shadow on The Wall

THEODORE STURGEON

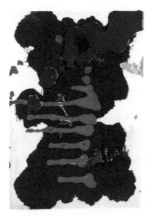

It was well after bedtime and Bobby was asleep, dreaming of a place with black butterflies that stayed, and a dog with a wuffly nose and blunt, friendly rubber teeth. It was a dark place, and comfy with all the edges blurred and soft, and he could make them all jump if he wanted to.

But then there was a sharp scythe of light that swept everything away (except in the shaded smoothness of the blank wall beside the door: someone *always* lived there) and Mommy Gwen was coming into the room with a blaze of hallway behind her. She clicked the high-up switch, the one he couldn't reach, and room light came cruelly. Mommy Gwen changed from a flat, black, light-rimmed set of cardboard triangles to a night-lit, day-time sort of Mommy Gwen.

Her hair was wide and her chin was narrow. Her shoulders were wide and her waist was narrow. Her hips were wide and her skirt was narrow, and under it all were her two hard silky sticks of legs. Her arms hung down from the wide tips of her shoulders, straight and elbowless when she walked. She never moved her arms when she walked. She never moved them at all unless she wanted to do something with them.

"You're awake." Her voice was hard, wide, flat, pointy too.

"I was asleep," said Bobby.

"Don't contradict. Get up."

Bobby sat up and fisted his eyes. "Is Daddy——"

"Your father is not in the house. He went away. He won't be back for a whole day—maybe two. So there's no use in yelling for him."

"Wasn't going to yell for him, Mommy Gwen."

"Very well, then. Get up."

Wondering, Bobby got up. His flannel sleeper pulled at his shoulders and at the soles of his snug-covered feet. He felt tousled.

"Get your toys, Bobby."

"What toys, Mommy Gwen?"

Her voice snapped like wet clothes on the line in a big wind. "Your toys—all of them!"

He went to the playbox and lifted the lid. He stopped, turned, stared at her. Her arms hung straight at her sides, as straight as her two level eyes under the straight shelf of brow. He bent to the playbox. Gollywick, Humpty-doodle and the blocks came out; the starry-wormy piece of the old phonograph, the cracked sugar egg with the peephole girl in it, the cardboard kaleidoscope and the magic set with the seven silvery rings that made a trick he couldn't do but Daddy could. He took them all out and put them on the floor.

"Here," said Mommy Gwen. She moved one straight-line arm to point to her feet with one straight-line finger. He picked up the toys and brought them to her, one at a time, two at a time, until they were all there. "Neatly, neatly," she muttered. She bent in the middle like a garage door and did brisk things with the toys, so that the scattered pile of them became a square stack. "Get the rest," she said.

He looked into the playbox and took out the old wood-framed slate and the mixed-up box of crayons; the English annual story book and an old candle, and that was all for the playbox. In the closet were some little boxing gloves and a tennis racket with broken strings, and an old ukulele with no strings at all. And that was all for the closet. He brought them to her, and she stacked them with the others.

"Those things too," she said, and at last bent her elbow to point around. From the dresser came the two squirrels and a monkey that Daddy had made from pipe cleaners, a small square of plate-glass he had found on Henry Street; a clockwork top that sounded like a church talking, and the broken clock Jerry had left on the porch last week. Bobby brought them all to Mommy Gwen, every one.

"Are you going to put me in another room?"

"No, indeed." Mommy Gwen took up the neat stack of toys. It was tall in her arms. The top fell off and thunked on the floor, bounced, chased around in a tilted circle. "Get it," said Mommy Gwen.

Bobby picked it up and reached it toward her. She stooped until he could put it on the stack, snug between the tennis racket and the box of crayons. Mommy Gwen didn't say thank you, but went away through the door, leaving Bobby standing, staring after her. He heard her hard feet go down the hall, heard the bump as she pressed open the guest-room door with her knee. There was a rattle and click as she set his toys down on the spare bed, the one without a spread, the one with dusty blue ticking on the mattress. Then she came back again.

"Why aren't you in bed?" She clapped her hands. They sounded dry, like sticks breaking. Startled, he popped back into bed and drew the covers up to his chin. There used to be someone who had a warm cheek and a soft word for him when he did that, but that was a long time ago. He lay with his eyes round in the light, looking at Mommy Gwen.

"You've been bad," she said. "You broke a window in the shed and you tracked mud into my kitchen and you've been noisy and rude. So you'll stay right here in this room without your toys until I say you can come out. Do you understand me?"

"Yes," he said. He said quickly, because he remembered in time, "Yes, ma'am."

She struck the switch swiftly, without warning, so that the darkness dazzled him, made him blink. But right away it was the room again, with the scythe of light and the shaded something hiding in the top corner of the wall by the door. There was always something shifting about there.

She went away then, thumping the door closed, leaving the darkness and taking away the light, all but a rug-fuzzed yellow streak under the door. Bobby looked away from that, and for a moment, for just a moment, he was inside his shadow-pictures where the rubber-fanged dog and the fleshy black butterflies stayed. Sometimes they stayed . . . but mostly they were gone as soon as he moved. Or maybe they changed into something else. Anyway, he liked it there, where they all lived, and he wished he could be with them, in the shadow country.

Just before he fell asleep, he saw them moving and shifting in the blank wall by the door. He smiled at them and went to sleep.

When he awoke, it was early. He couldn't smell the coffee from downstairs yet, even. There was a ruddy-yellow sun swatch on the blank wall, a crooked square, just waiting for him. He jumped out of bed and ran to it. He washed his hands in it, squatted down on the floor with his arms out. "Now!" he said.

He locked his thumbs together and slowly flapped his hands. And there on the wall was a black butterfly, flapping its wings right along with him. "Hello, butterfly," said Bobby.

He made it jump. He made it turn and settle to the bottom of the light patch, and fold its wings up and up until they were together. Suddenly he whipped one hand away, peeled back the sleeve of his sleeper, and presto! there was a long-necked duck. "Quack-ack!" said Bobby, and the duck obligingly opened its bill, threw up its head to quack. Bobby made it curl up its bill until it was an eagle. He didn't know what kind of noise an eagle made, so he said, "Eagle-eagle-eagle-eagle," and that sounded fine. He laughed.

When he laughed Mommy Gwen slammed the door open and stood there in a straight-lined white bathrobe and straight flat slippers. "What are you playing with?"

Bobby held up his empty hands.

"I was just——"

She took two steps into the room. "Get up," she said. Her lips were pale. Bobby got up, wondering why she was so angry. "I heard you laugh," she said in a hissy kind of whisper. She looked him up and down, looked at the floor around him. "What were you playing with?"

"A eagle," said Bobby.

"A what? Tell me the truth!"

Bobby waved his empty hands vaguely and looked away from her. She had such an angry face.

She stepped, reached, put a hard hand around his wrist. She lifted his arm so high he went on tiptoes, and with her other hand she felt his body, this side, that side. "You're hiding something. What is it? Where is it? What were you playing with?"

"Nothing. Reely, reely truly nothing," gasped Bobby as she shook and patted. She wasn't spanking. She never spanked. She did other things.

"You're being punished," she said in her shrill angry whisper. "Stupid, stupid, stupid . . . too stupid to know you're being punished." She set him down with a thump and went to the door. "Don't let me hear you laugh again. You've been bad, and you're not being kept in this room to enjoy yourself. Now you stay here and think about how bad you are breaking windows. Tracking mud. Lying."

She went out and closed the door with a steadiness that was like slamming, but quiet. Bobby looked at the door and wondered for a moment about that broken window. He'd been terribly sorry; it was just that the golf ball bounced so hard. Daddy had told him he should be more careful, and he had watched sorrowfully while Daddy put in a new pane. Then Daddy had given him a little piece of putty to play with and asked him never to do it again and he'd promised not to. And the whole time Mommy Gwen hadn't said a thing to him about it. She'd just looked at him every once in a while with her eyes and her mouth straight and thin, and she'd waited. She'd waited until Daddy went away.

He went back to his sunbeam and forgot all about Mommy Gwen.

After he'd made another butterfly and a dog's head and an alligator on the wall, the sunbeam got so thin that he couldn't make anything more, except, for a while, little black finger shadows that ran up and down the strip of light like ants on a matchstick. Soon there was no sunbeam at all, so he sat on the edge of his bed and watched the vague flickering of the something that lived in the end wall. It was a *different* kind of something. It wasn't a good something, and it wasn't bad. It just lived there, and the difference between it and the other things, the butterflies and dogs and swans and eagles who lived there, was that the something didn't need his hands to make it be alive. The something—stayed. Some day he was going to make a butterfly or a dog or a horse that would stay after he moved his hands away. Meanwhile, the only one who stayed, the only one who lived all the time in the shadow country, was this something that flickered up there where the two walls met the ceiling. "I'm going right in there and play with you," Bobby told it. "You'll see."

There was a red wagon with three wheels in the yard, and a gnarly tree to be climbed. Jerry came and called for a while, but Mommy Gwen sent him away. *"He's been bad."* So Jerry went away.

Bad bad bad. Funny how the things he did didn't used to be bad before Daddy married Mommy Gwen.

Mommy Gwen didn't want Bobby. That was all right—Bobby didn't want Mommy Gwen either. Daddy sometimes said to grown-up people that Bobby was much better off with someone to care for him. Bobby could remember 'way back when he used to say that with his arm around Mommy Gwen's shoulders and his voice ringing. He could remember when Daddy said it quietly, from the other side of the room, with a voice like an angry "I'm sorry." And now, Daddy hadn't said it at all for a long time.

Bobby sat on the edge of his bed and hummed to himself, thinking these thoughts, and he hummed to himself and didn't think of anything at all. He found a ladybug crawling up the dresser and caught it the careful way, circling it with his thumb and finger so that it crawled up on his hand by itself. Sometimes when you pinched them up they got busted. He stood on the windowsill and hunted until he found the little hole in the screen that the ladybug must have used to come in. He let the bug walk on the screen and guided it to the hole. It flew away, happy.

The room was flooded with warm dull light reflected from the sparkly black shed roof, and he couldn't make any shadow country people at all, so he made them in his head until he felt sleepy. He lay down then and hummed softly to himself until he fell asleep. And through the long afternoon the thing in the wall flickered and shifted and lived.

At dusk Mommy Gwen came back. Bobby may have heard her on the stairs; anyway, when the door opened on the dim room he was sitting up in bed, thumbing his eyes.

The ceiling blazed. "What have you been doing?"

"Was asleep, I guess. Is it nighttime?"

"Very nearly. I suppose you're hungry." She had a covered dish.

"Mmm."

"What kind of an answer is that?" she snapped.

"Yes ma'am I'm hungry Mommy Gwen," he said rapidly.

"That's a little better. Here." She thrust the dish at him. He took it, removed the top plate and put it under the bowl. Oatmeal. He looked at it, at her.

"Well?"

"Thank you, Mommy Gwen." He began to eat with the teaspoon he had found hilt-deep in the grey-brown mess. There was no sugar on it.

"I suppose you expect me to fetch you some sugar," she said

after a time.

"No'm," he said truthfully, and then wondered why her face went all angry and disappointed.

"What have you been doing all day?"

"Nothing. Playin'. Then I was asleep."

"Little sluggard." Suddenly she shouted at him. "What's the matter with you? Are you too stupid to be afraid? Are you too stupid to ask me to let you come downstairs? Are you too stupid to cry? Why don't you cry?"

He stared at her, round-eyed. "You wouldn't let me come down if I ast you," he said wonderingly. "So I didn't ast." He scooped up some oatmeal. "I don't feel like cryin', Mommy Gwen, I don't hurt."

"You're bad and you're being punished and it should hurt," she said furiously. She turned off the light with a vicious swipe of her hard straight hand, and went out, slamming the door.

Bobby sat still in the dark and wished he could go into the shadow country, the way he always dreamed he could. He'd go there and play with the butterflies and the fuzz-edged, blunt-toothed dogs and giraffes, and they'd stay and he'd stay and Mommy Gwen would never be able to get in, ever. Except that Daddy wouldn't be able to come with him, or Jerry either, and that would be a shame.

He scrambled quietly out of bed and stood for a moment looking at the wall by the door. He could almost for-sure see the flickering thing that lived there, even in the dark. When there was light on the wall, it flickered a shade darker than the light. At night it flickered a shade lighter than the black. It was always there, and Bobby knew it was alive. He knew it without question, like "my name is Bobby" and "Mommy Gwen doesn't want me."

Quietly, quietly, he tiptoed to the other side of the room where there was a small table lamp. He took it down and laid it carefully on the floor. He pulled the plug out and brought it down under the lower rung of the table so it led straight across the floor to the wall outlet, and plugged it in again. Now he could move the lamp quite far out into the room, almost to the middle.

The lamp had a round shade that was open at the top. Lying on its side, the shade pointed its open top at the blank wall by the door. Bobby, with the sureness of long practice, moved in the darkness to his closet and got his dark-red flannel bathrobe from a low hook. He folded it once and draped it over the large lower end of the lamp shade. He pushed the button.

On the shadow country wall appeared a brilliant disk of light, crossed by just the hints of the four wires that held the shade in place. There was a dark spot in the middle where they met.

Bobby looked at it critically. Then, squatting between the lamp and the wall, he put out his hand.

A duck. "Quackle-ackle," he whispered.

An eagle. "Eagle—eagle—eagle—eagle," he said softly.

An alligator. "Bap bap," the alligator went as it opened and closed its long snout.

He withdrew his hands and studied the round, cross-scarred light on the wall. The blurred center shadow and its radiating lines looked a little like a waterbug, the kind that can run on the surface of a brook. It soon dissatisfied him; it just sat there without doing anything. He put his thumb in his mouth and bit it gently until an idea came to him. Then he scrambled to the bed, underneath which he found his slippers. He put one on the floor in front of the lamp, and propped the other toe-upward against it. He regarded the wall gravely for a time, and then lay flat on his stomach on the floor. Watching the shadow carefully, he put his elbows together on the carpet, twined his forearms together and merged the shadow of his hands with the shadow of the slipper.

The result enchanted him. It was something like a spider, and something like a gorilla. It was a brand-new something that no one had ever seen before. He writhed his fingers and then held them still, and now the thing's knobby head had triangular luminous eyes and a jaw that swung, gaping. It had long arms for reaching and a delicate whorl of tentacles. He moved the

least little bit, and it wagged its great head and blinked at him. Watching it, he felt suddenly that the flickering thing that lived in the high corner had crept out and down toward the beast he had made, closer and closer to it until—whoosh!—it noiselessly merged with the beast, an act as quick and complete as the marriage of raindrops on a windowpane.

Bobby crowed with delight. "Stay, stay," he begged. "Oh, stay there! I'll pet you! I'll give you good things to eat! Please stay, *please!*"

The thing glowered at him. He thought it would stay, but he didn't chance moving his hands away just yet.

The door crashed open, the switch clicked, the room filled with an explosion of light.

"What are you doing?"

Bobby lay frozen, his elbows on the carpet in front of him, his forearms together, his hands twisted oddly. He put his chin on his shoulder so he could look at her standing there stiff and menacing. "I was—was just——"

She swooped down on him. She snatched him up off the floor and plumped him down on the bed. She kicked and scattered his slippers. She snatched up the lamp, pulling the cord out of the wall with the motion. "You were not to have any toys," she said in the hissing voice. "That means you were not to make any toys. For this you'll stay in here for—what are you staring at?"

Bobby spread his hands and brought them together ecstatically, holding tight. His eyes sparkled, and his small white teeth peeped out so that they could see what he was smiling at. "He stayed, he did," said Bobby. "He stayed!"

"I don't know what you're talking about and I will not stay here to find out," snapped Mommy Gwen. "I think you're a mental case." She marched to the door, striking the high switch.

The room went dark—except for that blank wall by the door.

Mommy Gwen screamed.

Bobby covered his eyes.

Mommy Gwen screamed again, hoarsely this time. It was a

sound like a dog's bark, but drawn out and out.

There was a long silence. Bobby peeped through his fingers at the dimly glowing wall. He took his hands down, sat up straight, drew his knees up to his chest and put his arms around them. "Well!" he said.

Feet pounded up the stairs. "Gwen! Gwen!"

"Hello, Daddy."

Daddy ran in, turning on the light. "Where's Mommy Gwen, Bob boy? What happened? I heard a——"

Bobby pointed at the wall. "She's in there," he said.

Daddy couldn't have understood him, for he turned and ran out of the door calling, "Gwen! Gwen!"

Bobby sat still and watched the fading shadow on the wall, quite visible even in the blaze of the overhead light. The shadow was moving, moving. It was a point-down triangle thrust into another point-down triangle which was mounted on a third, and underneath were the two hard sticks of legs. It had its arms up, its shadow-fists clenched, and it pounded and pounded silently on the wall.

"Now I'm never going into the shadow country," said Bobby complacently. "*She's* there."

So he never did.

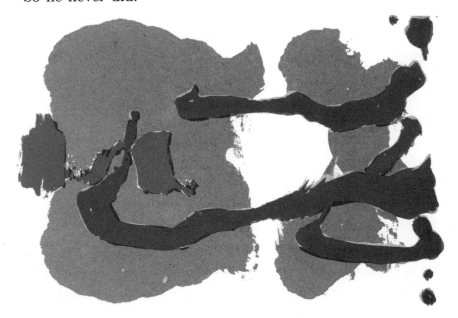

The Desrick on Yandro

MANLY WADE WELLMAN

It might could be true there's a curse on that house. It's up a mountain cove not many know of, and those who do know won't talk to you about it. So if you want to go there you'll have to find the place yourself.

When you find it you won't think at first it's any great much. Just a little house, half logs and half whipsawed planks, standing quiet and gray and dry, the open door daring you to come in.

But don't you go taking such a dare. Nor don't look too long at the three different-colored flowers on the bush by the doorstone. Those flowers look back at you like faces, with eyes that hold your eyes past the breaking away.

In the trees over you will be wings flapping, but not bird wings. Round-about you will sound voices, so soft and faint they're like voices you recollect from some long-ago time, saying things you wish you could leave forgotten.

If you get past the place, look back and you'll see the path wiggle behind you like a snake after a lizard. Then's when to run like a lizard, run your fastest and hope it's fast enough.

The folks at the party clapped me such an encore, I sang that song.

The lady had stopped her car when she saw my thumb out and my silver-strung guitar under my arm. Asked where I was headed, I told her nowhere special. Asked could I play the guitar, I played it as we rolled along. Asked me my name, I told her John. Then she invited me, most kindly, to her big country house to sing to her friends. They'd be obliged, she said. So I went there with her.

There were ladies and men in costly clothes, and they liked what I played and sang. Staying off the wornout songs, I smote out what they'd never heard before—*Rebel Soldier* and *Well I Know That Love Is Pretty* and *When the Stars Begin to Fall.* When they clapped me and hollered me for more, I sang the Yandro song, like this:

"I'll build me a desrick on Yandro's high hill
Where the wild beasts can't reach me nor hear my sad cry,
For you've gone away, gone to stay a while.
But you'll come back if you come ten thousand miles . . ."

Then they strung all round and made me more welcome than just any stranger could call for, and the hostess lady said I must stay for supper and sleep there that night. But at that moment, everybody sort of pulled back, and one man came up and sat down by me.

I'd been aware that, when first he came in, things stilled down. It was like when a big bully shows himself among little boys. He was built short and broad, his clothes were cut hand-some and costly. His buckskin hair was combed across his head to baffle folks he wasn't getting bald. His round pink face wasn't soft, and his big smiling teeth reminded you he had a skull under the meat. His pale eyes, like two gravel bits, made me recollect I needed a haircut and a shoe shine.

"You said Yandro, young man," said this fellow, almost like a charge in court, with me the prisoner.

"Yes, sir. The song's not too far from the Smokies. I heard it in a valley, and the highest peak over that valley's named Yandro. Now," I said, "I've had scholar-folks argue me it really means yonder, yonder high hill. But the peak's named Yandro, not a usual name."

"No," and he smiled toothy and fierce, "not a usual name. I'm like the peak. I'm named Yandro, too."

"How you, Mr. Yandro?" I said.

"I've never heard of that valley or peak, nor, I imagine, did my father. But my grandfather—Joris Yandro—came from the Southern mountains. He was young, with small education, but lots of energy and ambition." Mr. Yandro swelled up inside his fancy clothes. "He went to New York, then Chicago. His fortunes prospered. His son—my father—and then I, we contrived to make them prosper still more."

"You're to be honored," I said, my politest; but I judged, with no sure reason, that he might could not be too honorable about how he made his money, or either used it. How the others pulled back from him made me reckon he scared them, and that breed of folks scares worst where their money-pocket's located.

"I've done all right," he said, not caring who heard the brag. "I don't think anybody for a hundred miles around here can turn a deal or make a promise without asking me first. John, I own this part of the world."

Again he showed his teeth.

"You're the first one ever to tell me where my grandfather might have come from. Yandro's high hill, eh? How do we get there, John?"

I tried to recollect the way from highway to side way, side way to trail, and so in and round and over. "I fear I could show you better than I could tell you," I said.

"All right, you'll show me," he said, with no notion I might could have something different to do. "I can afford to make up my mind on a moment's notice, like that. I'll call the airport and charter a plane and we'll leave right now."

"I've asked John to stay here tonight," said my hostess lady.

"We leave now," said Mr. Yandro, and she hushed right up, and I saw how everybody was scared of him. Maybe they'd be pleasured if I got him out of there for a spell.

"Get your plane," I said. "I'll go with you."

He meant that thing he'd said. Not many hours had died before the hired plane set us down at the airport betwixt Asheville and Hendersonville. A taxi rode us into Hendersonville. Mr. Yandro found a used car man still at his place, and bought a

fair car from him. Then, on my guiding, Mr. Yandro took out
in the dark for that part of the mountains I told him about.

The sky stretched over us with no moon at all, only a many
stars like little stitches of blazing thread in a black quilt. For sure-
enough light, only our head-lamps—first on a paved road twin-
ing round one slope and over another and behind a third, then
a pretty good gravel road, then a pretty bad dirt road.

"What a stinking country!" said Mr. Yandro as we chugged
along a ridge top as lean as a butcher knife.

I didn't say how I resented that word about a country that
stoops to none on earth for prettiness. "Maybe we should ought
to have waited for daytime," was all I said.

"I don't ever wait," he sniffed. "Where's the town?"

"There's nary town. Just the valley. Three-four hours away, I
judge. We'll be there by midnight."

"What's a desrick, exactly?" he asked.

"That's a word only old-timey folks use these days. It's the
kind of cabin they used to make, strong logs and a door you can
bar, and loophole windows. So maybe you might could stand off
Indians."

"Or the wild beasts can't reach you," he quoted, and snickered. "What wild beasts do you have up here in the Forgotten
Latitudes?"

"Can't rightly say all of them. A few bears, a wildcat or two.
Used to be wolves, and a bounty for killing them. And so on."

True enough, I wasn't certain sure about the tales I'd heard,
and didn't love to tell them if Mr. Yandro would say they were
foolish for the lack of sense.

The narrow road climbed a great rocky slant one way, then
doubled back to climb the other way, and petered out into just
a double rut with an empty, scary-as-heck drop thousands of feet
beside the car. Finally Mr. Yandro edged us onto a sort of notch
beside the trail and cut off the power. He shook. Fear must have
been a new feel to his bones.

"We walk from here," I said. "Beyond's the valley."

He grumped about that, but out he got. I took a flashlight and

my guitar and led out. It was a down way from there, on a narrow trail where even a mule would be nervish. And not quiet
enough to be an easy trip.

You don't get used to that breed of mountain night noises, not
even if you're born and raised there and live and die there.
Noises too soft and sneaky to be real whispering voices. Noises
like big slow wings, far off and then near. And, above and below
the trail, noises like heavy soft paws keeping pace with you,
sometimes two paws, sometimes four, sometimes many. They stay
with you, such noises as that, all the hours you grope the night
trail, all the way down to the valley so low, till you're ready to
bless God for the little bitty crumb of light that means a human
home, and you ache and pray to get to that home, be it ever so
humble, so you can be safe inside with the light.

It's wondered me since if Mr. Yandro's constant chatter was a
string of curses or, for maybe the first time in his proud life, a
string of prayers.

The light we saw was a pine-knot fire inside a little cabin
above the stream that giggled along the valley bottom. The door
was open and somebody sat on the stoop.

"Is that a desrick?" panted and puffed Mr. Yandro.

"No, sir, it's newer made. Yonder's Miss Tully at the door, sitting up to think."

Miss Tully recollected me and welcomed us. She was eighty
or ninety, without ary tooth in her mouth to clamp her stone-
bowl pipe, but she stood straight as a pine on the split-slab floor,
and the firelight showed no gray to her neatly combed black
hair. "Rest your hats," she bade us. "So this here stranger man
is named Yandro. Funny, sir, you coming just now. You looking
for the desrick on Yandro? It's right where it's been," and she
pointed with her pipe stem off across the valley and up the far
side.

She gave us two chairs bottomed with juniper bark by the fire,
and sat on a stool next the shelf with herbs in pots and one-two
old paper books, *The Long Lost Friend* and *Egyptian Secrets,* and
Big Albert, the one they tell you can't be flung away or given

away or burnt, only to be got rid of by burying with a funeral prayer, like a human corpse.

"Funny," she said again, not laughing, "you coming along just as the seventy-five years run out."

"I was just a pigtail girl back then, when Joris Yandro courted Polly Wiltse, the witch girl. Mr. Yandro, you favor your grand-sire a right much. He wasn't nowhere as stout-built as you, and younger by years when last I saw him, though."

Though I'd heard it all before, I harked at it. It was like a many such tale at the start. Polly Wiltse was sure enough a witch, not just a study-witch like Miss Tully, and Polly Wiltse's beauty would melt the heart of nature and make a dumb man cry out, "Praise God Who made her!" But none dared court her save only Joris Yandro, who was handsome for a man as she was lovely for a woman. For it was his wish to get her to show him the gold on top of the mountain named for his folks, that only Polly Wiltse and her witchings could find.

"Sure enough there's gold in these mountains," I answered Mr. Yandro's interrupting question. "The history books tell that before even the California rush, folks mined and minted gold in these parts."

"Gold," he repeated me, both respectful and greedy. "I was right to come."

Miss Tully told that Joris Yandro coaxed Polly Wiltse to fetch down gold to him, and then he carried it off and never came back. And Polly Wiltse pined and mourned like a sick bird, and on Yandro's top she built her desrick. She sang the song, the one I'd sung, it was part of a long charm-spell. Three quarters of a century would pass, seventy-five years, and her love would come back.

"But he didn't," said Mr. Yandro. "My grandfather died up North."

"He sent his grand-boy, who favors him." Miss Tully thumbed tobacco into her pipe. "All the Yandros moved out, purely scared of Polly Wiltse's singing. But the song fetched you back here, just at the right time, to where maybe she's waiting."

"In her desrick, where the wild beasts can't reach her," Mr. Yandro quoted, and laughed. "John says they have bears and wildcats up here." He expected her to say I was wrong.

"Other things, too. Scarced-out animals like the Toller."

"The Toller?" he said.

"The hugest flying thing there is, I reckon," said Miss Tully. "It tolls its voice like a bell, to tell other creatures their feed is come near. And there's the Flat. It lies level with the ground and not much higher, and it can wrop you like a blanket." She lighted the pipe with a splinter from the fire. "And the Bammat. Big, the Bammat is."

"You mean the Behemoth," he suggested.

"No, the Behemoth was in Bible times. The Bammat's hairy-like, with big ears and a long wiggly snaky nose and twisty white teeth sticking out its mouth."

"Oh!" and Mr. Yandro trumpeted his laugh. "You've heard some story about the Mammoth. Why, it's been extinct for thousands of years."

"Not for such a long time, I hear tell," she said, puffing.

"Anyway," he argued on, "the Mammoth, the Bammat as you call it, was of the elephant family. How would it get up in these mountains?"

"Maybe folks hunted it up here," said Miss Tully, "and maybe it stays here so folks'll reckon it's dead and gone these thousand years. Then there's the Behinder."

"And what," inquired Mr. Yandro, "might the Behinder look like?"

"Can't rightly say. For it's always behind the one it's a-fixing to grab. And there's the Skim, it kites through the air. And the Culverin, that can shoot pebbles with its mouth."

"And you believe all that?" sneered Mr. Yandro, the way he always sneered at everything, everywhere.

"Why else do I tell it? Well, sir, you're back where your kin used to live, in the valley where the mountain was named for them. I can let youins sleep here on my front stoop this night."

"I came to climb the mountain and see the desrick," said Mr.

Yandro with that anxious hurry to him I kept wondering on.

"You can't climb there till it's light," she said, and she made us up two quilt pallets on the stoop.

I was tired, glad to stretch out, but Mr. Yandro fussed, as if it was wasting time. At sunup, Miss Tully fried us some side meat and some slices of cold-set hominy grits and fixed us a snack to carry, and a gourd for water. Mr. Yandro held out a ten-dollar bill.

"No, I thank you," said Miss Tully. "I bade you stay. I don't take money for such as that."

"Oh, everybody takes money from me," he snickered, and flung it on the door sill at her feet. "Go on, it's yours."

Quick as a weasel, her hand grabbed a big stick of stove wood. "Stoop down and take that money bill back, Mr. Yandro," she said.

He did as she said to do. She pointed the stick out across the stream in the thickets below, and up the height beyond. She acted as if there'd been no trouble a second before.

"That's Yandro Mountain," she said, "and up at the top, where it looks like the crown of a hat, thick with trees all the way up, stands the desrick built by Polly Wiltse. Look close with the sun rising, and you can maybe make it out."

I looked hard. There for sure it was, far off and high up. It looked a lean sort of building. "How about trails up?" I asked.

"There's trails up, John, but nobody walks them."

"Now, now," said Mr. Yandro. "If there's a trail, somebody walks it."

"Maybe, but I don't know ary soul in this here valley would set foot to such a trail, not with what they say's up there."

He laughed, as I wouldn't have dared. "You mean the Bammat," he said. "And the Flat and the Skim and the Culverin."

"And the Toller," she added for him, "and the Behinder. Only a gone gump would climb up yonder."

We headed down to the waterside, and crossed on a log. On the far bank led a trail along, and when the sun was an hour up we were at the foot of Yandro's hill and a trail went up there too.

We rested. He needed rest worse than I did. Moving most of the night before, unused to walking and climbing, he had a gaunted look to his heavy face and his clothes were sweated and dust dulled out his shiny shoes. But he grinned at me.

"So she's waited seventy-five years," he said, "and so I look like the man she's waiting for, and so there's gold up there. Gold my grandfather didn't carry off."

"You truly believe what you heard," I said, surprised.

"John, a wise man knows when to believe the unusual, and know how it will profit him. She's waiting up there, and so is the gold."

"What when you find it?" I inquired him.

"My grandfather went off and left her. Sounds like a good example to me." He grinned toothier. "I'll give you some of the gold."

"No, I thank you, Mr. Yandro."

"You don't want pay? Why did you come here with me?"

"Just made up my mind in a moment, like you."

He scowled up the height. "How long will it take to climb?"

"Depends on how fast we keep the pace."

"Let's go," and he started up.

Folks' feet hadn't worn that trail. We saw a hoof mark.

"Deer," grunted Mr. Yandro, and I said, "Maybe."

We scrambled up a rightward slant, then leftward. The trees marched in close with us and their branches filtered just a soft green light. Something rustled. A brown furry shape, bigger than a big cat, scuttled out of sight.

"Woodchuck," wheezed Mr. Yandro, and again I said, "Maybe."

After working up for an hour we rested, and after two hours more we rested again. Around 10 o'clock we got to an open space with clear light, and sat on a log to eat the corn bread and smoked meat Miss Tully had fixed. Mr. Yandro mopped his face with a fancy handkerchief and gobbled food and glittered his eye at me.

"What are you glooming about?" he said. "You look as if

you'd call me a name if you weren't afraid to."

"I've held my tongue by way of manners, not fear," I said. "I'm just thinking how and why we came so far and sudden to this place."

"I heard that song you sang and thought I'd see where my people originated. Now I've a hunch about profit. That's enough for you."

"You're more than rich enough without that gold," I said.

"I'm going up," said Mr. Yandro, "because, by God, that old hag down there said everyone's afraid to. And you said you'd go with me."

"Right to the top with you," I promised.

I forebore to say that something was looking from among the trees right behind him. It was big and broad-headed, with elephant ears, and white tusks like banisters on a spiral staircase, but it was woolly-shaggy, like a buffalo bull. How could a thing as big as the Bammat move without making noise?

On we climbed. We heard noises from the woods and brush, behind rocks and down little draws, as if the mountain side thronged with live things, thick as fleas on a possum dog and another sight sneakier.

"Why are you singing under your breath?" he grunted.

"I'm not singing. I need my wind for climbing."

"But I hear it." We stopped on the trail, and I heard it too.

Soft, almost like a half-remembered song in your mind, it was the Yandro song, all right:

> "Look away, look away, look away over Yandro
> Where them wild things are a-flyin',
> From bough to bough, and a-mating with their mates,
> So why not me with mine? . . ."

"It comes from above us," I said.

"Then we must be nearly at the top."

As we started to climb again, I heard the noises to right and left, and realized they'd gone quiet when we stopped. They moved when we moved, they waited when we waited. Soft noises, but lots of them.

Which is why I, and Mr. Yandro probably, didn't pause any more on the way up, even on a rocky stretch where we had to climb on all fours. It was about an hour before noon when we got to the top.

There was a circle-shaped clearing, with trees thronged all the way round except toward the slope. Those trees had mist among and betwixt them, quiet and fluffy, like spider webbing. And at the open space, on the lip of the way down, perched the desrick.

Old-aged was how it looked. It stood high and looked higher, because it was so narrow built of unnotched logs, four set above four, hogpen fashion, tall as a tall tobacco barn. Betwixt the logs was chinking, big masses and wads of clay. The steep roof was of long-cut, narrow shingles, and there was one big door of one axe-chopped plank, with hinges inside, for I saw none. And one window, covered with what must have been rawhide scraped thin, with a glow of soft light soaking through.

"That's the desrick," puffed Mr. Yandro.

Looking at him then, I know what most he wanted on this earth. To be boss. Money just greatened him. His greatness was bigness. He wanted to do all the talking and have everybody else do all the listening. He licked his lips.

"Let's go in," he said.

"Not where I'm not invited," I told him, flat. "I said I'd come with you to the top, and I've done that."

"Come with me. My name's Yandro, and this mountain's name is Yandro. I can buy and sell every man, woman and child in this part of the country. If I say it's all right to go in, it's all right."

He meant that thing. The world and all in it was just there to let him walk on it. He took a step toward the desrick. Somebody hummed inside, not the words of the song, just the tune. Mr. Yandro snorted at me, to show how small he reckoned me to hold back, and headed toward the big door.

"She's going to show me the gold," he said.

Where I stood at the clearing's edge, I was aware of a sort of closing in round the edge, among the trees and brush. Not that it could be seen, but there was a *gong-gong* somewhere, the voice of the Toller saying to the other creatures their feed was near. Above the treetops sailed a round flat thing like a big plate being flung high. A Skim. Then another Skim. And the blood in my body was as solid cold as ice, and for voice I had a handful of sand in my throat.

Plain as paint I knew that if I tried to back up, to turn round even, my legs would fail and I'd fall down. With fingers like sleety twigs I dragged forward my guitar to touch the silver strings, for silver is protection against evil.

But I never did. For out of some bushes near me the Bammat stuck its broad woolly head and shook it at me once, for silence. It looked me betwixt the eyes, steadier than a beast should ought to look at a man, and shook its head again. I wasn't to make any noise, and I didn't. Then the Bammat paid me no more mind, and I saw I wasn't to be included in what would happen then.

Mr. Yandro knocked at the big plank door. He waited, and knocked again. I heard him rough out that he wasn't used to waiting for his knock to be answered.

The humming had died inside. Mr. Yandro moved around to the window and picked at that rawhide.

I saw, but he couldn't, how around from back of the desrick flowed something. It lay on the ground like a broad, black, short-furred carpet rug. It humped and then flattened, the way a measuring worm moves. It came up pretty fast behind Mr. Yandro. The Toller said *gong-gong-gong*, from closer to us.

"Anybody home?" bawled Mr. Yandro. "Let me in!"

That crawling carpet brushed its edge on his foot. He looked down at it, and his eyes stuck out like two doorknobs. He knew what it was, he named it at the top of his voice.

"The Flat!"

Humping against him, it tried to wrap round his foot and leg. He gobbled out something I'd never want written down for my last words, and pulled loose and ran toward the edge of the clearing.

Gong-gong, said the Toller, and just in front of Mr. Yandro the Culverin slid into sight on its many legs. It pointed its needly mouth and spit a pebble. I heard the pebble ring on Mr. Yandro's head. He staggered and half fell. And I saw what nobody's ever supposed to see.

The Behinder flung itself on his shoulders. Then I knew why nobody's supposed to see one. I wish I hadn't. To this day I can see it, plain as a fence at noon, and forever I'll be able to see it. But telling about it is another matter. Thank you, gentlemen, I won't try.

Everything else was out—the Bammat, the Culverin, all the others—hustling Mr. Yandro across toward the desrick, and the door moved slowly and quietly open to let him in.

As for me, I hoped and prayed they wouldn't mind if I just went down the trail as fast as I could put one foot below the other.

Scrambling down, without a noise to keep me company, I reckoned I'd probably had my unguessed part in the whole thing. Seventy-five years had to pass, and then Mr. Yandro return to the desrick. It needed me, or somebody like me, to put it in his head and heart to come to where his grandsire had courted Polly Wiltse, just as though it was his own whim.

I told myself this would be a good time to go searching for another valley, a valley where there was a song I wanted to hear and learn, a right pretty song named *Vandy, Vandy*. But meanwhile—

No. No, of course Mr. Yandro wasn't the one who'd made Polly Wiltse love him and then had left her. But he was the man's grand-boy, of the same blood and the same common, low-down, sorry nature that wanted the power of money and never cared who was hurt so he could have his wish. And he looked enough like Joris Yandro so that Polly Wiltse would recognize him.

So I headed out of the valley. I was gone by sundown.

I've never studied much about what Polly Wiltse might could be like, welcoming him into her desrick on Yandro, after waiting there inside for three quarters of a hundred years. Anyway, I never heard that he followed me down. Maybe he's been missed by those who knew him. But I'll lay you any amount of money you name that he's not been mourned.

The Wheelbarrow Boy

RICHARD PARKER

"Now see here, Thomis," I said. "I've just about had enough of you. If you haven't settled yourself down and started some work in two minutes' time I shall turn you into a wheelbarrow. I'm not warning you again."

Of course, Thomis was not the only one: the whole class had the fidgets: he just happened to be the one I picked on. It was a windy day, and wind always upsets kids and makes them harder to handle. Also, I happened to know that Thomis's father had won a bit of money on the Pools, so it was easy to understand the boy's being off balance. But it's fatal to start making allowances for bad behavior.

After about three minutes I called out, "Well, Thomis? How many sums have you done?"

"I'm just writing the date," said the boy sullenly.

"Right," I said. "You can't say I didn't warn you." And I changed him into a wheelbarrow there and then—a bright red metal wheelbarrow with a pneumatic tyre.

The class went suddenly quiet, the way they do when you take a strong line, and during the next half-hour, we got a lot of work

done. When the bell for morning break went I drove them all
out so as to have the room to myself.

"All right, Thomis," I said. "You can change back now."

Nothing happened.

I thought at first he was sulking, but after a while I began to
think that something had gone seriously wrong. I went round to
the Headmaster's office.

"Look," I said, "I just changed Thomis into a wheelbarrow
and I can't get him back."

"Oh," said the Head and stared at the scattering of paper on
his desk. "Are you in a violent hurry about it?"

"No," I said. "It's a bit worrying, though."

"Which is Thomis?"

"Scruffy little fellow—pasty-faced—always got a sniff and a
mouthful of gum."

"Red hair?"

"No, that's Sanderson. Black, and like a bird's nest."

"Oh yes. I've got him. Well, now," he looked at the clock.
"Suppose you bring this Thomis chap along here in about half
an hour?"

"All right," I said.

I was a bit thoughtful as I went upstairs to the Staff Room.
Tongelow was brewing the tea, and as I looked at him I remembered that he had some sort of official position in the Union.

"How would it be if I paid my Union sub?" I said.

He put the teapot down gently. "What've you done?" he asked.
"Pushed a kid out of a second-floor window?"

I pretended to be hurt. "I just thought it was about time I
paid," I said. "It doesn't do to get too much in arrears."

In the end he took the money and gave me a receipt, and when
I had tucked that away in my wallet I felt a lot better.

Back in my own room Thomis was still leaning up in his chair,
red and awkward, a constant reproach to me. I could not start
any serious work, so after about ten minutes I set the class something to keep them busy and then lifted Thomis down and
wheeled him round to the Head.

"Oh, good," he said. "So the gardening requisition has started to come in at last."

"No," I said, dumping the barrow down in the middle of his carpet. "This is Thomis. I told you . . ."

"Sorry," he said. "I'd clean forgotten. Leave him there and I'll get to work on him straight away. I'll send him back to you when he's presentable."

I went back to my class and did a double period of composition, but no Thomis turned up. I thought the Old Man must have forgotten again, so when the bell went at twelve I took a peep into his room to jog his memory. He was on his knees on the carpet, jacket and tie off, with sweat pouring off his face. He got up weakly when he saw me.

"I've tried everything," he said, "and I can't budge him. Did you do anything unorthodox?"

"No," I said. "It was only a routine punishment."

"I think you'd better ring the Union," he said. "Ask for Legal Aid—Maxstein's the lawyer—and see where you stand."

"Do you mean we're stuck with this?" I said.

"You are," said the Head. "I should ring now, before they go to lunch."

I got through to the Union in about ten minutes and luckily Maxstein was still there. He listened to my story, grunting now and then.

"You are a member, I suppose?"

"Oh yes," I said.

"Paid up?"

"Certainly."

"Good," he said. "Now let me see. I think I'd better ring you back in an hour or so. I've not had a case quite like this before, so I'll need to think about it."

"Can't you give me a rough idea of how I stand?" I said.

"We're right behind you, of course," said Maxstein. "Free legal aid and all the rest of it. But . . . but I don't fancy your chances," he said and rang off.

The afternoon dragged on, but there was no phone call from

Maxstein. The Head got fed up with Thomis and had him wheeled out into the passage. At break-time I phoned the Union again.

"Sorry I didn't ring you," said Maxstein when I got through to him again. "I've been very busy."

"What am I to do?" I asked.

"The whole thing," said Maxstein, "turns on the attitude of the parents. If they decide to prosecute I'll have to come down and work out some line of defense with you."

"Meanwhile," I said, "Thomis is still a wheelbarrow."

"Quite. Now here's what I suggest. Take him home tonight—yourself. See his people and try to get some idea of their attitude. You never know; they might be grateful."

"Grateful?" I said.

"Well, there was that case in Glasgow—kid turned into a mincing machine—and the mother was as pleased as could be and refused to have him changed back. So go round and see, and let me know in the morning."

"All right," I said.

At 4 o'clock I waited behind and then, when the place was empty, wheeled Thomis out into the street.

I attracted quite a lot of attention on the way, from which I guessed the story must have preceded me. A lot of people I did not know nodded or said, "Good evening," and three or four ran out of shops to stare.

At last I reached the place and Mr. Thomis opened the door. The house seemed to be full of people and noise, so I gathered it was a party in celebration of the Pools.

He stared at me in a glazed sort of way for a moment and then made a violent effort to concentrate.

"It's Teddy's teacher," he bawled to those inside. "You're just in time. Come in and have a spot of something."

"Well, actually," I said, "I've come about Teddy . . ."

"It can wait," said Mr. Thomis. "Come on in."

"No, but it's serious," I said. "You see, I turned Teddy into a wheelbarrow this morning, and now . . ."

"Come and have a drink first," he said urgently.

So I went in, and drank to the healths of Mr. and Mrs. Thomis. "How much did you win?" I asked politely.

"Eleven thousand quid," said Mr. Thomis. "What a lark, eh?"

"And now," I said firmly, "about Teddy."

"Oh, this wheelbarrow caper," said Mr. Thomis. "We'll soon see about that."

He dragged me outside into the yard and went up to the wheelbarrow. "Is this him?" he said.

I nodded.

"Now look here, Teddy," said Mr. Thomis fiercely. "Just you come to your senses this minute, or I'll bash the daylights out of you." And as he spoke he began to unbuckle a heavy belt that was playing second fiddle to his braces.

The wheelbarrow changed back into Teddy Thomis and nipped smartly down the garden and through a hole in the fence.

"There you are," said Mr. Thomis. "Trouble with you teachers is you're too soft with the kids. Here, come in and have another drink."

Homecoming

RAY BRADBURY

"Here they come," said Cecy, lying there flat in her bed. "Where are they?" cried Timothy from the doorway. "Some of them are over Europe, some over Asia, some of them over the Island, some over South America!" said Cecy, her eyes closed, the lashes long, brown, and quivering.

Timothy came forward upon the bare plankings of the upstairs room. "Who are they?"

"Uncle Einar and Uncle Fry, and there's Cousin William, and I see Frulda and Helgar and Aunt Morgiana and Cousin Vivian, and I see Uncle Johann! They're all coming fast!"

"Are they up in the sky?" cried Timothy, his little gray eyes flashing. Standing by the bed, he looked no more than his fourteen years. The wind blew outside, the house was dark and lit only by starlight.

"They're coming through the air and traveling along the ground, in many forms," said Cecy, in her sleeping. She did not move on the bed; she thought inward on herself and told what she saw. "I see a wolf-like thing coming over a dark river—at the shallows—just above a waterfall, the starlight shining up his pelt.

193

I see a brown oak leaf blowing far up in the sky. I see a small bat flying. I see many other things, running through the forest trees and slipping through the highest branches; and they're *all* coming this way!"

"Will they be here by tomorrow night?" Timothy clutched the bedclothes. The spider on his lapel swung like a black pendulum, excitedly dancing. He leaned over his sister. "Will they all be here in time for the Homecoming?"

"Yes, yes, Timothy, yes," sighed Cecy. She stiffened. "Ask no more of me. Go away now. Let me travel in the places I like best."

"Thanks, Cecy," he said. Out in the hall, he ran to his room. He hurriedly made his bed. He had just awakened a few minutes ago, at sunset, and as the first star had risen, he had gone to let his excitement about the party run with Cecy. Now she slept so quietly there was not a sound. The spider hung on a silvery lasso about Timothy's slender neck as he washed his face. "Just think, Spid, tomorrow night is Allhallows' Eve!"

He lifted his face and looked into the mirror. His was the only mirror allowed in the house. It was his mother's concession to his illness. Oh, if only he were not so afflicted! He opened his mouth, surveyed the poor, inadequate teeth nature had given him. No more than so many corn kernels—round, soft and pale in his jaws. Some of the high spirit died in him.

It was now totally dark and he lit a candle to see by. He felt exhausted. This past week the whole family had lived in the fashion of the old country. Sleeping by day, rousing at sunset to move about. There were blue hollows under his eyes. "Spid, I'm no good," he said, quietly, to the little creature. "I can't even get used to sleeping days like the others."

He took up the candleholder. Oh, to have strong teeth, with incisors like steel spikes. Or strong hands, even, or a strong mind. Even to have the power to send one's mind out, free, as Cecy did. But, no, he was the imperfect one, the sick one. He was even—he shivered and drew the candle flame closer—afraid of the dark. His brothers snorted at him. Bion and Leonard and Sam. They laughed at him because he slept in a bed. With Cecy it was different; her bed was part of her comfort for the composure necessary to send her mind abroad to hunt. But Timothy, did he sleep in the wonderful polished boxes like the others? He did not! Mother let him have his own bed, his own room, his own mirror. No wonder the family skirted him like a holy man's crucifix. If only the wings would sprout from his shoulder blades. He bared his back, stared at it. He sighed again. No chance. Never.

Downstairs were exciting and mysterious sounds. The slithering sound of black crêpe going up in all the halls and on the ceilings and doors. The smell of burning black tapers crept up the banistered stair well. Mother's voice, high and firm. Father's voice, echoing from the damp cellar. Bion walking from outside the old country house lugging vast two-gallon jugs.

"I've just got to go to the party, Spid," said Timothy. The spider whirled at the end of its silk, and Timothy felt alone. He would polish cases, fetch toadstools and spiders, hang crêpe, but when the party started he'd be ignored. The less seen or said of the imperfect son the better.

All through the house below, Laura ran.

"The Homecoming!" she shouted gaily. "The Homecoming!" Her footsteps everywhere at once.

Timothy passed Cecy's room again, and she was sleeping quietly. Once a month she went belowstairs. Always she stayed in bed. Lovely Cecy. He felt like asking her, "Where are you now, Cecy? And *in* who? And what's happening? Are you beyond the hills? And what goes on there?" But he went on to Ellen's room instead.

Ellen sat at her desk, sorting out many kinds of blond, red and black hair and little scimitars of fingernail gathered from her manicurist job at the Mellin Village beauty parlor fifteen miles away. A sturdy mahogany case lay in one corner with her name on it.

"Go away," she said, not even looking at him. "I can't work with you gawking."

"Allhallows' Eve, Ellen; just think!" he said, trying to be

friendly.

"Hunh!" She put some fingernail clippings in a small white sack, labeled them. "What can it mean to you? What do you know of it? Go back to bed."

His cheeks burned. "I'm needed to polish and work and help serve."

"If you don't go, you'll find a dozen raw oysters in your bed tomorrow," said Ellen, matter-of-factly. "Good-by, Timothy."

In his anger, rushing downstairs, he bumped into Laura.

"Watch where you're going!" she shrieked from clenched teeth.

She swept away. He ran to the open cellar door, smelled the channel of moist earthy air rising from below. "Father?"

"It's about time," Father shouted up the steps. "Hurry down, or they'll be here before we're ready!"

Timothy hesitated only long enough to hear the million other sounds in the house. Brothers came and went like trains in a station, talking and arguing. If you stood in one spot long enough the entire household passed with their pale hands full of things. Leonard with his little black medical case, Samuel with his large, dusty ebony-bound book under his arm, bearing more black crêpe, and Bion excursioning to the car outside and bringing in many more gallons of liquid.

Father stopped polishing to give Timothy a rag and a scowl. He thumped the huge mahogany box. "Come on, shine this up, so we can start on another. Sleep your life away."

While waxing the surface, Timothy looked inside.

"Uncle Einar's a big man, isn't he, Papa?"

"Unh."

"How big is he?"

"The size of the box'll tell you."

"I was only asking. Seven feet tall?"

"You talk a lot."

About nine o'clock Timothy went out into the October weather. For two hours in the now-warm, now-cold wind he walked the meadows collecting toadstools and spiders. His heart began to beat with anticipation again. How many relatives had Mother

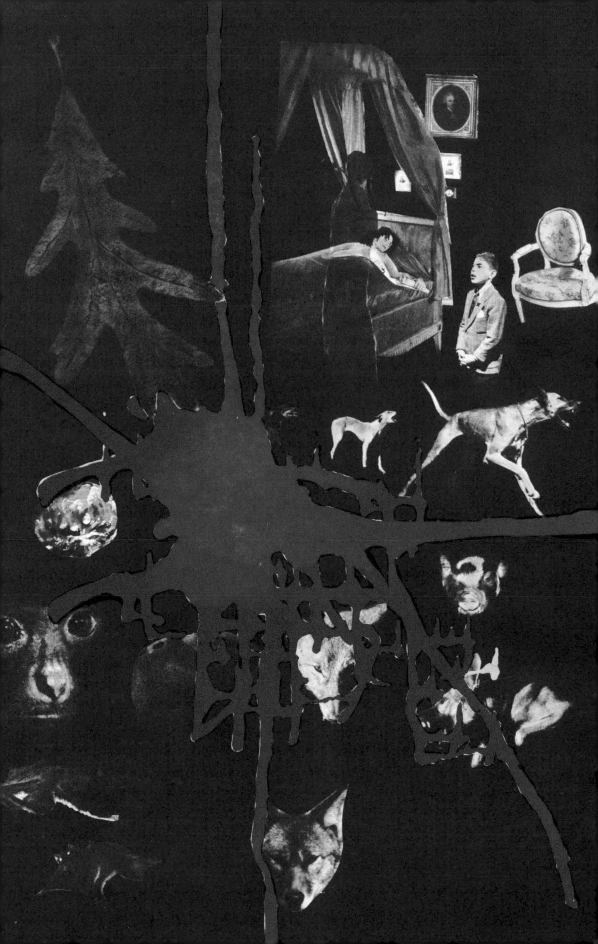

said would come? Seventy? One hundred? He passed a farm-house. If only you knew what was happening at our house, he said to the glowing windows. He climbed a hill and looked at the town, miles away, settling into sleep, the town hall clock high and round white in the distance. The town did not know, either. He brought home many jars of toadstools and spiders.

In the little chapel belowstairs a brief ceremony was celebrated. It was like all the other rituals over the years, with Father chant-ing the dark lines, Mother's beautiful white ivory hands moving in the reverse blessings, and all the children gathered except Cecy, who lay upstairs in bed. But Cecy was present. You saw her peering, now from Bion's eyes, now Samuel's, now Mother's, and you felt a movement and now she was in you, fleetingly, and gone.

Timothy prayed to the Dark One with a tightened stomach. "Please, please, help me grow up, help me be like my sisters and brothers. Don't let me be different. If only I could put the hair in the plastic images as Ellen does, or make people fall in love with me as Laura does with people, or read strange books as Sam does, or work in a respected job as Leonard and Bion do. Or even raise a family one day, as Mother and Father have done. . . ."

At midnight a storm hammered the house. Lightning struck outside in amazing, snow-white bolts. There was a sound of an approaching, probing, sucking tornado, funneling and nuzzling the moist night earth. Then the front door, blasted half off its hinges, hung stiff and discarded, and in trooped Grandmama and Grandpapa, all the way from the old country!

From then on people arrived each hour. There was a flutter at the side window, a rap on the front porch, a knock at the back. There were fey noises from the cellar; autumn wind piped down the chimney throat, chanting. Mother filled the large crystal punch bowl with a scarlet fluid poured from the jugs Bion had carried home. Father swept from room to room lighting more tapers. Laura and Ellen hammered up more wolfsbane. And Timothy stood amidst this wild excitement, no expression to his face, his hands trembling at his sides, gazing now here, now there. Banging of doors, laughter, the sound of liquid pouring, darkness, sound of wind, the webbed thunder of wings, the padding of feet, the welcoming bursts of talk at the entrances, the transparent rattlings of casements, the shadows passing, coming, going, wavering.

"Well, well, and *this* must be Timothy!"

"What?"

A chilly hand took his hand. A long hairy face leaned down over him. "A good lad, a fine lad," said the stranger.

"Timothy," said his mother. "This is Uncle Jason."

"Hello, Uncle Jason."

"And over here——" Mother drifted Uncle Jason away. Uncle Jason peered back at Timothy over his caped shoulder, and winked.

Timothy stood alone.

From off a thousand miles in the candled darkness, he heard a high fluting voice; that was Ellen. "And my brothers, they *are* clever. Can you guess their occupations, Aunt Morgiana?"

"I have no idea."

"They operate the undertaking establishment in town."

"What!" A gasp.

"Yes!" Shrill laughter. "Isn't that priceless!"

Timothy stood very still.

A pause in the laughter. "They bring home sustenance for Mama, Papa, and all of us," said Laura. "Except, of course, Timothy . . ."

An uneasy silence. Uncle Jason's voice demanded, "Well? Come now. What about Timothy?"

"Oh, Laura, your tongue," said Mother.

Laura went on with it. Timothy shut his eyes. "Timothy doesn't —well—doesn't *like* blood. He's delicate."

"He'll learn," said Mother. "He'll learn," she said very firmly. "He's my son, and he'll learn. He's only fourteen."

"But I was raised on the stuff," said Uncle Jason, his voice passing from one room on into another. The wind played the trees

outside like harps. A little rain spatted on the windows——
"raised on the stuff," passing away into faintness.

Timothy bit his lips and opened his eyes.

"Well, it was all my fault." Mother was showing them into
the kitchen now. "I tried forcing him. You can't force children,
you only make them sick, and then they never get a taste for
things. Look at Bion, now, he was thirteen before he . . ."

"I understand," murmured Uncle Jason. "Timothy will come
around."

"I'm sure he will," said Mother, defiantly.

Candle flames quivered as shadows crossed and recrossed the
dozen musty rooms. Timothy was cold. He smelled the hot tallow
in his nostrils and instinctively he grabbed at a candle and walked
with it around and about the house, pretending to straighten the
crêpe.

"Timothy," someone whispered behind a patterned wall, hissing
and sizzling and sighing the words, *"Timothy is afraid of the dark."*

Leonard's voice. Hateful Leonard!

"I like the candle, that's all," said Timothy in a reproachful
whisper.

More noise, more laughter, and thunder. Cascades of roaring
laughter. Bangings and clickings and shouts and rustles of clothing. Clammy fog swept through the front door. Out of the fog,
settling his wings, stalked a tall man.

"Uncle Einar!"

Timothy propelled himself on his thin legs straight through the
fog, under the green webbing shadows. He threw himself across
Einar's arms. Einar lifted him.

"You've wings, Timothy!" He tossed the boy light as thistles.
"Wings, Timothy; fly!" Faces wheeled under. Darkness rotated.
The house blew away. Timothy felt breezelike. He flapped his
arms. Einar's fingers caught and threw him once more to the
ceiling. The ceiling rushed down like a charred wall. "Fly, Timothy!" shouted Einar, loud and deep. "Fly with wings! Wings!"

He felt an exquisite ecstasy in his shoulder blades, as if roots
grew, burst to explode and blossom into new, moist membrane.

He babbled wild stuff; again Einar hurled him high.

The autumn wind broke in a tide on the house, rain crashed down, shaking the beams, causing chandeliers to tilt their enraged candle lights. And the one hundred relatives peered out from every black, enchanted room, circling inward, all shapes and sizes, to where Einar balanced the child like a baton in the roaring spaces.

"Enough!" shouted Einar, at last.

Timothy, deposited on the floor timbers, exaltedly, exhaustedly fell against Uncle Einar, sobbing happily. "Uncle, uncle, uncle!"

"Was it good, flying? Eh, Timothy?" said Uncle Einar, bending down, patting Timothy's head. "Good, good."

It was coming toward dawn. Most had arrived and were ready to bed down for the daylight, sleep motionlessly with no sound until the following sunset, when they would shout out of their mahogany boxes for the revelry.

Uncle Einar, followed by dozens of others, moved toward the cellar. Mother directed them downward to the crowded row on row of highly polished boxes. Einar, his wings like sea-green tarpaulins tented behind him, moved with a curious whistling sound through the passageway; where his wings touched they made a sound of drumheads gently beaten.

Upstairs, Timothy lay wearily thinking, trying to like the darkness. There was so much you could do in darkness that people couldn't criticize you for, because they never saw you. He *did* like the night, but it was a qualified liking; sometimes there was so much night he cried out in rebellion.

In the cellar, mahogany doors sealed downward, drawn in by pale hands. In corners, certain relatives circled three times to lie down, heads on paws, eyelids shut. The sun rose. There was a sleeping.

Sunset. The revel exploded like a bat nest struck full, shrieking out, fluttering, spreading. Box doors banked wide. Steps rushed up from cellar damp. More late guests, kicking on front and back portals, were admitted.

It rained, and sodden visitors laid their capes, their water-pelleted hats, their sprinkled veils upon Timothy who bore them to a closet. The rooms were crowd-packed. The laughter of one cousin shot from one room, angled off the wall of another, ricocheted, banked and returned to Timothy's ears from a fourth room, accurate and cynical.

A mouse ran across the floor.

"I know you, Niece Leibersrouter!" exclaimed Father.

The mouse spiraled three women's feet and vanished into a corner. Moments later a beautiful woman rose up out of nothing and stood in the corner, smiling her white smile at them all.

Something huddled against the flooded pane of the kitchen window. It sighed and wept and tapped continually, pressed against the glass, but Timothy could make nothing of it, he saw nothing. In imagination he was outside staring in. The rain was on him, the wind at him, and the taper-dotted darkness inside was inviting. Waltzes were being danced; tall thin figures pirouetted to outlandish music. Stars of light flickered off lifted bottles; small clods of earth crumbled from casques, and a spider fell and went silently legging over the floor.

Timothy shivered. He was inside the house again. Mother was calling him to run here, run there, help, serve, out to the kitchen now, fetch this, fetch that, bring the plates, heap the food—on and on—the party happened around him but not to him. The dozens of towering people pressed in against him, elbowed him, ignored him.

Finally, he turned and slipped away up the stairs.

He called softly. "Cecy. Where are you now, Cecy?"

She waited a long while before answering. "In the Imperial Valley," she murmured faintly. "Beside the Salton Sea, near the mud pots and the steam and the quiet. I'm beside a farmer's wife. I'm sitting on a front porch. I can make her move if I want, or do anything or think anything. The sun's going down."

"What's it like, Cecy?"

"You can hear mud pots hissing," she said, slowly, as if speaking in a church. "Little gray heads of steam push up the mud like bald men rising in the thick syrup, head first, out in the broiling channels. The gray heads rip like rubber fabric, collapse with noises like wet lips moving. And feathery plumes of steam escape from the ripped tissue. And there is a smell of deep sulphurous burning and old time. The dinosaur has been abroiling here ten million years."

"Is he done yet, Cecy?"

"Yes, he's done. Quite done." Cecy's calm sleeper's lips turned up. The languid words fell slowly from her shaping mouth. "Inside this woman's skull I am, looking out, watching the sea that does not move, and is so quiet it makes you afraid. I sit on the porch and wait for my husband to come home. Occasionally, a fish leaps, falls back, starlight edging it. The valley, the sea, the few cars, the wooden porch, my rocking chair, myself, the silence."

"What now, Cecy?"

"I'm getting up from my rocking chair," she said.

"Yes?"

"I'm walking off the porch, toward the mud pots. Planes fly over, like primordial birds. Then it is quiet, so quiet."

"How long will you stay inside her, Cecy?"

"Until I've listened and looked and felt enough; until I've changed her life some way. I'm walking off the porch and along the wooden boards. My feet knock on the planks, tiredly, slowly."

"And now?"

"Now the sulphur fumes are all around me. I stare at the bubbles as they break and smooth. A bird darts by my temple, shrieking. Suddenly I am in the bird and fly away! And as I fly, inside my new small glass-bead eyes I see a woman below me, on a boardwalk, take one two three steps forward into the mud pots. I hear a sound as of a boulder plunged into molten depths. I keep flying, circle back. I see a white hand, like a spider, wriggle and disappear into the gray lava pool. The lava seals over. Now I'm flying home, swift, swift, swift!"

Something clapped hard against the window. Timothy started.

Cecy flicked her eyes wide, bright, full, happy, exhilarated.

"Now I'm *home*!" she said.

After a pause, Timothy ventured, "The Homecoming's on. And everybody's here."

"Then why are you upstairs?" She took his hand. "Well, ask me." She smiled slyly. "Ask me what you came to ask."

"I didn't come to ask anything," he said. "Well, almost nothing. Well, oh, Cecy!" It came from him in one long rapid flow. "I want to do something at the party to make them look at me, something to make me good as them, something to make me belong, but there's nothing I can do and I feel funny and, well, I thought you might . . ."

"I might," she said, closing her eyes, smiling inwardly. "Stand up straight. Stand very still." He obeyed. "Now, shut your eyes and blank out your thoughts."

He stood very straight and thought of nothing, or at least thought of thinking nothing.

She sighed. "Shall we go downstairs now, Timothy?" Like a hand into a glove, Cecy was within him.

"Look, everybody!" Timothy held the glass of warm red liquid. He held up the glass so that the whole house turned to watch him. Aunts, uncles, cousins, brothers, sisters!

He drank it straight down.

He jerked a hand at his sister Laura. He held her gaze, whispering to her in a subtle voice that kept her silent, frozen. He felt tall as the trees as he walked to her. The party now slowed. It waited on all sides of him, watching. From all the room doors the faces peered. They were not laughing. Mother's face was astonished. Dad looked bewildered, but pleased and getting prouder every instant.

He nipped her, gently, over the neck vein. The candle flames swayed drunkenly. The wind climbed around on the roof outside. The relatives stared from all the doors. He popped toadstools into his mouth, swallowed, then beat his arms against his flanks and circled. "Look, Uncle Einar! I can fly, at last!" Beat went his hands. Up and down pumped his feet. The faces flashed past him.

At the top of the stairs before knowing it, flapping, Timothy heard his mother cry, "Stop, Timothy!" far below. "Hey!" shouted

Timothy, and leaped off the top of the well, thrashing.

Halfway down, the wings he thought he owned dissolved. He screamed. Uncle Einar caught him.

Timothy flailed whitely in the receiving arms. A voice burst out of his lips unbidden. "This is Cecy! This is Cecy!" it announced shrilly. "Cecy! Come see me, all of you, upstairs, first room on the left!" Followed by a long trill of high laughter. Timothy tried to cut it off with his tongue, his lips.

Everybody was laughing. Einar set him down. Running through the crowding blackness as the relatives flowed upstairs toward Cecy's room to congratulate her, Timothy banged the front door open. Mother called out behind him, anxiously.

"Cecy, I hate you, I hate you!"

By the sycamore tree, in deep shadow, Timothy spewed out his dinner, sobbed bitterly and threshed in a pile of autumn leaves. Then he lay still. From his blouse pocket, from the protection of the matchbox he used for his retreat, the spider crawled forth. Spid walked along Timothy's arm. Spid explored up his neck to his ear and climbed in the ear to tickle it. Timothy shook his head. "Don't, Spid!" He sobbed somewhat less.

The feathery touch of a tentative feeler probing his eardrum set Timothy shivering. "Don't, Spid!" He sobbed somewhat less.

The spider traveled down his cheek, took a station under the boy's nose, looked up into the nostrils as if to seek the brain, and then clambered softly up over the rim of the nose to sit, to squat there peering at Timothy with green gem eyes until Timothy filled with ridiculous laughter. "Go away, Spid!"

Timothy sat up, rustling the leaves. The land was very bright with the moon. In the house he could hear the faint ribaldry as Mirror, Mirror was played. Celebrants shouted, dimly muffled, as they tried to identify those of themselves whose reflections did not, had not ever appeared in a glass.

"Timothy." Uncle Einar's wings spread and twitched and came in with a sound like kettledrums. Timothy felt himself plucked up like a thimble and set upon Einar's shoulder. "Don't feel badly, Nephew Timothy. Each to his own, each in his own way.

How much better things are for you. How rich. The world's dead for us. We've seen so much of it, believe me. Life's best to those who live the least of it. It's worth more per ounce, Timothy, remember that."

The rest of the black morning, from midnight on, Uncle Einar led him about the house, from room to room, weaving and singing. A horde of late arrivals set the entire hilarity off afresh. Great-great-great-great and a thousand more great-greats Grandmother was there, wrapped in Egyptian cerements. She said not a word, but lay straight as a burnt ironing board against the wall, her eye hollows cupping a distant, wise, silent glimmering. At the breakfast, at four in the morning, one-thousand-odd-greats Grand-mama was stiffly seated at the head of the longest table.

The wind got higher, the stars burned with fiery intensity, the noises redoubled, the dances quickened, the drinking became more positive. To Timothy there were thousands of things to hear and watch. The many darknesses roiled, bubbled, the many faces passed and repassed. . . .

"Listen!"

The party held its breath. Far away the town clock struck its chimes, saying six o'clock. The party was ending. As if at a cue, in time to the rhythm of the clock striking, their one hundred voices began to sing songs that were four hundred years old, songs Timothy could not know. They twined their arms around one another, circling slowly, and sang, and somewhere in the cold distance or morning the town clock finished out its chimes and quieted.

Good-bys were said, there was a great rustling. Mother and Father and the brothers and sisters lined up at the door to shake hands and kiss each departing relative in turn. The sky beyond the open door colored and shone in the east. A cold wind entered.

The shouting and the laughing bit by bit faded and went away. Dawn grew more apparent. Everybody was embracing and crying and thinking how the world was becoming less a place for them. There had been a time when they had met every year, but now decades passed with no reconciliation. "Don't forget, we meet in

Salem in 1990!" someone cried.

Salem. Timothy's numbed mind turned the word over. Salem, 1990. And there would be Uncle Fry and Grandma and Grandfather and a thousand-times-great Grandmother in her withered cerements. And Mother and Father and Ellen and Laura and Cecy and Leonard and Bion and Sam and all the rest. But would he be there? Would he be alive that long? Could he be certain of living until then?

With one last withering wind blast, away they all went, so many scarves, so many fluttery mammals, so many sere leaves, so many wolves, loping, so many whinings and clustering noises, so many midnights and ideas and insanities.

Mother shut the door. Laura picked up a broom.

"No," said Mother, "we'll clean up tonight. We need sleep first."

Father walked down into the cellar, followed by Laura and Bion and Sam. Ellen walked upstairs, as did Leonard.

Timothy walked across the crêpe-littered hall. His head was down, and in passing a party mirror he saw himself, the pale mortality of his face. He was cold and trembling.

"Timothy," said Mother.

He stopped at the stair well. She came to him, laid a hand on his face. "Son," she said, "we love you. Remember that. We all love you. No matter how different you are, no matter if you leave us one day," she said. She kissed his cheek. "And if and when you die, your bones will lie undisturbed, we'll see to that. You'll lie at ease forever, and I'll come see you every Allhallows' Eve and tuck you in the more secure."

The house was silent. Far away the wind went over a hill with its last cargo of small dark bats echoing, chittering.

He walked up the steps, one by one, crying to himself all the way.

M